A Searing Faith

––

The Heart Pyre - Book One

Audrey Martin

A SEARING FAITH

Paperback edition ISBN: 9789998797208

EBook edition ISBN: 9789998797215

Copyright © 2023 by Audrey Martin

All rights reserved. Audrey Martin asserts the moral right to be identified as the author of this work.

No part of this publication may be reproduced, distributed, or transmitted in any form or by any means, including photocopying, recording, or other electronic or mechanical methods, without the prior written permission of the publisher, except as permitted by Luxembourg copyright law.

This is a work of fiction. All of the characters, organizations, and events portrayed in this novel are either products of the author's imagination or are used fictitiously. Any resemblance to actual persons, living or dead (except for satirical purposes), is entirely coincidental.

A SEARING FAITH

Book Cover Design by Audrey Martin

Book Cover Illustration by Mona May

1st edition 2023

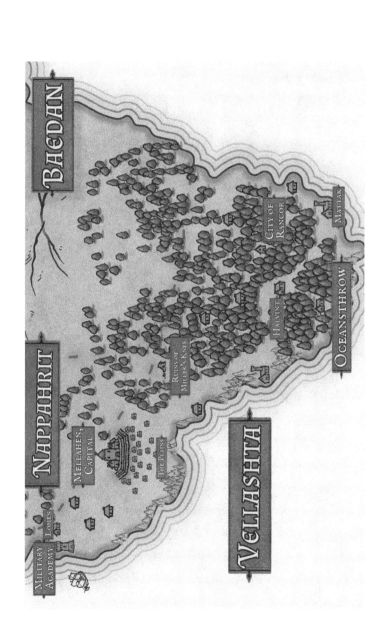

Chapter One

Rena's siblings ran around her in a whirlwind of giggles, almost knocking down the two plates she was holding.

"Sit down!" she told them, unable to hold in her laughter. She knew she had to be sterner, but how could she yell at them when their joy was so infectious?

"Stop being so loud," her third brother, Valerio, mumbled as he sat at the table — having outgrown childish glee over the last couple of months.

"Did you wake up Mom like I told you to?" Rena asked, managing to step around her younger brothers and place the plates on the table.

"Yeah, yeah," Valerio replied, breaking a bread roll in two and letting the steam rise up from its centre.

"I'm awake, stop worrying," Rena's mother called, stepping into the kitchen, her curly brown hair sticking out in every direction. "Thank you for preparing everything, my love," she said, leaning in to kiss Rena's cheek.

"I made you some anchovy paste," Rena told her mother, nodding towards the bowl sitting next to the sink.

"What luck it is to have you in our lives," her mother replied, putting the bowl on the table in front of her designated seat, before stepping out of the kitchen again.

"Maya, breakfast is ready!" Rena shouted, leaning over to glance down the corridor.

"Did you know—" Lino, the youngest of the bunch, said, arriving at the table. "—that if you feed cows nothing but carrots, they make orange milk. Or maybe purple, depending on the carrots."

"Is that so?" Rena said with a smirk, turning towards her brothers again.

"What if you feed them both carrots?" Savio, the last of her brothers, asked. "Would the milk be orange *and* purple, or would it make brown?"

"You are both so stupid," Valerio mumbled into his bread.

"Be nice," Rena whispered as she placed the jug of olive oil next to him.

The front door opened, and Rena's uncle stepped into the room. He was a tall, burly man, almost filling the entirety of the doorframe. The resemblance to her father could be seen in the wide amber eyes, and the dimple in his right cheek, but his skin was much darker than her father's — a deep golden brown from working outside in the sun most days, which also showed in the wrinkles around his eyes.

"Good morning everyone!" He bellowed with a wide smile, stepping closer to stand behind Lino's chair. "Ready for the new week?"

"Why are you already here, Simón?" Rena's mother asked, as she walked back into the kitchen, tying a red and purple scarf around her hair.

Rena tried to meet her mother's eyes, to beg her to not start another argument with her uncle, but her mother simply stepped past her.

"The sun rose an hour ago. You should be happy I didn't arrive when it was still night."

He leaned forward and picked up the bread roll from Lino's plate.

"Hey!" Lino cried out, turning to try to get the bread back.

"Where's my lovely brother, then?" Simón asked, tearing a piece of bread off the roll before popping it into his mouth. He passed the roll back to Lino with a ruffle of his nephew's hair, smudging him with flour residue.

"In the bakery," Rena answered, placing mugs of fresh milk on the table in front of her siblings. "He's had a new idea."

"Hopefully something useful," her uncle chuckled nervously.

"Either way, it smells delicious!" Rena's mother replied, sitting down next to her eldest son. "Valerio, put something on the bread, don't just eat it naked like that."

"Doesn't matter how delicious it smells to you if people won't buy it, my dear Amalia." Simón sat down on the chair that usually belonged to his brother. "We just talked about this last week. We're not in the big cities here. People don't buy things they've never heard of before, they buy what they know and can trust. They can't afford to waste money on something their children won't eat."

Rena closed her eyes for a moment, bracing herself for what was to come. She had hoped they wouldn't have to start the week like this, but with how tense the situation in her family had become over the last couple of months, she felt stupid for ever wishing for calm.

"You take everything too seriously," Rena's mother replied, waving him off. "The situation is nowhere near as dire as you make it out to be. People don't want to eat the same old food day in, day out."

"Can we at least eat before we start fighting again?" Rena muttered.

"We're not fighting," Amalia said, shooting her brother-in-law a quick smile that didn't reach her eyes.

"So how many of those do you actually sell full-price?" Simón continued, ignoring his niece's request. He stared at Rena's mother, his smile gone, his fingers tapping rhythmically against the table. "How many do you have to put on sale at the end of the day because they didn't sell? Excuse me if I don't want the mill and the bakery that my great-grandfather already operated to be sold off because you couldn't bother making the right kind of bread."

The children had fallen silent, all pretending to be enraptured by the food. Rena put a plate in front of her uncle, and smiled at him.

"We're not going to lose either of them," Rena replied, forcing her voice to sound cheerful. "I'm going to help out more after school. I can bake the regular loafs, and Dad can continue making his new recipes, then people can choose which ones they like best. We'll just reduce the amount we produce so we won't need to throw any of them out."

He looked up at her, opening his mouth as if he wanted to say something. Instead, he sighed, and glanced down at his plate.

"I'm just saying," he started again in a softer voice, looking up at Rena's mother. "If you would relinquish at least one of the two to me—"

"Stop it." Amalia pushed away from the table, standing in the same motion. "We already talked about this, the mill and the bakery can't be separated, they operate as one. We can't just give up one of them."

"They only operate as one because of the way you work," Simón snapped back. "They could very easily be separated."

"They have operated like this for twenty years, they will continue operating like this for twenty more. And look at us, we can't even eat breakfast together without fighting. How do you think it would be if we had to work together?"

"I know money has been a bit tight lately," Rena interjected, a knot forming in the pit of her stomach. "But we can fix that. I've got a plan for the following weeks, and I made sure it was to everyone's liking. It's going to be fine, just give us a chance to show you."

She stared deeply into her uncle's eyes, pleading for him to finally relent. He held her gaze for a moment, then quickly raised his eyebrows and looked away. The tightness in his jaw, however, revealed that this would not be the last time he brought up the subject.

"She even went around and asked people which goods they liked the most," her mother added, gesturing widely with her hands. "And then she made us a schedule of when to bake what. Never before have we baked with a *schedule*, but if my dear Rena thinks that's what we need to do, then that's what we'll do."

She came over to Rena and took her daughter's face in her hands, smooshing it together before planting a big kiss on both cheeks. Rena couldn't help herself but break out in a big grin, and the tightness in her stomach slowly unfurled.

Her uncle didn't say anything for a while, just observed them, before getting up — the chair screeching as it pushed back.

"Don't put too much pressure on her," he said wearily.

"I'll be fine," Rena told him, the smile still on her face. "I like the work, and if I want to take over the bakery one day I need the experience anyway."

"Really hope you can take over," he muttered before turning to Rena's mother. "So, what is this big plan of yours? Shouldn't you already be baking? People are starting to get hungry."

"Yes, yes, yes, stop pressuring me," her mother waved him off, turning around to walk out of the kitchen. "I'm already on my way."

Rena finally sat down, breaking open the bread roll on her plate and pouring a small trickle of olive oil and sprinkled some salt on it.

"How are you guys doing?" her uncle asked, coming to stand behind Lino again. "Everything all right with school?"

He opened the flood gates, and Rena's younger brothers started rattling off, in minute detail, all of the events of the previous week.

"Where's your sister, by the way?" Rena's uncle asked when conversation had clearly moved past his initial question.

"Still in her room, like always," Rena answered before taking a bite from her breakfast, relishing in the warmth of the fresh bread and the salty aroma of the olive oil. The last knot in her stomach loosened at the prospect of finally touching food.

"Rena, my love, come here for a second," her mother called from the hallway.

Rena swallowed quickly and excused herself from the table. Her mother was in the big pantry, next to the entrance to the bakery, where they kept all the ingredients they needed for their products. Rena and Maya had just spent all of Saturday afternoon cleaning it and rearranging the containers, but somehow her mother had managed to undo all of their hard work. Half of the boxes were now laying on the ground, a large portion of them opened, their contents spilled onto the ground.

"I can't find the rosemary," her mother told her, pulling another box off of the shelf and opening it.

"Are you sure we still have some?" Rena asked as she walked around the room, finding the empty box labelled "rosemary" and picking it up to put it back on the shelf.

"I thought we did."

"I didn't see any on Saturday when I was cleaning."

Her mother chuckled, handing Rena the box she'd just opened.

"Maybe we should have checked which herbs we still had before finalising your lovely plan."

"We'll just have to change some things around and make another kind of bread today. We still have a lot of wild garlic and basil. We can just make what we had planned for Friday instead."

Rena put the box back onto the shelf, and reached down to pick up the next box while her mother busied herself trying to find rosemary.

"No, no, no. I told Carmen and Irma that we would have the rosemary bread today. They're already waiting. And I'm sure half the village knows about it by now."

"Mother! You need to make sure we can actually bake the breads before telling everyone we're going to sell them."

She shut her eyes and dug her nails into her palms to calm herself before more words could tumble from her mouth. Getting angry at her mother wouldn't help the situation either.

"Oh, don't be like your uncle," her mother chastised.

Rena took in a long, deep breath and opened her eyes again, reminding herself that soon she would be done with school and then she could manage the bakery full-time.

"I suppose I could go into the forest and collect some," Rena sighed. "Miss Kaari would understand. I'll just ask Tala if I missed anything important."

"Oh Rena," her mother whispered, stepping away from the shelf to take Rena's hand. "You don't have to miss school because of my carelessness."

"It's okay," Rena said softly, smiling to hide her disappointment. "We're only doing reading in the mornings. I'm pretty good at it already. Usually I just help out the younger pupils."

Her mother took her face in both hands and smiled at her.

"You are such a blessing to this family, my love," she said and kissed her slowly on both cheeks, before stepping away and picking up one of the boxes from the ground. "Take your sister with you. If it's the two of you, you'll be done quicker, and then you can go to school in the afternoon. She doesn't pay attention when she's there anyway."

"I'll go ask her." Rena nodded and stepped out of the pantry.

Maya was sitting on the floor of their bedroom, a box of jewellery in front of her, the necklaces and rings strewn across her lap. She looked closer to their father's side of the family, her skin a touch darker than Rena's light copper colour, although her eyes were the golden hazel of their mother's side, while Rena's eyes had the same amber colour her father and uncle had. They had both, however, inherited their father's thick, dark brown hair, that Rena wore in long waves beyond her shoulders, and Maya wore only to her chin.

"I'm going out to gather some rosemary in the forest, would you come with me?" Rena asked, stepping closer to her sister.

Maya held a leaf-shaped pendant up to the light, turning it from side to side, before bringing it back down to her lap and rubbing the rag she was holding in the other hand over the side of the pendant.

"Busy," she finally mumbled, not looking up.

Rena crouched down next to her, wrapping her arms around her knees, and observed her sister.

"What are you doing?"

"Cleaning some old stuff."

Rena tilted her head, her gaze wandering over the dirty and corroded jewellery.

"Those are grandma's old necklaces," Rena said, reaching out to pick up one of the necklaces.

"Mmhmm. Found them in a box in one of the cupboards."

Rena observed her sister for a while without saying anything. She liked the spontaneity in Maya's heart — that she could see something and decide on the spot what had to be done – even though it could be frustrating at times when she ignored her responsibilities for it. It was a refreshing contrast to their parents — who said they would remember to do something later, and then forget about it.

Rena didn't actually need help gathering the herb from the forest. It might take her a bit longer, but she really didn't mind. The jewellery didn't deserve to be forgotten in an old box anyway.

"Here, for you," Maya said, finally looking up to hand Rena the necklace she had just polished.

"Thank you." Rena smiled and put the necklace on. The pendant made of green enamel was in the shape of an alder tree leaf — almost the outline of a heart — and hung on a simple brass chain. She picked the pendant up to look down at it, her thumb stroking its outline. "It's so pretty."

Maya riffled through the rest of the jewellery.

"I'm trying to figure out which one to give to Mom. That one's the prettiest, but I'm keeping this for me." She picked up a golden ring with a square green gemstone that looked like it had barely been worn, and slipped it on her right middle finger, even though the ring was clearly too big.

"Maybe this one," she added, picking up another golden ring, this one with dents and a corner of the gem chipped. "I'll have to clean it a bit more though."

"I remember Grandma wearing that to a wedding once," Rena replied.

She smoothed the necklace and pulled her long hair away from it.

"Don't forget to go to school, okay?" Rena told Maya as she rose to leave. "Miss Kaari will be cross with you if you keep missing classes."

"I know how to read. I don't need to waste my time waiting for the others to catch up."

"You could help them, you know," Rena mentioned, placing her hand on the door frame.

"That's your job," Maya muttered, her eyebrows knitting together in concentration as she tried to bend the links of a chain back into place.

"Right." Rena chuckled softly, and turned away.

Chapter Two

Rena walked through the forest, avoiding the young seedlings and puddles that had formed the night before. She lifted the hem of her beige dress with one hand, an old basket filled with various herbs in the other. A chilly breeze flowed through her hair, her fringe braided back so it wouldn't constantly fall into her face.

She couldn't really tell how long she had been in the forest, but by the way her stomach grumbled she had probably already missed lunch. She navigated her way back to the road, taking the long way around to avoid the larger puddles. When she reached the road, however, it seemed different from how it had looked it the morning. The dirt and gravel had been stirred up, forcing Rena to walk on the thin strip where the grass started growing so she wouldn't get stuck in the mud. She cursed whichever king or lord or margrave had decided to march their battalion through these forests instead of using the well-paved roads further north. She slipped and almost fell, but managed to catch herself without losing too many of the herbs. Why did the military have to ride on these roads when all of the big, important cities in their province were in the west — and she knew it had to have been the military, because who else travelled in such large groups without leaving wagon tracks?

It began with the smell. Something biting and acrid crawled its way down her nose, her hand automatically shooting up to cover her face. She couldn't place the stench, but as she continued walking it grew stronger. Her frown deepened as she realised she was smelling fire. Not a cosy, wooden fire that fills your heart with warm feelings of home. It was a vile scent that brought horrible news with it. It smelled of burned wood, scorched dirt, hot metal, and behind it all was a smell that Rena's mind didn't dare place. Something that made her stomach tighten and turn. It tore its way past her hand and down her throat and clutched itself to her lungs so it would never leave her mind again. She tried to imagine what could emit such a smell. Maybe the butcher's shop in town had burnt down. Maybe someone's field had caught fire and their life stock had tragically been involved. Her mind didn't dare wander further than that.

Next came the light. With every step she took, with every bend in the road, the horizon grew brighter. The trees were lit up by a pulsing orange glow, its heart blazing up into an engulfing white that seemed to suck any last hope out of Rena's heart. Her lower jaw dropped open, and the stench crept its way over her tongue as vomit rose up her throat. She dropped the basket, the herbs spreading across the road in front of her. She straightened back up, pressing the heel of her hand against her mouth as tears rolled down her cheeks. Her father's friend, Jesper, had a field with goats close to this road. If it had caught fire, it could explain the bright light and propagating smoke. She wanted to turn around and run away, to never find out where the smoke that was covering the road in front of her was coming from, but she forced herself to press on.

Last came the sound. The sound of cracking wood, falling roofs, searing haystacks, and popping bones. But in some ways, it was very silent. No wind, no birds, no mice. Like nothing dared come near this forsaken place. Maybe they were right. Maybe it was a bad idea to continue on this path. Maybe she should trust her instincts, turn around and never look back.

The heat finally reached her when she approached the last bend before her village. From this far away, the heat caressed her like the warm embrace of a campfire on an autumn evening. A speck of dust landed on her nose. Dust? She frowned, and glancing upward, realized it was ashes falling from the sky. Her eyes grew wide and she frantically tried to wipe the specks of ash away, tried to shake them out of her hair, but she couldn't avoid their relentless descent. Her breaths came in quick and shallow, the heat and the smoke clawing at her being with every gasp. She couldn't blink anymore, her eyes staring at the outlines of the trees in front of her, prickling and burning. She tried to swallow, but her throat was too dry. Her tongue stuck to the roof of her mouth, fat and swollen. Her palms were sweaty, and although everything else on her felt scorching hot, her fingers were ice cold.

She pressed on, her left hand holding her dress so tightly that her fingers were going numb. Her feet were taking her faster and faster, evolving into a trot until, finally, she ran towards the fire. The end of the road came into view, and with it, the inferno where her village should have been. She came to a halt a few meters before the entrance to the village, her legs weak and buckling under her. She fell to the ground, her hands and knees hitting the mud hard. She didn't mind the dirt getting on her clothes anymore; she was shutting out the heat that scorched her eyebrows, and completely forgot about the smell that tugged on every fibre of her being. She barely even noticed the sting on her skin as the leaf-shaped pendant Maya had given her only hours before burned its shape onto her. She looked up, taking quick, shallow breaths, her eyes wide, set on the remains of the first house beyond the path — the one that belonged to her father's friend, Jesper. Only two thick, vertical beams remained, engulfed in smoke and flame.

Her whole existence was in that village, her whole existence *was* that village. And now it was standing in front of her, brighter than the sun could have ever been, and there was nothing she could do about it. Her body stood still for an instant, frozen in the heat surrounding her, and then a deafening scream escaped her, tearing at her throat, as if everything she was, everything she had ever been, and everything she would ever be tried to leave her at once.

Chapter Three

Slowly, over time, the heat and the smoke that surrounded Rena subsided, making it easier for her to breathe again. The flames that had licked their way up the church tower were slowly retreating as they found less and less material to latch onto.

Rena still sat on the ground, the cold of the muddy road finally seeping through her dress and creeping up her legs and back. Her mouth was dry, her throat throbbing from the smoke and screaming. Every time she blinked it felt like a million needles were meticulously stabbing every millimetre of her eyes.

None of this felt real. Not what her skin could feel, or her eyes could see, or her nose could smell. But she couldn't claim it felt like a nightmare either. A nightmare would have ended by now. She would have woken up, drenched in sweat, and her mother would be comforting her. Her mother, who had surely been behind the counter at the bakery when the fire broke out. Who might still be in the bakery, unable to escape without her help.

She pushed herself up, her body shaking with the effort. Her fingers were ice cold, and moving them hurt her joints. She almost slipped and fell back down, but she managed to brace herself on her hands, the shock sending a wave of pain through her body. As she stood up she wrapped her arms around her chest, her beige dress caked in mud and falling heavily around her legs.

She looked out over the village, her breaths coming in shaky and shallow. She turned around to look at the forest around her, her arms drawing tighter. Her surroundings were getting dimmer, the sun low on the horizon. She had been sitting on the ground for so long, waiting for the fire to ease off. A tightness formed in her stomach, her eyes going blurry, thinking that if she had acted quicker, gotten up right away, she might have been able to help someone but that it might now be too late. That she might arrive at her home, her family dead, reaching out for her, waiting for her to save them.

Bile clawed its way up her throat and she vomited acid, her stomach having been empty for a while. She wiped her mouth with the back of her hand and forced herself to stand upright, her gaze ahead to where her home should be. Her eyes were wide open, unblinking, tears quietly streaming down her face, as she pushed ahead and started walking. From the corners of her eyes, she could see what little remained of her village. How the front of Maggie's soap shop still stood upright even though there was only debris behind the windows and she could see the sky through them. How the produce stands in front of the ruins of the food store remained untouched, the vegetables and fruits covered in ash. How Tala's home was nothing more than a smouldering mass.

She followed the faint outline of the streets until she reached the eastern side of the village, her uncle's house in front of her. The roof had caved in, taking with it most of the building. What remained of the white façade had turned black around the door and windows, the green-painted wooden frames still smouldering. Her throat tightened up, making it impossible for her to breath until a long wail escaped from its hold. She folded in on herself, crouching down and putting her head between her knees, her arms wrapping over her.

She couldn't do this, couldn't take this anymore. She didn't want to face her own home in this state. Didn't want to find her family lying underneath all of the rubble. She should have left, just run away and never looked back. Start a new life and live with the belief that, somehow, her family had survived and were living a happy life somewhere.

The call of a crow broke through the silence, answered shortly after by a second crow. Rena slowly looked up, her jaw trembling uncontrollably. Another caw, this time from a different side. She glanced around herself, realising that soon the animals would dare to come closer to the village. Realising what these animals would do to the people when they found them.

She stood and turned away from her uncle's house, walking down the row of her neighbours' collapsed houses until she stood in front of the all too familiar light-yellow façade of her family's home and bakery. The mill stood a few meters behind the house, still mostly intact as it was made of solid stone, only the roof and the blades having crumpled.

As she stepped closer, the pungent smell of burned flesh that she had managed to block out until now became stronger, threatening to make her vomit again, but there was nothing left in her that could escape.

The roof of her house had caved in on the left side, although it seemed mostly unharmed over the bakery. The windows had burst open, black columns running up the exterior wall. Both doors were still closed and barely damaged, as if she could open them and just step into an undamaged building. She reached a shaky hand towards the door to her house but quickly flinched back when she touched the scalding hot metal of the handle. She stopped then, unsure what to do. She tried to simply push the door open with her shoulder but it didn't budge. She looked around herself, trying to find something that could help her, wondering for a second if she should climb through the broken windows.

She walked over to door of the bakery, touching the handle carefully with the tips of her fingers before grasping it and slowly opening the door. A wall of smoke drifted out, making her cough. She pushed the door open wider to let the smoke escape and tried to peer into the room, but the light from outside didn't penetrate very far. She pulled the collar of her dress over her nose and stepped inside. The front of the room seemed mostly intact, but the further she got the more chaos there was. The shelves behind the counter had collapsed, spilling the loaves of bread all over the floor. The glass panes of the counter had exploded, shards mixing with the bread on the ground. She stepped forward towards the door that lead to her house, careful not to step on any shards and have the glass pierce through her canvas shoes. One of the shelves had collapsed in front of the door, although the fire didn't seem to have touched it. With great effort she pulled it aside, just enough to be able to open the door. She wrapped the hem of her dress around her hand and pulled the door open, another wall of smoke hitting her.

She waited a bit for the smoke to calm down, then squeezed herself through the opening. The floor was littered with ash, dust and debris from the roof, a collapsed beam blocking her way to the other door.

She looked up and was able to see the sky, only a few beams remaining above her.

She knew that it wasn't safe to stay inside the house, that something might fall down on her at any moment, but she had to at least try to find her family.

"M-mom?" She croaked out, her throat aching from the effort. "Mom," she called out a second time, louder. Her voice echoed back to her but no one answered.

She stepped over the rubble lying on the floor, almost slipping on the ashes, and made her way to the kitchen at the end of the hallway. The door wasn't closed completely and she was able to push it open. She froze when she saw the outline of a foot lying on the ground. She stopped breathing and just stared at her mother's shoes.

Rena's hand slowly came up to her mouth, her jaw trembling as her breaths came in shakily, faster and faster and faster, her vision going blurry. She had to hold on to the doorframe or she would have collapsed. She pushed the door open further to reveal the rest of her mother's body, lying face down on the ground, buried under two large beams. The fire had barely touched her but like the rest of the house she was covered in soot and ashes.

"Mom," Rena said weakly, knowing full well that she wouldn't get a reply.

She stepped closer until she saw a smaller body buried underneath her mother's arm, his face buried in their mother's chest.

"No no no no no," she repeated under her breath as she tried to approach them.

She stepped onto one of the beams but it croaked and groaned, dust drizzling down from the ceiling. She tried to step over it, to get closer to her mother and brother, but no matter how she approached the beam, it threatened to shift and bring the rest of the roof down with it.

A large sob escaped her throat and suddenly she couldn't stop herself from wailing, a long cry escaping her throat. She cried until her lungs burnt and her throat ached and no sound escaped her mouth anymore. She could taste the ashes on her tongue, could feel them clinging to the inside of her nose.

Somewhere in the back of the house something collapsed, the deafening *thud* accompanied by a wave of heat and dust. When the smoke had settled again she glanced around, panic suddenly overtaking her that she might end up buried in the house with her family. She straightened and turned around, every muscle in her body aching. She wrapped her arms tightly around her as she walked away from the lifeless bodies of her mother and brother.

She had thought she would be strong enough. That she would be able to bury them, to give them the dignity they deserved after death, but she couldn't do it. Her heart ached too much. Never in her life had she felt this much and this little at the same time. Like her entire being was composed of grief that there was no space left for anything else. She squeezed her way through the door again, the glass on the floor of the bakery cutting through her shoes.

She turned left as she exited the bakery, her gaze fixed on the ground, unwilling to look up at the destruction that surrounded her. Something caught her eye, a glint on the ground to her right. She paused and frowned as her eyes scanned the area until they landed on something metallic. She stepped closer and reached down to pick it up. It was a dull, golden ring, its socket empty from the gemstone it once held. Her eyes grew wide as she recognised it. Her grandmother's ring, the one Maya had said she would keep to herself.

Rena looked up, her hand automatically reaching towards her new pendant as she frantically glanced around at anything that could indicate that Maya was still around. How could the ring have ended up here, on the street outside her house? Had Maya dropped it? Had someone tried to steal it?

She noticed that what looked like drag marks lead away from her and only a few metres up ahead lay the green gemstone. Rena rushed towards it, picking it up and holding it tightly in her fist next to the ring. She followed the drag marks towards the centre of town before they vanished. She looked around desperately, trying to find where they picked up again, but the ground was so stirred up and covered in ashes that she couldn't find them anywhere.

The church tower suddenly collapsed in on itself, sending a cloud of ashes into the sky with a loud, dull crash. A wave of heat hit Rena a heartbeat later, pain radiating over her skin. She closed her eyes tightly and turned her face away, her hand coming up to cup her nose so she wouldn't breathe in the ashes. She drew her face towards her lap, waiting for the blast to wash over her.

After a moment, she carefully opened one eye, and peaked out at the ruins in front of her. She shot up when she saw a hand poking out of the ruins of the church. She hurried closer, careful to avoid the rubble of the tower that had spread over the streets. Small pieces of paper floated through the air and covered the ground — some empty, some with printed letters, and some with the shaky script of children's handwriting.

She kept her eyes fixed on the hand, determined to at least help whoever was stuck beneath the church. As she approached, her whole body started to shake and go stiff at the same time. She stopped in front of it, looking down at the red flesh the fire had exposed, flecks of ashes covering the open wounds. Whoever the hand belonged to was stuck underneath a thick wooden beam, their body hidden underneath the rubble.

"Don't worry, I'm here to help," she told the hand in a barely audible voice. "Everything's going to be all right. I'll get you out of here and then we can look for help together."

The words failed to reassure even herself as she crouched down and reached a hand out, forcing it to advance and touch the wooden beam that trapped the body. Her hand was shaking so badly that it took her a while before her fingers made contact with the wood. Its surface was still warm. She breathed in and the stench of burnt flesh flooded her senses, forcing her to turn around and gag. She started sobbing silently, her hand covering her mouth, the other clenching down on the ground, her fingers digging through the layers of ash and debris and gravel.

"I'm sorry," she muttered over and over as she got up.

Slowly, stiffly, she reached down, holding her breath while both her hands came to grip the edge of the beam. She tried to lift it, but her body hurt and her muscles were too tense and the beam didn't even creak with her effort. She stood up and turned away to breathe in, before turning back around and trying again, putting all of her remaining force into the attempt. This time she managed to lift the beam slightly, not enough for anyone to be able to crawl out, but enough that the other beams lying on top shifted, and the one she was holding onto slid back, making her lose her footing and fall on it. She tried to catch herself and push herself back up but her shoe slipped on the layer of ash and she tripped, bumping her elbow on a sharp rock.

The wooden beam had fallen onto the arm again, and because of its displaced location the arm was now sticking up towards the sky, the edge of the beam burying into the soft flesh of the forearm, cutting a wide gash into it.

"Oh stars, I'm so sorry," Rena muttered, scrambling back towards the beam, pushing against it to try to move it backwards. But her effort caused the beam to further open the wound, revealing bone, and trickles of blood fell to the ground.

"No, no, no," Rena murmured, her hands reaching towards the wound, but never quite touching it, unsure what she should do. "I'm so sorry, I'm so sorry," she repeated over and over as she scrambled upright and backed away, her breath coming in quick and ragged.

Her foot stepped on something hard and Rena stopped, glancing down before she could tell herself it might not be a good idea. Her muddy shoe covered whatever it was, so she carefully stepped back, revealing what looked like a wooden figurine — a bird of some sort — the body long and pointed with the wings spread out to its side, almost like a cross. She looked out over the ruins around her, noticing that similar figurines were sticking out of the mud as if they had deliberately been placed in a circle around the old church. Her eyes grew wide in horror at what this could mean. That someone had arranged them here, willingly, while the fire was raging. That that person might be responsible for setting the fire in the first place.

She shook her head violently, reaching down to pick up the figurine, before backing away from the church, turning around, and running towards the road that would lead her to the nearest town, Halvint. There was no point in thinking such horrible thoughts. This must just have been a terrible accident. An unintended fire that spread from house to house. Luck had simply abandoned them. Once she reached Halvint she was sure to meet someone else who had escaped the fire, maybe even someone from her family. Maya might have escaped, simply dropping the ring while running away.

She stumbled over the road as the sun hung low on the horizon, barely visible above the tree tops. Her eyes had glazed over as she stared out into the endlessly repeating road in front of her. She had wrapped her arms tightly around herself, her feet aching from the gashes she had received in the bakery and the long distances she had had to walk. She felt empty inside, like her being had left her and only her body remained on this wretched road.

She heard something approaching, something that sounded like a badly made machine, with a lot of clanking and humming and buzzing. She looked at the end of the road in confusion and saw a light approach, slowly, and as her eyes adjusted, she could make out the outline of a caravan, but where there should have been horses there was nothing. A chimney jutted out of the wagon's rear, smoke coming out of it in thick clouds. In the front, in the driver seat, sat a person, with an unruly white beard and dishevelled hair.

Rena stopped in the middle of the road, unsure what to do with this approaching contraption; afraid of this stranger but relieved that she wasn't alone anymore.

"Oh, hello there," the man called out to her in surprise before she could make a decision, and the wagon slowly came to a halt with a loud screech.

Chapter Four

Rena stood only a few metres from the strange caravan that rumbled and rattled and sputtered out clouds of smoke. The driver stared at her, first with a friendly smile, then, slowly, his eyebrows drew together in concern.

"Are you all right?" he asked, pushing down a lever and the machine finally fell silent.

He was close enough for her to finally get a good look at him – a lantern at the top of the caravan illuminating him from above. He had a gentle, round face with wrinkles weaving across his pale skin, and a long, bushy white beard with matching eyebrows. Round, golden goggles above his forehead kept his wild hair in check. His clothes were made of thick leather, like traveller's clothes, but unlike a regular traveller, his were clean, undamaged and adorned with brightly shining golden buttons.

His caravan was even stranger. It looked like he had taken one of the ornate horse-drawn carriages you only saw in big cities and had added a chimney to it. It was made of dark wood and its side had been painted green with ornate, bronzen swirls. Rena had never seen anything like it, at least the part where it seemed to operate without horses. She'd heard of all the marvels people were creating in the big cities — that they now had tools and gadgets that worked without muscle power and that they were building a giant vehicle that worked through steam and moved on tracks. She had been doubtful about most of these stories however – especially when people started talking about how these machines were alive – but she couldn't ignore the reality that stood before her.

The man got up and stepped down the few steps to his left. He headed towards Rena, but stopped when she flinched, unsure about this stranger that was so different than anyone she had ever met. She had been raised to always be polite to people, even when they seemed different to you, but her mind was clouded from the exhaustion and her whole body was screaming for her to be careful, no matter how unlikely it was that this man had anything to do with the fire.

"Are you all right?" the man repeated. "My name is Rodrick. You look cold. Let me go get you a blanket and some hot tea." He turned around and hurried towards the back of the caravan. "Or maybe some soup, if you'd prefer."

From the footrest of the driver's seat a dog emerged and jumped down onto the road. It was reddish-brown with long, thin, black legs and a bushy tail that ended in white fur. The tip of its long snout was black and it had big, arching ears with white fur inside — although one of its ears had been bitten off. Rena took another step back when she saw the dog — it looked so different from the ones she had seen in her village — too long and too thin. It slowly crept towards Rena, head bowed as it looked at her. It was tall enough to come up to her hips and she was certain that if it wanted to, it could easily push her to the ground.

But then its head pricked up and its tail started wagging, and Rena recognised those signs. She slowly knelt down, keeping her eyes on the dog, and held her hand out towards it. The dog lifted its head higher and she could see its nostrils working furiously. It approached her carefully until it was close enough to stretch its head and sniff her hand.

"Hi there," Rena murmured.

The dog carefully pushed its nose against her fingertips. Rena obliged and stretched herself closer to run her hand over the dog's head and pet it behind its ear. The dog seemed all too happy with this development and nuzzled its head into her hand. The heat from its body tingled against her ice-cold fingers and at the same time the knot that was lodged tightly between her ribs slowly started to unfurl.

"I've seen you've met Vincent," the man said as he came back towards them, and Rena instinctively pulled her hand away from the dog, scared she had done something wrong. The dog, however, did not agree with her decision, and pushed its head back into her hand.

"He's lovely, isn't he?" The man continued, holding out a thick, dark, woollen blanket which Rena gladly accepted. "When I left on my little journey I thought to myself, "Rodrick, you shouldn't be out on the road all by yourself, it's dangerous out there, get yourself a dog that can protect you," and look what I ended up with." He paused and chuckled. "But I am quite happy with him, nonetheless. He brings me a lot of comfort. It makes missing home a bit more bearable."

She wrapped the blanket tighter around her shoulders. The dog came closer, sniffing at the blanket, and poking her legs with his nose until Rena relented and started petting him again.

"Let me get you that soup," Rodrick muttered and turned around.

A moment later, Rodrick came back with two wooden chairs and two mugs. The chairs looked completely out of place on the open road, with their ornate carvings and mother-of-pearl details. They looked like they belonged in a royal palace. Their presence on this mud road leading from one small town to another, in one of the most rural corners of Vellashta — which was in its part one of the most rural provinces of the kingdom — felt like a transgression in and of itself.

"Here you go," Rodrick said as he put the chairs down before handing her one of the mugs.

She got up, scratching the dog's chin one last time before sitting down on one of the chairs, delicately, so as not to break it. Instantly, her body sagged, her back hitting the back of the chair, as if it had just been waiting to stop. She reached a hand out to take the mug of soup but she was trembling so much and her arm was so weak that she couldn't clasp it. Instead, tears filled her eyes again and a loud sob escaped her throat. Her hand shot up to cover her mouth but she couldn't stop the wailing. Her lungs seized up again, making it almost impossible for her to breath. The exhaustion had distracted her enough to make her mind go blank, but now it all rushed back to her – the smell and the heat and the hand trapped under the church and her mother and brother's lifeless bodies in their demolished kitchen.

"Oh, no, no, no, no, no," Rodrick muttered, his hands coming up towards her but stopping before he actually touched her. "Did something happen? Please don't cry, I can help you. We can fix this. Did you get lost? Did someone hurt you?"

He looked her over, searching for injuries.

Rena swallowed and shook her head. She opened her mouth but nothing came out, her breath coming in ragged bursts.

"Take your time," Rodrick told her.

She closed her eyes and breathed in deeply, trying to stop her tears.

"I'm from Oceansthrow," she managed to gasp out. "And it's gone. The whole town is gone. My whole family—"

Her throat seized up again and she bent forward, hiding her face in her lap.

"Oh, my child," Rodrick said quietly, sorrow drenching his throat. "I saw smoke in the distance earlier, does it have anything to do with that?"

She nodded in response, shutting her eyes tightly to make the tears stop.

"We should get you to safety, and then we can get help," Rodrick continued. "Did you see anyone else escape? Maybe they went to Halvint or Mattak."

"Everyone's dead," Rena moaned, gasping for breath. "There's no one left. The fire took everything. It's all just ashes now, and I don't know what happened. I'm all alone and I don't even understand why."

Her lips trembled so she pressed them together and bit down, hard.

"I am so very sorry," Rodrick repeated. "I wish there was anything I could tell you that would make it easier for you. Life can be cruel sometimes, and we must carry that burden alone. But if there is anything you need or want, you can tell me and I will try with all of my power to help you."

She took a few deep, shaky breaths, trying to calm herself enough to continue talking.

"I couldn't help them," she murmured. "I wanted to see if I could find anyone who was still alive, or at least bury the people I could find, because I didn't want wild animals to find them, but I'm not strong enough. I couldn't get my family out of the rubble and I could help the person trapped under the church. I just made it all worse."

Another wail escaped her lips, and she brought her hand up to muffle it.

"My child, fear not, they will find peace in their slumber, but you cannot do this by yourself," Rodrick said, his hand coming to rest gently on Rena's back. "Even for just the two of us the task is too big, it would take us a whole day to bury everyone, and I don't think it is safe to go back to your village during the night. The buildings might be unstable. We need to get you to safety first and make sure you can rest. Our best option would be to go to Halvint, ask for help, and come back in the morning. The situation might not be as dire as you think it is."

Rena nodded faintly. She told herself that he was right, that going back to Oceansthrow right away wouldn't be a good idea, even if it left a sour taste in her mouth that she would be able to rest in safety while her town still lay in embers. But maybe it wasn't the entire town. Maybe parts of it survived and she simply hadn't seen it. Maybe someone else did escape and she would meet them in Halvint. It might even be Maya.

She resolved herself and took in a deep breath. She shook her head slightly to clear her head, then looked up at Rodrick.

"Do you think someone did this?" Rena asked, burying her hands into the fabric of her dress. "An entire village, destroyed by fire. That doesn't seem right to me. If it would have occurred naturally, someone would have noticed and warned everyone else, right? And they would have managed to save at least some of the buildings. And it isn't even the dry season yet, fire shouldn't be spreading this quickly."

"Well," he started, then cleared his throat and shifted in his chair. "I cannot say anything for certain until I have seen the village myself. There is always the possibility of accidental fires spreading from one building to the next, but, you're right, the chance of it taking over the entire village is rather low. However," he took a break and sighed, "I have heard of similar events before."

Rena's eyes shot up to him.

"Similar events?"

Rodrick frowned at the ground, before waving her off and standing up.

"You shouldn't preoccupy yourself with such dark theories right now." He picked up the mug of soup and handed it to her, smiling warmly. "How about you eat a little and then we head over to Halvint? You deserve some rest. Hopefully we'll run into more people from your village there. You might have just missed each other while escaping the fire."

She accepted the mug but didn't drink from it.

"Were the other fires accidents? O-or was someone responsible for them?"

He shot her an apologetic smile, but waited before answering, clearly evaluating how much he should tell her.

"There are some indications that they weren't accidental."

She stared at him for a moment, acid creeping up the back of her throat again. It became difficult for her to breath, imagining what kind of person would be willing to cause such a tragedy.

"Who would do something like that?" she rasped, her eyes drifting unfocused to the ground.

Rodrick shook his head and looked down at the dog.

"I cannot tell you more. I do not want to sell you false beliefs. As I've said, we cannot be certain someone was responsible for this before we actually investigated the origin of the fire. And even then, it would be difficult to say if this tragedy is actually linked to the other events I mentioned. It's better if we simply assumed it was a tragic accident until proven otherwise. It would be better for your peace of mind."

She nodded slowly and looked down and the mug in her hands, even though she couldn't bring herself to believe him. The thought of someone being responsible for this tragedy terrified her, but at least it would explain the situation. At least there would be someone to find and interrogate about it. It wouldn't simply mean that the entire town's luck had turned sour.

She took a sip of the warm soup – a creamy, white liquid made of potatoes and leek.

"If someone's responsible for the fire, we need to notify the guards," she said quietly between sips.

"Yes, my child, we can do all of that once we've reached Halvint," Rodrick answered calmly. "Do you have family nearby? Someone you can stay with afterwards?"

"I have an aunt in Lomen, west of here, but she's sick and I don't want to be a burden," Rena replied, her finger stroking over a notch in the rim of the mug.

"I am sure your aunt wouldn't see you as a burden," Rodrick answered with a smile. "I can accompany you until you have reached her house, and even if you decide that you don't want to stay there, I wouldn't mind having another companion on my travels."

Rena nodded and took another sip. She had no intentions of going to her aunt's until she had figured out what had happened to her village. Whether with Rodrick or alone, she would find a way to uncover this mystery and find her sister.

Chapter Five

As they steered the caravan around to head to Halvint, Rena sat on the bench next to Rodrick, with Vincent laying on the floor between their feet. Her butt started hurting after only ten minutes as the entire wagon trembled and shook. And then there was the noise. Not just the sound of whatever machinery Rodrick had added to his caravan to get it to move on its own, but the clanking and banging of everything he kept inside of it. She couldn't imagine why he had created this monstrosity. He had somehow made it more uncomfortable, slower and louder than a regular horse-drawn carriage.

They arrived in Halvint when the sun had set and the moon was illuminating their way. Halvint was slightly bigger than her hometown, which just meant it had an actual inn, and visitors had somewhere comfortable to stay that wasn't a refurbished church tower. The town was quiet, the streets empty, as if no one had noticed yet what had happened to their neighbouring town.

The calm didn't bode well. If someone else from Oceansthrow had arrived before her, the town should be in uproar. They should have run into someone travelling back to Oceansthrow on their way to Halvint. But the fact the town seemed quiet and serene told Rena that she truly had to be the only survivor, and that realisation cramped itself tightly around her heart.

"What are we going to do?" Rena whispered, unsure if Rodrick could hear her above the sound of his machine. Her blood was running cold again. She clutched the ends of the blanket, still draped around her shoulders, her knuckles turning white.

"First of all, we're getting you a place to rest and a warm bed," Rodrick told her. "Don't worry about anything else, I will take care of it. I will find people who can ride back to your town and assess the situation, but that should be none of your concern. At least not until tomorrow."

He drove them right to the inn, parking his caravan between two others. Even its size looked so out of place, towering over the two old, battered carts besides it. Rodrick climbed down and came to the other side of the wagon, holding a hand up to help Rena down, which she gladly accepted.

The inn was warm and lively when they pushed through the door. Rodrick strode right up to the counter at the opposite side to the entrance where the innkeeper stood. Rena looked over the jovial faces sitting at tables around her and a weird feeling came over her, as if she wasn't really there at the moment. Like she could see them, but they couldn't see her. Slowly, she advanced to where Rodrick stood, looking from one face to the next, trying to recognise anyone in the crowd.

"Good evening, sir," Rodrick said with a wide smile at the innkeeper over the noise of the crowd.

"You're back already?" the innkeeper asked, frowning at Rodrick.

"Yes, an unforeseeable occurrence changed my plans. I would like to request your finest room for my companion here." With this, he gestured at Rena who finally looked up at the innkeeper, their eyes meeting.

The innkeeper's frown deepened, putting the mug he had been cleaning on the counter. He was a stout man, with dark brown skin, a short-cropped, black beard, and tired eyes.

"You all right?" he asked, glancing at her filthy clothes.

She didn't react at first, the words not wanting to register correctly in her mind. When she had finally processed what he had asked she nodded once, weakly, almost as if it was meant as a question. The innkeeper's eyes darted back and forth between her and Rodrick.

"There has been an incident," Rodrick murmured, leaning closer so the innkeeper could hear him.

The man stared at him with apprehension and only leaned forward when Rodrick waved him closer.

"I don't want to alarm everyone and cause panic," Rodrick continued, Rena having to step closer to understand what he was saying – the blood rushing in her ears making it difficult to hear anything. "My young friend here is from Oceansthrow. I found her distressed wandering alone on the road between both towns. I'm sad to report that there has been a terrible tragedy. We had hoped to find someone else from town here, but I suppose there would be more of an ongoing commotion if another survivor had arrived before us. You see, there was a fire in Oceansthrow. A rather terrible one."

"What do you mean?" The innkeeper leaned in closer, bracing his elbows against the counter.

"According to my friend, the fire ravaged through the entire town. She thinks she might be the only who survived."

"Like those other fires you're looking into?"

"Potentially," Rodrick said with some hesitation.

Rena momentarily snapped out of her haze and looked at Rodrick in confusion. He had mentioned having heard of these other fires, he hadn't mentioned investigating them however.

"I want to discuss how to proceed with the correct authorities here," Rodrick continued, not having noticed Rena's gaze, "but I thought the first priority was to get my companion to a place where she could rest."

"What happened?" the innkeeper asked, his attention switching to Rena.

"I don't know," Rena croaked out. "I was out gathering herbs in the forest and when I came home everything was in flames. D-did you happen to see someone else from Oceansthrow? Did anyone arrive before me?"

The innkeeper stared at her and shook his head, his mouth slightly open in reflection, his tongue poking at his lower lip. Rena's heart sank to her stomach and she diverted her eyes from the man.

"I wanted to discuss with your guards and the people of your village what should be done, because I myself have not seen the damage yet, and I think my friend is too shocked to deliver a full report on the situation."

The innkeeper leaned back before shouting, "Devon!"

Half the heads in the room turned to look at them, and even though Rena could only see them from the corner of her eyes, she immediately tensed up, a cold shudder running down her spine.

"What?" A man replied from a round table to their left, where a game of cards was in full swing. Rena turned her head slightly to the side to glance at the man. He was short and burly, with a thick, copper beard and a crooked scar along his right temple.

"Come here," the innkeeper shouted, waving the man over.

The man looked down at his cards then back up again.

"Why?" he shouted back.

"Just come here, you lazy bastard."

The man huffed, and pushed his chair back with force, before carefully putting his cards face-down on the table.

"Nobody touch these!" he told his companions while pointing at the cards, before walking over to where Rodrick and Rena were standing.

He nodded as a greeting before addressing the innkeeper.

"What do you want?"

The innkeeper leaned forward.

"Oceansthrow burned down," he whispered.

"What?" Devon replied, apparently not having understood this situation required hushed voices.

"Shut it," the innkeeper hissed and leaned even closer. "We need to figure out what to do before proclaiming what happened to the whole room. You need to send someone over to check it out. I'll get some people together and see what can be done in the morning."

Devon frowned at him before shifting his gaze over to Rodrick and Rena and looking them over, stopping to inspect Rena's muddy and ash-covered clothes, wrinkling his nose at the smell that still clung to her.

"Did you come from there?" he asked with a nod in Rena's direction.

Rena wrapped her arms tighter around herself and nodded. She suddenly felt very exposed, as if the world had shifted to stare her down, and she disliked this feeling even more than the one she had felt before.

"What happened?" Devon asked the both of them.

"They don't know," the innkeeper replied for them. "Go fetch your nephew and ride out to the town. You'll know best what to look for."

Devon nodded reluctantly before answering.

"Fine."

He knocked on the counter twice before turning away and striding out of the building. The people he had previously been playing cards with turned to the innkeeper in confusion – one of them daring to peek at Devon's cards – but the innkeeper just waved them off.

He leaned down to grab something from under the counter before placing a long key with a wooden pendant attached to it in front of Rena.

"I'm putting you in room 4," he said and slid the key to Rena. "It's the best room we have. I'll tell my wife to draw you a bath and bring you some new clothes, she'll come and get you when the bath is ready. Just go down that corridor and you'll find it, the number's written on the door."

He pointed to a swinging door to their left which led to a corridor behind the counter. Rena picked up the key with ice cold fingers and mouthed a quick "thank you."

A few minutes later Rena was set up in her room, waiting for the innkeeper's wife to tell her the bath was ready. Rodrick had brought Vincent to her room and then left again to join the discussion about how to proceed. The dog was lying curled up in front of the lit fireplace, happily napping. Rena eyed the fire warily, her whole body tensing up each time the wood crackled and popped.

The room was small, but hers was the only bed in it. It was a large, soft bed, although the linens were coarse from usage. A small, copper wash basin stood in the corner with enough water that Rena could at least wash the dirt off her face and hands. The innkeeper had hung a singular painting above the bed, a landscape of the ocean sketched on a wooden board with thick paint.

The silence of the room hung heavy around her. She could only hear the noise of the inn if she really concentrated on it, like she was lying beneath a pile of blankets, and most of the time the fire still drowned it out. Suddenly, she regretted having chastised her siblings for being loud and raucous all the time, for having been playful and happy and alive. Tears welled up in her eyes, wishing that she could hear their screams just once more. That she could hear them laughing and arguing and prattle on about the most meaningless things. Her chest ached, and she could feel the pain spread across her already sore body.

Her hands clutched onto her dress, and she shut her eyes and lips tight, desperately trying not to cry again, but it didn't work. The tears started rolling down her face and she gasped before succumbing to her sobs. She wanted to go home, and sleep in her own bed, and wake up in the morning to the smell of freshly baked bread, and go to the kitchen to make breakfast for everyone. She wanted to meet up with

Tala and listen to her ramble on about all the rumours she'd heard about the royal court, and fantasize about what the citadel in Mak-Hemma looked like. She wanted to sit down with her brothers and teach them how to read, and she wanted to stay up late with Maya without their parents noticing, and she wanted to go to her uncle's house to eat his delicious honey cake — but none of it would ever happen again.

She struggled to breathe, heavy tears falling to her lap and staining her dress. She tried to force herself to take deep breaths so she wouldn't succumb to her hiccups, but it barely worked. She leaned down and pressed her forehead against her knees, bunching the fabric of her dress around her face, not caring about the mud and dirt and ashes still covering it, and screamed into it. Screamed until her throat hurt and there was no air left in her lungs. She stayed like that for a moment, breathing in the smell of the fire that still lingered on her dress, the images from that afternoon playing on repeat in her mind. The collapsing church tower, her uncle's destroyed house, Maya's ring in the mud, the arm trapped underneath the church, her family's lifeless bodies.

Something bumped against her leg and she shot upright in surprise, but it was only Vincent. He glanced up at her, nudging her leg with his snout again. Rena stared at him for a moment, her mouth hanging open, blinking rapidly. She slowly lifted her right hand and placed it on the dog, his fur pleasantly warm from the fire he had been napping next to. Rena forced herself to smile at him and took his head in both her shaky hands, petting the side of his snout with her thumbs. She leaned forward and planted a soft kiss to his forehead.

"Thank you," she murmured into his fur.

As she sat back up, something shifted against her stomach. She patted around on the folds of her dress to see what it could be, then instantly remembered the figurine she had found near the church and stowed away in the pocket of her dress. She fished it out and held it in both hands, running her thumbs over it. It didn't look like much — crude shapes that vaguely resembled a bird with outstretched wings. The surface was smooth and the wood had been burned to give it a polished black colour. Lines had been carved into its front, from one tip of the wing to the other. They looked like they meant something — straight lines connected by triangles — but it wasn't in a script she had ever seen.

The door to the room opened and Rena jerked up, but it was only Rodrick coming in with two small rolls of dark bread in one hand, and a bone in the other.

"Is everything all right?" he asked when his eyes landed on Rena, his eyebrows knitting together in concern.

Rena nodded, pressing her lips shut tightly and wiping the tears away from her cheeks.

"I'm just not used to being alone like this," she murmured, looking back down at the figurine in her lap where her dress was now covered in wet spots.

"Oh, child," Rodrick muttered, closing the door with his elbow before coming over to her.

He put the bread rolls on the nightstand before sitting next to Rena. They sat in silence for a while, only Vincent stirring to sniff the bone in Rodrick's hand. The dog gently nibbled at the bone until Rodrick let go of it.

"You know," Rena murmured, turning the figurine in her hands. "If my mother hadn't forgotten to get rosemary, I would have been in school today. And I was supposed to take my sister to the forest with me, but she was busy doing something else, so I didn't insist."

She closed her eyes tightly and took a few long, shaky breaths so she wouldn't unravel again.

"You cannot start thinking like this," Rodrick told her quietly. "Do not blame yourself for any of their deaths. There is nothing we can change about how life will play out. You couldn't have known what would happen today, so how could you ever blame yourself for it? Concentrate on the fact that you are alive and that there is someone left to remember them."

Rena nodded and blinked her eyes open, looking down at the figurine in her hands.

"You know," Rodrick continued, shifting next to her. "I had a son once. He was a brilliant young man, full of amazing ideas, but he was taken from me much too soon. For years I blamed myself, trying to figure out what I could have changed, how I could have made sure no harm would come to him. But the only thing you gain from thoughts like these are loneliness and heartache."

"I'm so sorry," Rena said, looking up at him, but he just waved her off.

"I am an old man now, there is no use in remembering all of the instances where I wishes I had acted differently. But I know that these feelings can eat you alive and stop you from living. I just want you to keep this in mind, that you did nothing wrong and that blaming yourself for this tragedy isn't what your family would have wanted."

Rena sighed heavily and looked out over the room. She knew he was right, but knowing it was different than feeling it. She told herself that she just needed time, that of course it still felt too raw and too painful when she hadn't even had the opportunity to rest. That tomorrow or in a week or in a month she wouldn't feel this broken anymore.

"What if not all of them are dead?" Rena said, barely audible, her mind inescapably coming back to the ring in the mud over and over again.

"Like I said, there is always the possibility that someone else escaped. Maybe tomorrow we will hear of someone having escaped to Mattak."

"I think my sister might still be alive."

From the corner of her eyes she could see Rodrick's eyebrows furling and unfurling, as if he was trying to comprehend what she had said.

"That would be wonderful, but why specifically your sister?" he finally asked.

Rena straightened and took a deep breath.

"I found her ring on the ground outside our house. She didn't go to the forest with me because she was cleaning my grandmother's old jewellery, and she showed me one specific ring, one with a green gem in it, and I stumbled upon in it the mud. The gem had been knocked out of its socket, but I'm sure it is the same ring."

She put the bird figurine on the bed between her and Rodrick and rummaged around in her dress pocket until she found the ring and the loose gem. She held them in both hands and looked down at them.

"I know it is the same ring," she continued while pressing the gem back into its socket, until it snapped into place. "I just don't understand what it was doing outside our house."

"Oh, child," Rodrick sighed. "It might have just been tossed outside during the commotion. I don't think you should interpret too much into this discovery."

"I know, but what if Maya lost it when she ran away? O-or what if whoever is responsible for the fire kidnapped her? I think I saw some drag marks on the ground next to the ring. They might have taken her with them."

"No, no, no," Rodrick muttered, turning towards her to take her hands in his. "We can't know something like this for certain. We don't know what happened. The fire still might have been a tragic accident. We just don't have enough evidence to know one way or the other."

"I don't think it was an accident. I found these strange figurines near the church." She slid one hand out of his grasp and picked up the bird figurine.

"What's that?" Rodrick asked, frowning down at it.

"I'm not sure. They were planted in a wide circle around the church. Someone must have placed them there during the fire."

"May I see it?" Rodrick asked, releasing her other hand.

Rena placed the figurine in his hands. He held it up to the light then held it close to his face.

"Fascinating," Rodrick muttered.

"What is it?"

"Did you, perchance, grow up religious?" Rodrick asked her.

"Not particularly," Rena replied, not sure what the old faiths had to do with any of this. "We didn't dismantle our church like other places did, but we also didn't exactly use it for its intended purpose. Why? Does it have something to do with the old gods?"

"It bears resemblance to artefacts that have been found in old monasteries and such. Well, at least like a crude imitation of one. Like someone could only remember the basic shape of it, or was really bad at carving," he chuckled and handed the figurine back to Rena.

"You've said you've been investigating the other villages that were destroyed by fire, right? Did you find anything similar there?"

"The villages I visited had been destroyed years, if not decades ago. There was nothing left of them, I'm afraid. And I also didn't hear of any stories or rumours of anyone else finding such relics after the fires, but in general it is difficult to find any information about these tragedies."

"And the writing?" Rena asked, letting her thumb run over the carvings.

"I'm not sure. I've seen the script before, I think it resembles some old writing used in this part of the world ages ago, but I'm really not an expert in languages. I do know someone who is, but they live up in the very north. I've been meaning to visit them for a while now, but it would take us over a week to reach them."

Rena was silent for a while, turning the crude figurine around in her hands, feeling the coarse smoothness of the burned wood under her fingers.

"Why do you think it was there?" she asked, placing the figurine on the nightstand next to her.

She undid the clasp of her necklace, then slid the ring onto the chain so it could sit next to the leaf-shaped pendant.

"Who knows," Rodrick said and got up, picking up the bread rolls and handing one to Rena. "It seems strange that they had been deliberately placed in a circle around the church, but it could be as easy as someone from your village still believing in the old faiths and trying to communicate with their god during the most frightful time of their life. But we can talk about it more in the morning. For now, it would do you good to eat something and take a bath before going to sleep."

"I just don't get why this happened," Rena muttered, glancing up at Rodrick and taking the bread roll he was handing her.

Chapter Six

Rena jolted awake, drenched in sweat, her heartbeat hammering in her head. She didn't recognise the room she was in, kept looking around to find the second bed in which Maya should have been sleeping. But it wasn't there. And the wash basin was in the wrong corner. And there shouldn't have been a fire place or a painting above her bed.

Slowly the memories of the previous day flooded her mind and the loneliness crept back into her bones, spreading across all of her being until it was all she could feel. She pulled her knees closer, bending over to burry her face in the blanket and screamed until her lungs were empty and her throat ached.

Once she had quieted down again, it felt like the room was caving in on her, silence pressing down to the point where she couldn't breathe, and she knew she had to get out of this room as quickly as possible.

She threw the blanket off and slung her legs over the bed in one fluid motion. She put on the new dress she had been given – similar to hers but with a red vest instead of a green one – and in a few quick steps she was out of the room and down the hallway.

A SEARING FAITH

She slowed before entering the inn's tavern, but she couldn't hear any sounds coming from it so she picked up her pace again — her stomach tightening at the thought of having been abandoned.

As she entered the room, her vision went blurry at the sight of the empty tables, and she had to blink multiple times to recognise that she wasn't actually alone. At the opposite side of the room, near the fireplace, sat Rodrick, hunched over a journal, too engrossed to notice her. At his feet, beneath the table, Vincent was curled up, seemingly asleep.

She noticed two other people sitting at the counter — one younger guy with a bowl of food in front of him, and an older woman writing a letter. She walked past them, her eyes fixated on the floor in front of her, her heartbeat hammering in her chest.

"Hi," she breathed as she walked up to Rodrick, hearing her own voice muffled by the blood rushing through her ears.

Rodrick jerked up, looked at her with wide eyes, then relaxed and smiled.

"Good morning. Sit down."

He gestured to the chair opposite, the one Rena was standing next to.

"How are you feeling?" he asked.

Rena didn't answer right away, sitting and brushing her dress down before looking back up at him, forcing at least a small, trembling smile to her lips.

"I'm all right," she finally said, her voice thin, and she knew that it must have been plainly visible that it was a lie.

"It is perfectly normal to not feel well after such events," he told her, his smile turning softer and more apologetic. "Please don't think that you have to force your feelings down for the sake of others."

She nodded and looked down, trying desperately not to break this early in the day.

"Do you want anything to eat? Something to drink?" Rodrick asked, not waiting for her answer before getting up. "I'll go ask Darian what he could make us, he's in the kitchen, I'll be back in a second."

Before Rena even had time to process everything he had said, he was already gone. She watched him go around the counter and disappear behind a door, and thought to herself that she wasn't actually all that hungry.

Her gaze drifted back to the table – her eyes itching with pain every time she blinked – and landed on Rodrick's journal. It was still laying open. The pages were filled with tight handwriting, and even smaller letters in the margins around the initial block of text. The inks used didn't all have the same shade, giving the impression the notes hadn't all been written at the same time. She couldn't make out any words, since the journal was upside down from her vantage point, but in the margins of the left page she spied symbols drawn in green ink. She quickly glanced over at the door, ensuring Rodrick wasn't on his way back, and leaned closer to the journal, craning her neck to better see the symbols. On one side were five intricate circles with flower patterns in the middle, similar to ones she had seen carved into older stone buildings. On the other side were simpler motifs – different triangles and rectangles that were linked together. Her eyes drifted over the rest of the page, and only then did she notice that the text wasn't written in a language she knew.

At the bottom of the page, her eyes fell on a different script, something that looked similar to the carvings from her figurine. Before she could lean closer to have a proper look, the door to the kitchen opened and she jerked back, turning her head to glance away — as if she had just been admiring the room's decor and nothing else.

"Here we go," Rodrick muttered, as he placed two wooden bowls on the table between them. The bowls were filled with what people often had for breakfast in Vellashta — a mix made of eggs, spelt flour, milk, and whichever herbs grew around town. Rena pulled the bowl closer and took the spoon Rodrick offered.

"Did you hear anything new about the village?" Rena asked between bites.

Rodrick sat down and closed his journal, pulling it aside so he had enough space to eat.

"Not much. Devon came back during the night but sadly not with any good news. He said with the darkness of the night and the still smoldering buildings they didn't find much and didn't dare enter any buildings, but that sadly also means that they didn't find any survivors. He already left again this morning with a larger group of people. Hopefully they will at least we able to bury the deceased. Apparently, he also met some travellers from Mattak who had seen the smoke from far away. I wish I could tell you they had brought news of other survivors with them, but sadly they didn't."

Rena sighed heavily and put her spoon down, having lost the little appetite she had had.

"You mentioned yesterday that this wasn't the first time you heard of an entire village burning down like this," Rena asked.

"I'm afraid not," Rodrick said ruefully. "I've been wandering the kingdom these last few years, observing how people lived in each province and recording any interesting stories I came across. I've heard of a lot of catastrophes and tragic accidents that caused the death of a lot of people, and I've heard of a multitude of fires that destroyed parts of towns or cities. Especially in bigger cities when the buildings are close to each other, a fire can spread very easily. But it is rare that the entirety of a town is destroyed through such means, or that none of the inhabitants managed to escape. Over the years, however, I've heard of a few of these destructive fires. A town called Miller's Knee was destroyed west of here about two years ago. A few years before that, a small town on the western coast of Napahrit was destroyed, not far from Vellashta's military academy of actually. The one before that happened about ten years ago in Mashod. There's always several years between each incident, although they seem to be happening more frequently. And it is always small, remote towns that are affected."

"Do you know how the fires happen?" Rena asked.

"Most people seem to think that they were just dreadful accidents. An oven that had been left unsupervised, an old machine that malfunctioned, children not being careful enough. But these explanations never sat quite right with me."

Darian — who Rena recognised as the innkeeper from last night — brought them mugs of elderflower tea, and Rena welcomed the smell and taste of something that didn't remind her of home. She picked up the mug in both hands and concentrated on the warmth, pulling the mug up to her face to warm the tip of her nose, before taking a careful sip.

"What do you think happened to the towns?" Rena asked, putting the mug back down on the table.

Rodrick looked down at his own mug, pensively turning it in his hands.

"I don't have any leading theories on it yet. Maybe claiming that I've been investigating these fires is a bit of an exaggeration. I'm a scribe of the land, I'm interested in a lot of different topics at the same time, and there are a lot of events and occurrences I find intriguing."

"But do you think someone is responsible for the fires?" Rena insisted, leaning forward.

"I really don't want to establish any hypotheses before having more authentic information."

"But the figurines would indicate that someone was there, right?"

"Like I already said yesterday," Rodrick noted slowly, putting weight behind each word, "there might be a multitude of reasons why these figurines were arranged in a circle around the church."

"Why have I never heard about any of these fires?" Rena sighed heavily and leaned back in her chair again, picking up her mug to take another sip.

"I suppose because people don't like to talk about such tragedies. And since most of them happened so far away, news might just not have travelled all the way down here. There's also always the possibility that your parents didn't want to burden you with the knowledge of such events."

Rena's frown deepened, unable to believe that news of towns burning down wouldn't have reached them, especially if it happened in their own province. And even if her parents hadn't wanted to tell their children about it, it was impossible to keep such momentous events secret throughout an entire town. It didn't feel right that she had never heard of the other fires before. The thought of no one outside their own little part of the kingdom ever hearing about what happened to Oceansthrow made her stomach twist in a strange way. Her fingers grew cold and sweaty, even though they were still touching the warm mug. She took another sip of tea but her mouth remained dry, her tongue lying heavily against her palate.

"We should talk to the guards," she burst out, pushing herself upright again, her whole body waiting for her to do *something*.

"I don't know if they will be able to help much," Rodrick noted. "Especially in such a small town. I'm not even sure there is a guard station here."

"I know there is one. Even if they can't help us, they can still tell us where we need to go and who we need to talk to to find out more."

Chapter Seven

The guard station was a small building near the centre of town, with one bigger room in the front that contained desks, chairs, and cabinets, and two empty holding cells in the back. Only one person was currently in the building, a middle-aged man with greying hair, who had his feet up on one of the desks and was eating something out of a bowl.

"Excuse me," Rena said around the knot forming in her throat as she walked up to him.

"Yes?" he asked with a mouth full of food.

"You might have already heard of me. I'm from Oceansthrow."

Her heart was beating quickly, and her palms were starting to sweat, as if the anticipation of potentially learning more about what had happened to her family was just too much to handle.

"Right." He took his feet off of the desk and put the bowl down.

He gestured for Rena to sit on the chair opposite him, while Rodrick had to drag one over from another desk.

"I was just wondering if you could help me and whether you knew what had happened?" Rena asked, interlacing her trembling fingers in her lap. "I've heard that some people went to investigate the town this morning. Did they report anything back? D-do you know who could be responsible for this?"

The man cleared his throat and sniffled, running the side of his hand over his mouth.

"Right, well, first of all, as a representative of the province of Vellastha and the kingdom of Kal-Hemma, I extend to you our deepest condolences and we profoundly regret that such events happened."

"Thank you," Rena murmured instinctively, taken aback by the monotony in his voice.

"Yes, some people went to Oceansthrow, and some are still currently there," he continued, leaning forward on the desk and interlacing his fingers. "No, I cannot tell you what they have reported and what we potentially do or do not know."

"O-okay," Rena replied, blinking in confusion.

"I talked to Devon last night," Rodrick interjected. "I know that they didn't find much yesterday, and I'm sure you haven't yet heard anything from the people who rode to the village this morning. I understand that you might not be able to tell us much about what happened, but would it be possible to know if you have heard of similar events from other parts of the province or even the kingdom? Maybe it would be possible to tell us more about those?"

"I'm not at liberty to discuss current investigations with civilians."

"B-but, that doesn't make any sense," Rena stammered, her frown deepening. "I'm not just a civilian. I was present during the fire. I'm a victim. Shouldn't I be kept informed?"

The man sighed, and looked past them towards the door before addressing them again.

"Anyone who is not part of the guard corps or another military facility is considered a civilian."

"Should you not at least try to find out if I know anything?" Rena asked, her voice getting louder and more desperate. "Since I was there when the fire was still going?"

"Right. Do you know anything?" He asked, barely any emotions in his voice, as if he wished she would just leave him alone.

"Well, I didn't see who started it, but I'm fairly certain a person or a group of people is responsible for the fire."

"That is a hypothesis we can neither confirm nor deny," he interrupted her with the same monotonous voice, as if he had simply memorized a list of phrases. "In the vast majority of cases such tragedies occur because of an unfortunate accident or because of unlucky weather conditions, and if the incident was started intentionally by a human being, it was most likely someone from town who held a personal grudge against its inhabitants, such as someone who has been wronged or ostracized by their neighbours."

"That doesn't make any sense," Rena murmured.

"From our professional point of view, which clearly has more experience in such matters than any civilian's, it definitely does make sense." He said the last part mockingly, imitating her tone of voice.

Rena mouth ran dry and the knot in her throat made it really difficult for her to swallow. This was not how she had imagined the visit to go. She had thought that even if the guards wouldn't know anything yet, they would at least be willing to help her. She hadn't expected to be looked down upon.

"Listen, young man," Rodrick said, scooting forward on his chair, "I know that there are protocols about who exactly is allowed to know certain types of information, but would it be possible to make an exception just this once to comfort a young girl who lost her home and her family a day ago."

"I'm not allowed to make exceptions," the guard replied with a shrug.

"B-but I found something in the mud," she managed to stammer out, her eyes starting to prickle.

"You found something in the mud," the man repeated, shacking his head slightly from side to side with each word.

"A little figurine," she stuttered as she scrambled to get the object out of her dress pocket. "A little bird. With something carved into its front."

She held the figurine in both hands towards the guard, who just looked at it without any real interest.

"So, you found a toy," he finally said.

"N-no!" Rena stuttered, her mouth hanging open for an instant, unsure how he could have come to that conclusion. "There were at least five or six of them, I think even more. Arranged in a circle around the church."

The door behind them opened and three more guards wandered in, all covered in dirt and ash.

"Finally," the man they had been talking to muttered and got up.

"Devon!" Rena exclaimed and shot up, rushing over to him. "We met last night, you remember, right?"

Devon sighed and stopped. His eyes were streaked with red veins and dark circles had formed underneath. He stank of smoke, which made Rena recoil with memories of the previous day.

"Yeah, I know you," Devon replied, his voice gruff from use.

"Did you find anything? D-did anyone else survive?"

He shook his head and ran a hand over his hair, making ash drizzle down onto the stone floor.

"No, I'm really sorry, we didn't find any one other survivors."

"Okay," Rena replied quietly.

She had known how unlikely it would be to find anyone else alive, especially a day after the fire started. But in the depths of her heart she had still hoped, desperately wishing she wasn't the only one who had gotten away. Even after hearing Devon's reply she couldn't stop herself from believing, thinking that maybe someone was stuck in the basement of a collapsed house and the rescuers simply hadn't gotten to them yet. That someone had managed to escape into the woods and they would be found soon. That Maya might still be out there somewhere.

"For what it's worth," Devon continued in his tired voice, "I *am* truly sorry this happened to you. I wish we had found more survivors. I had friends in Oceansthrow, some that I'd known for decades. I still can't wrap my head around them being gone, even after spending the whole day wading through the ruins. So, I can't even imagine how you must feel. We'll continue looking, but I don't think we will actually find anyone."

Tears welled in her eyes and she blinked them away, clearing her throat before addressing Devon again.

"Did you find any more of these figurines?" she asked, her hands trembling as she presented the bird to Devon.

He looked down at it for a while, before turning around and walking away.

"Current investigations are not to be discussed with civilians," he said as he sat down behind a desk.

"B-but, I'm not a civilian," she replied, confused by his sudden shift in attitude.

"From my current point of view, you are," he told her and unlaced his shoes.

"Why can't you tell me what you found?" she pleaded, the tears finally running down her cheeks.

"Listen, child. I would love to tell you more," Devon said, finally looking up at her as he let his shoes drop to the ground, "and I understand that it must be frustrating to not know what happened to your family and friends. I wish I could tell you more, but if I tell you too much I can get discharged from the guard corps, or worse. I would suggest you wait until the investigation is over, and ask again. But even then, I can't guarantee that I would be allowed to tell you anything specific. We need to wait for the big guys to tell us what to do."

"So how can I find out more?" Rena replied, desperation drenching her voice.

"You'd have to talk to someone higher up. Either try the military academy or the archives or something. But, just so you know, it's pretty unlikely they'll actually talk to you."

"B-but–"

"Rena, I think we should go back to the inn," Rodrick said calmly, putting a hand on her back. "They are clearly not at liberty to tell us anything more about their investigation."

Rena took a deep breath and sighed, nodding slightly.

"You're right," she murmured, and with a heavy heart she turned around.

They got back to the inn for lunch, and sat at the same table. More people were seated around them now, and Rena could feel their stares on her.

She absentmindedly pet Vincent with one hand, using the other to prop up her head, her mind feeling like it had been wrapped in wool.

"What do we do now?" she asked, her eyes wandering over the grainy white wall behind Rodrick.

"Well, we could try my method and simply talk to people. You'd be astonished how much you can find out by being friendly and willing to listen to what people have to say. And as Devon mentioned, there's also the official records that might hold information, but it is indeed rather difficult to get access to these."

She sighed, mulling her options over. She didn't know how Rodrick had been conducting his previous investigation, or how serious he had been about it, but it didn't seem like he had gained much knowledge just from talking to people. She didn't want to wait until Devon got the permission to maybe tell her more about their investigation, and she didn't want to wait to find someone else who might perhaps be able to tell them a tiny shred of the truth. Not if they'd still have to figure out if the information was valid or just an unfounded rumour.

"We could at least try to get to the official reports," Rena said listlessly.

"Well," Rodrick started, tilting his head from side to side while frowning. "Like I said, it is rather difficult to get access to them. And as Devon mentioned, it might be unlikely that anyone at the military academy or the archives would talk to us. To access these kinds of reports you need a special decree which you can only obtain under specific circumstances. I don't think they count "curiosity" as a good enough reason."

"But we aren't just curious about it." She leaned back in her chair, annoyed by constantly having to reiterate the same facts. "My entire family died, and I have no idea why, isn't that enough of a reason?"

"I know," Rodrick said calmly, pushing his hands towards hers on the table, palms up so she could place her own hands in his. "I know. We can try to plead your case. I just want you to know they are very strict and secretive with this kind of information, and we might not be able to access the records. I don't want you to get your hopes up for nothing. You saw how the guards can be to outsiders."

Rena nodded and breathed in deeply, leaning forward to place her hands in Rodrick's.

"Hi," a voice suddenly sounded next to them. Rena looked up in shock, having not heard the man approach. She didn't recognise him at first but then remembered seeing him sitting at the counter eating breakfast that morning. "You're the girl from Oceansthrow, right? I didn't mean to pry, but I couldn't help overhearing your conversation."

He looked about ten years older than Rena, and wore dark trousers with a long-sleeved, blue shirt, both covered in patches where someone had hastily tried to cover up some holes. His curly, dark brown hair had been tied into a bun, though some strands had already abandoned ship, and his face was peppered with light stubble.

"Hi, I'm Logan," he said, dragging a chair over from another table, its back facing the table, before sitting on it. He held out a hand to Rena and she shook it automatically, too stunned to go against her manners. "As I said, I didn't mean to pry, but if you're looking for information, I'm pretty good at finding the right people for that," he continued, and shook Rodrick's hand. "Or finding someone who can get you one of those special decrees," he added with a wink.

Chapter Eight

Soon after, Rena found herself inside Rodrick's caravan, sitting on the floor with her back against the wall of the driver's seat, the dog's head in her lap. The caravan was filled with big, wooden furniture that was strapped to the walls and pots, vials and tools dangling from the ceiling, clanking together and making the journey almost unbearable. To her left was a sort of oven that Rodrick had warned her no to get too close to. Rena was exhausted, her perception clouded by a thick fog, her head pulsing with every jolt of the wagon.

Logan was sitting in the front with Rodrick, telling him where they had to go. He had said he knew how to get them access to the records, they would just have to go to a different city to meet one of his acquaintances. At first it had sounded perfect, like they had finally found someone who was willing to help them, but the longer the journey took, the more time Rena had to think of all of the ways this could go wrong.

Logan had seemed friendly enough, but that might just be a façade and he was actually part of the group who caused the fire and had been tasked with eliminating her before she could find out too much. He hadn't told them where this informant of his was located, just that it was a small town they probably had never heard of before. She hadn't even asked him why he was willing to help them, and the more time passed, the more she kept wondering about it. Maybe he expected payment, but what would happen once he found out she had no money or other possessions? He might have seen Rodrick's caravan and simply wanted to rob them, luring them into the forest so that no one would find them.

Despite the loud noise surrounding her and the uncomfortable position she was in, she quickly fell asleep, only jolting awake once the caravan rumbled to a stop. Without waiting for her, Vincent got up, wriggling his way out of her grip and went over to the door, which swung open only a moment later. Rena took a deep breath before pushing herself up. She brushed her new dress down and finally joining the rest of the group outside. Rodrick had driven the caravan off the road and into the forest between some trees, but not far. Rena could still see the road a few metres away. She looked down at the damp earth underneath her feet, holding the hem of the dress up, unsure if it had been a good idea to drive the caravan off the road like this. But Rodrick looked unperturbed, smiling and nodding at her as their eyes met.

Rena looked at the forest surrounding them, trying to find a road leading to a town or the hint of buildings between the trees, but there was nothing. A knot tightened in her stomach, her fears and suspicions about Logan getting louder in the back of her mind.

"All right, so," Logan said, clapping his hands together to get everyone's attention. "You guys don't look like you've ever been to the camp before, so let me set out some ground rules. Don't fuck anyone over while inside the camp, you will get thrown out and barred from ever coming back, if not worse. If you want to fuck someone over, wait until you're outside again. If you tell any guards or military dogs about where to find the camp or what you saw while here, people will hunt you down, and you don't want to imagine what they'll do to you once they've got you. And don't stare at anyone when you're inside the camp, that's just rude. Other than that, we'll have a great time." He beamed a wide smile at them.

"I thought you were bringing us to a city?" Rena asked, looking around nervously, the knot in her stomach tightening.

Logan vaguely gestured around before saying, "it's kind of a city. You just can't really find it on a map, and sometimes it's not where you saw it last time but people live there and there are shops and even a school, so it's basically a city."

"Oh, interesting," Rodrick replied, his face lighting up. "I've never been to one of the cities of outlaws before."

"One of the what?" Rena exclaimed, practically snapping her neck to look over at Rodrick.

"Ok, so technically, the entrance is a bit down the road," Logan told them, pointing to his left, completely ignoring Rena's distress. "But I know a way that's faster, through the forest, and then we don't have to go through the whole hassle of officially entering the camp since we're only here to ask someone for a favour."

"We're sneaking into a camp full of criminals?" Rena asked with growing unease.

"I wouldn't call it sneaking," Logan replied, waving her worries away. "There's so much surveillance in the trees around the camp they probably already know we're here. But I know them, and they know me, so it's all fine. And the camp isn't full of criminals. The criminals' families also live there."

Rena's head snapped up to stare at the top of the trees with wide open eyes, before looking back down at Logan, waiting for him to tell her it was all just a joke. He simply grinned, which didn't actually help quell her fears.

"A-are we allowed to enter the city without announcing our arrival first?" Rena asked with a trembling voice. "I wouldn't want to be a bother or seem rude."

"We're not staying very long, they probably won't even notice."

"B-but we're strangers. Wouldn't it be easier if you went in alone to find your acquaintance? We'll just slow you down because we've never been to the city. What if we get lost?"

Logan chuckled, his eyebrows knitting together for an instant.

"The camp's really not big enough for you to get lost in."

"I don't have anything to repay you with. I wouldn't want to accept your help without compensating you for your time and effort."

"I'm sure we can come to an arrangement," Rodrick replied.

Rena's eyes snapped to him, wide with shock and betrayal.

"Yeah, I had to come here anyway for something else, and I know how difficult it is to, like, get to the truth when you're trying to talk to Devon and his posse of donkeys. You can just see this as my good deed for the year."

He winked at Rena, and then turned to the caravan, nodding towards the vehicle.

"You sure you want to leave your machine out here in the open without supervision?" he asked.

Rena swallowed hard, but her throat was cramped shut so tightly that the movement hurt.

"Vincent's perfectly capable of looking after it," Rodrick answered, petting the dog's head. "And it's not that easy to pick the lock. It wouldn't be the first time I leave it somewhere in the wild. I can't be next to it at all times after all." He chuckled lightly, as if that was the strangest thought anyone could have.

"It's up to you, friend," Logan said, raising his hands as if he wasn't convinced of the situation. "Just saying, people out here are pretty good at stealing."

"It'll be fine," Rodrick said with a small smile and turned around. He snapped his fingers and pointed at the ground, and the dog jumped to attention and followed him. Rodrick patted the seat of the driver's cabin twice, and Vincent jumped up onto the footrest.

"Stay," Rodrick told him before petting his head. "Good boy."

As Rodrick came back, he rummaged in one of the pockets of his coat and pulled out a strange key, one with a long shaft and different sized half-circles wrapping around the end of it. He slid the key into the keyhole, turned it halfway to one side, pushed it further in, then turned it the other way. A loud *clonk* resounded, as if multiple bolts had just snapped shut.

He turned around to Rena and Logan and clasped his hands behind his back.

"Now, if you wouldn't mind," he said, nodding at Logan. "Please lead the way."

"Sure thing," Logan answered, and turned, waving at them to follow.

A SEARING FAITH

Rena looked to the front of the caravan, worried about leaving Vincent alone, but when she turned back around to ask Rodrick about whether it was truly safe, the two men had already advanced into the forest. She glanced around one more time, the knowledge that she was about to follow two strangers deep into a forest to find a supposed clandestine settlement sinking in. Her fingers grew stiff and ice-cold as she stared at the sliver of road next to the caravan. She could turn around and follow it to the nearest town, find her way back to Halvint and seek shelter in the inn. It wouldn't bring her closer to finding out what had happened to Oceansthrow, but it would bring her closer to safety. There had to be other ways of learning the truth, of knowing whether Maya was still alive or not.

She balled her hands into fists and looked back into the forest. Rodrick and Logan had disappeared between the trees, so Rena had to jog to catch up to them. As she came up besides Rodrick, he shot her a friendly smile, and she forced herself to smile back at him.

She glanced up into the trees surrounding them to find the so-called surveillance Logan had talked about, but all she could see was the blue sky beyond the treetops. It wasn't long before Rena couldn't see the road or the caravan behind them anymore. It was like the forest had swallowed them, was increasing encroaching on them with every step. It was a new feeling for her. Forests had always been her refuge — a friend she had known all her life – but now its overbearing presence made her want to crumble to the ground and sob. With each step, the sinking feeling that something bad was about to happen spread through her being, that they would pass a tree and stumble upon something horrific.

She kept her eyes fixed on Logan's shoes in front of her and wrapped her arms tightly around her chest.

They kept marching and marching, never stumbling upon the aforementioned camp, as if they were stuck walking circles in this forest for the rest of eternity.

Logan slowed down and raised his hand, gesturing about as if sending hand signals to someone. Rena looked up but still couldn't tell whether they were being observed or not. Faintly, she could hear sounds of human activity, like a murmur getting louder the further they got. A few more steps and Rena was finally able to see something between the trees — structures, somewhere between shacks and tents.

"Okay," Logan whispered, stopping and turning to face them. "Once we enter, you need to stay as quiet as possible until I tell you we're clear. I'm not one hundred percent sure where my informant currently is, but I know where he *might* be, so we'll go look at those places first and hope we find him quickly."

Rodrick nodded, a serious expression on his face. Rena's heart hammered in her chest, her eyes darting between each sliver of fabric she could see between the trees. The tents formed a wall between them and the city, running along to either side until the darkness of the forest swallowed them.

"Is this safe?" she whispered quietly.

"Yeah, sure," Logan waved her off. "Like I said, I know the people who live here, so just don't be an ass to anyone and everything's gonna be fine. Okay? Let's go."

He turned around before Rena could voice any more of her concerns, and snuck up to one of the structures — what looked like the backside of a light brown, rectangular tent that had been attached to some trees. It was bigger than the two tents surrounding it, high enough that a person could comfortably stand in it, but the fabric had been mended in various places, revealing its age. He lay flat on the ground, and pulled the hem up just enough to peer inside. After a moment, he sprung back up and pulled the edge higher, waving for Rodrick and Rena to enter — even though the gap was barely high enough for anyone to fit through. Groaning, Rodrick lay on the ground and rolled himself through.

Rena glanced around one last time, the feeling laying heavy on her heart that she either had to run away now or follow Rodrick and hope she hadn't made the mistake of trusting the wrong people.

She inhaled deeply before laying on her belly, and crawling through the opening. She stood back up inside the tent and tried to dust off the new dress she had gotten from Darian's wife – although the dirt had already managed to stain the fabric. She sighed, thinking how the dress didn't belong to her and she'd had it for less than a day before muddying it. Logan rolled in after her and the tent closed behind him.

"Welcome to my humble abode," he whispered as he passed Rena.

She looked up, taking in the sparse furnishing around her. To her left lay a straw mattress on the floor next to a wicker chest. To her right was a thick rug with a low, wooden table, pillows surrounding it on the ground. On the table stood a single, half-burnt candle — the only lamp or decoration in the entire space. Along the edge of the tent lay an assortment of clay and metal pots, half-stacked in each other.

The only object that appeared sturdier and more valuable was a wooden chest to the right of the mattress. It was made of dark wood, decorated with intricate carvings, and the faint remains of blue paint flecked its top.

"This is your home?" Rodrick asked, his gaze drifting across the dim room.

Logan waved his hand around as he walked up to the wooden chest.

"Sometimes," he replied, crouching in front of it. "When I feel like it."

Something clicked, and the chest sprang open. A heartbeat later, Logan had closed the lid again, and stood back up.

"All right, we can go!" he told them, waving for them to follow him. He went to the front of the tent and knelt to slide his hands under the flap, working on something on the other side. He got back up and held it open, waving the other two through with a little bow.

Rena went out first, cautiously, glancing from side to side before stepping out. Tents stretched out in front of her and to both sides, a make-shift road weaving between the trees. The tents all looked different, some sturdier, some just blankets carelessly draped over a pole and attached to the trunk of a tree. The ground in front of the tents was well-travelled. She couldn't see far ahead – her view blocked by the forest – but the darkness dissipated a few metres in front of her, indicating that they were near a clearing.

A group of people stood talking in front of a tent to her right, far enough so she couldn't understand their conversation. One man laughed at whatever the second had said, and clapped him on the shoulder as the other broke into a wide smile. She turned her back to them, hoping they hadn't seen her face, her heart racing.

Rodrick came to stand next to her, then Logan peered out and looked both ways before hurrying outside and kneeling to re-tie the knot of the tent's entrance. In one motion he straightened, and stood between Rodrick and Rena, looped his arms around their shoulders, and pressed them forward.

"All right," he whispered. "First we g—"

"Welcome back, Logan," a voice arose from behind them and made Logan flinch.

"Ah, f—. Hi!" Logan turned around, a big smile on his face, letting go of Rena's and Rodrick's shoulders. "What a coincidence!"

"What a coincidence to find me in my own neighbourhood?" the woman said, one eyebrow raised with a light smile on her lips.

She was leaning against one of the trees, her arms crossed in front of her chest. Rena could have sworn she hadn't been there a second ago. Rena froze, unsure if they were in trouble now that they had been caught sneaking into the camp, but the woman barely even acknowledged Rodrick and her.

She was somewhere in her thirties, with dark skin, and long, thin, black braids that tightly hugged her scalp. Two patches of lighter skin – almost white – covered her face, both going from her eyes towards her temple, and running down the length of some of the braids. She was thin but muscular, with worn-out leather trousers, and a dark leather vest that fastened a loose green shirt tightly to her waist.

"Well, yeah, you know," Logan trailed off, looking everywhere but at her.

"Were you trying to sneak in?" the woman asked with a playful smile on her lips.

"Pfft, no," Logan replied, and shook his head, the muscles in his face not exactly sure which emotion to emulate.

The woman sighed, and her eyes finally drifted towards Rodrick, looking him up and down before her gaze landed on Rena. She had beautiful black eyes, round and wide, reflecting the few rays of sunshine that managed to pierce through the treetops above.

Heat rose in Rena's cheeks while a strange feeling trailed its way up from her stomach into the rest of her body, and she had to look away from the woman's intense gaze.

"I suppose no one has welcomed you to the camp yet if you're sneaking around with this idiot," she said, nodding at Logan, who raised his arms in mock offence.

She pushed herself away from the tree trunk and stepped towards Rena. She took Rena's face in both hands – more white marks dotting the back of her hands – and touched their foreheads together. Rena's breath hitched at the unexpected warm touch.

"The stars welcome you to the city of Rancor. Every human is welcome here, no matter their past or future deeds. May the dark obscure you from your enemies, and grant you rest."

The woman lifted her head and smiled softly at Rena.

"Thank you," Rena replied, unsure of how she was supposed to respond and unable to look the woman in the eyes.

"You're supposed to say "May the light brighten your resolve and lead your way to justice,"" Logan muttered, leaning closer to her.

Rena repeated the words, although they felt foreign in her mouth, and it came out more as a question than a statement.

"Don't let our name frighten you," the woman told her, winking before repeating the welcome with Rodrick.

She stepped back and looked at both of them, as if trying to decipher who they were.

"I don't get a welcome?" Logan asked, stretching his arms to the side as if for a hug.

"No darkness could obscure *your* problems," the woman replied, side-eyeing him for a second before glancing back at Rena and Rodrick.

"My name is Kalani. Would you be so kind as to tell me yours?"

"My name is Rodrick Hal'Varika. I am a tinkerer and scribe of the land. We meant no disrespect when we entered your city through an unorthodox entrance. Our common friend here told us he was accustomed to the region, and that our unannounced arrival would not be a problem."

Kalani regarded him for an instant before nodding and turning to Rena.

"I'm Rena of Oceansthrow," she muttered, and bowed her head.

"You are awfully young to be a scribe of the land," Kalani remarked, slightly tilting her head to the side.

"Oh, I'm not," Rena stammered, shaking her head. "I, umm, have personal reasons why I'm accompanying Rodrick at this moment," she replied, unsure how much she was allowed to tell anyone in this city about what had happened — though, it felt silly to hide the fact that an entire village had burned down.

Kalani's eyes narrowed slightly, but she didn't ask any further questions.

Her friendly demeanour fell as she turned towards Logan.

"And why are you here?"

"They need help with something, and I gain self-worth through helping other people?" Logan tried, but Kalani's eyebrows arched up in doubt.

"Curiosity?" He tried again. Kalani's expression didn't change.

"I may need help with something," he finally admitted, pursing his lips and glancing away.

Rena glanced over at Logan, her eyebrows knitting together. He hadn't told them anything about what he needed from them, and he certainly hadn't asked if they would be willing or even able to help him.

"With what?" Kalani asked.

"Now see, I only divulge that information to people who agree to help."

Kalani sighed and closed her eyes before turning back to Rena and Rodrick.

"I hope you didn't promise him too much," she told them dryly.

"Be that as it may," she continued, without letting anyone have a chance to reply. "I will need you to follow me. The Sovereign Outcast is waiting for you."

"Oh come on, do we have to?" Logan sighed.

"They're especially happy to see you again," Kalani replied, smiling faintly at Logan.

"Why?" Logan asked Kalani, squinting at her in distrust as he took a small step back. "I haven't been here in forever. Whatever happened, it wasn't me. Did you talk to Deacon? What did he say? I swear, whatever he said, it was probably a lie. I had nothing to do with any of it. And since when does Cass act so high and mighty? Are they trying to emulate the Royal Council? Are we becoming like our enemies now?"

Kalani had already half-turned to walk the group to their new destination, but stopped in her tracks to stare back at Logan.

"Cass will tell you themselves what they want from you," she said, deliberately enunciating each word.

Kalani and Logan stared at each other for a while, unblinking. The knot that had formed in Rena's stomach unravelled and tightened again in a more familiar pattern, the one where tense silence made her want to crawl out of her skin. At home she would have known what to say to calm everyone down. Would have known which compromises needed to be taken to avoid a fight. But here? In a new environment surrounded by strangers? People who were probably used to fighting and standing their ground? She couldn't even start to imagine what the right response would be. Her mind raced with half-formed apologies and excuses, nothing seeming just the right fit for this situation. Her mouth opened slowly, her tongue sticking to the dry roof of her mouth.

"The Sovereign Outcast doesn't have to justify themselves to you," Kalani said, breaking the silence before Rena had come up with a suitable approach. "If they want to talk to you, you go and talk."

"Since when is it unreasonable to ask what they want to talk about?" Logan exclaimed, throwing his hands out to the side. "I thought we were all equal here."

"Oh my stars, I don't know what they want to talk about," Kalani burst out. "They didn't give me a detailed list of everything you have ever fucked up. You know yourself best. Pick whichever failure is the most recent and most likely to piss off Cass."

Rena crossed her arms and looked down. She forced her breaths to be long and shallow, to stay as still as possible. The laughter of the men behind them had long since died down, and it felt like the fight in front of her could be heard throughout the entire camp.

"All right, all right," Logan put his hands up in defence, taking another step back. "No need to get personal. I just wanted to be prepared for my big audience with their holy majesty."

Kalani closed her eyes and took in a long breath.

"Just shut up and follow me," she said in defeat, and turned to walk away.

"Excuse me?" Rodrick interjected, and Kalani stopped instantly, slowly turning back to stare him down. "I wouldn't want to inconvenience you further, but this affair sounds like a serious, personal matter that might take some time to resolve, and we wouldn't want to be a hindrance to the proper advancement of this debate."

Kalani didn't answer, just kept staring at Rodrick, the muscles in her jaw clenching and unclenching.

"And, uhm," Rena added, forcing her voice out, desperate to break the tension. "I'm sure the Sovereign Outcast has more important things to do than talk to us. I don't know what your discussion just now was about, and I'm sure I'm not entitled to know the details anyway, but I'm sure that a private audience would be more conductive to mending this situation. And, I mean, we aren't anyone important anyway. If it's just to give us an official welcome, then you already did, so I don't think it would be necessary for them to spend their valuable time on greeting us. We'll just be somewhere in town. I'm sure we stick out enough that everyone will notice where we're going, so we won't be too hard to find. If all that is okay with you?"

"They've got a point. Several even," Logan added, pointing a finger from Rodrick to Rena and back again.

Kalani looked at Rena before blinking and sighed in resignation, shaking her head slightly.

"Fine. I've got more important things to do with my day anyway. Let's go, Logan."

She turned around for the third time and started walking away.

"Let me just hug them goodbye real quick," he said and darted over to Rena, trapping her in a tight embrace before she even had the time to lift her arms. From over his shoulder Rena saw Kalani stop, her muscles tensed, clenching her hands into fists and then stretching them, but she didn't turn around.

Rena froze in Logan's arm, her breathing stopped, her blood running cold.

"Go find Sayaf," he whispered in her ear, "he's an old man living in a wooden shack near the bakery. Follow the smell of bread and you'll find him. Tell him I sent you."

He patted her on the back and let go of her, turning to Rodrick before she'd had the time to really register the hug. She started breathing again – pain shooting through her body as the air expanded her cramping lungs. She moved one finger after the other until she could finally unlock the rest of her joints.

Logan let go of Rodrick, patting his left cheek twice, and then jogged up to Kalani. He passed her, not waiting for her to catch up, and disappeared down the road.

Rena slowly turned to Rodrick, who looked more bemused than the panic she thought was appropriate for this situation.

Chapter Nine

"What a strange fellow," Rodrick chuckled and turned to Rena, his hands interlaced behind his back.

Rena took in a few shaky breaths and looked around. The men that had been behind them had disappeared, leaving Rena and Rodrick on a suspiciously calm, and empty road.

"I don't like it here," Rena muttered.

"I find it fascinating," Rodrick noted, glancing around at their surroundings. "Such a different way of living."

"Maybe we should just go home."

"There's no need for that." Rodrick shot her a small smile that was meant to reassure her. "We can find Logan's associate on our own, I'm sure of it. And don't worry, Logan will certainly be fine too, I don't think this lovely lady would have arrived to welcome him on her own if it was something truly serious."

Rena nodded slowly, even though her worries didn't lie with Logan's well-being.

"He told me something about cornflower blue drapes on the shack of his informant," Rodrick continued, squinting at the tents that surrounded them, "and that if he doesn't believe Logan sent us we should remind him of something called 'Nura's Pendant'. If we ask enough people I'm sure we'll find Logan's acquaintance in no time. Let's just go this way."

He stepped forward and headed in the same direction as Logan and Kalani had. Rena sighed heavily and followed him, glancing furtively between the tents to get a glimpse of what lay at the centre of the camp.

"He told me to look for a man named Sayaf and that he lives near a bakery," she said as she caught up to Rodrick. "But, I don't think we should just tell random people about who we're looking for, right? We're outsiders, maybe they don't trust us."

"Don't be so quick to judge, my dear. But you might be right, we should only ask people about Logan's informant as a last resort. I'm sure we can find the man's abode on our own with the information he has given us."

They weaved their way between the trees and makeshift homes, their eyes on the ground so they wouldn't trip over any ropes holding the structures in place. The city seemed to be made up of ever smaller circular rows of homes – small gaps between structures allowing the passage from one road to the next. The closer Rena and Rodrick got to the centre, the less trees blocked their passage and the more light shone through the treetops.

At first, they didn't meet anyone on the streets, though they could hear people going about their lives in their homes. At one point, they passed a tent where the flap had been rolled up, and as Rena glanced inside, she saw four people sitting on the ground around a low table. Her gaze washed over them, until her eyes locked with a woman sitting at the far-end of the table. Rena quickly averted her gaze, heat rushing to her cheeks. Logan had told them not to stare at anyone. How could she have let her curiosity get the better of her?

Her heart beat furiously in her chest as she waited for the woman to climb out of the tent and scream at her. She tried to listen for her footsteps, but all she could hear was blood rushing through her ears. She kept her gaze fixed on the ground in front of her, her eyes burning from staying open too long. But no one yelled after her, and no one came running for her, and soon she was far enough from the tent that she dared to look back. Her shoulders relaxed when she noticed that they were still the only people travelling these paths, and, as she turned back around, she wiped at her eyes to get rid of the burning sensation.

Rodrick suddenly stopped in the middle of the road and Rena almost ran into him. For a second, she thought he might have noticed her blunder, and wanted to chastise her, but he wasn't even looking at her.

"Do you smell that?" he asked, frowning and sniffing the air.

She closed her eyes and breathed in deeply. Beneath the smell of the forest was a faint whiff of sweet bread. Once she had noticed it, the smell jumped out at her, flooding all her senses with memories of her home. All the times she had opened a roll of fresh bread and the steam rose out of it, all the times her grandparents had let her help them knead the dough when she was still little, all the times she had slid the loafs into the oven with her mother.

Her eyes shot open and she instantly dropped into a crouch, her hands shooting up to cover her mouth and nose. Her heart was hammering in her ears so loudly that it drowned out Rodrick's enquiries on her wellbeing. All she could picture was the old stone oven at the back of her house, the flames in its centre growing and crawling out of it, inching forward until they had engulfed the entire house.

She bit down on her cheek until it was the only thing she could feel. She focused her eyes on the tents surrounding them, noting each detail that seemed unusual to her, anything that reminded her she wasn't in Oceansthrow.

"Rena, are you all right?" Rodrick's desperate pleads burst through to her and she finally dared looking up at him.

She slowly lifted her hands from her face and started breathing again – shallow breaths at first until she forced herself to take deeper ones. She nodded – the movement jerky, as if her muscles didn't want to obey.

"What happened?" Rodrick asked, leaning down towards her, one hand on her shoulder.

She took a deep breath and stood up, taking a small step away from his touch.

"My parents had a bakery," she muttered, wiping down her dress.

Her fingers felt numb, her vision was blurry. She blinked, trying to focus her eyes, but instead it just caused white bursts to appear.

"Oh child, why didn't you say anything?"

"I don't know, I just didn't really think of mentioning it. Maybe I just didn't want to think about it." She glanced over at him and shot him a small, apologetic smile. It felt unnatural, like her face had forgotten how the motion worked.

Rodrick smiled back at her, a softness surrounding his grey eyes.

"If this is too much for you and you, just let me know," he said in a low voice. "I can search for Logan's acquaintance on my own."

"No, it's okay, I'm going to be fine," she replied, more to herself than to Rodrick. She straightened her back and looked out at the structures surrounding them. "But this means we're getting closer," she continued, her mouth running dry at the thought of reaching the bakery.

Rodrick craned his neck to look over the tents. Rena tried doing the same – thinking she would at least be able to see some smoke from the oven – but the homes and trees were still too intertwined for her to see much.

"Let's go this way," Rodrick said, walking towards a gap between two tents, even though it didn't look like a path meant to be taken.

They had to clamber past trees – almost hugging the trunks at some point – and over ropes that anchored the tents to the ground, and Rena was horrified at the possibility of stumbling onto one of the tents and destroy someone's home.

The closer they got to the centre of the city, the busier the streets were. The structures got bigger and sturdier, more people stood outside their homes talking to each other, even kids were running through the streets. The heart of the camp had wider roads, and to either side of them vendors sold a myriad of goods on tables. People strolled through the streets looking at the wares and talking to each other as if they were in any other city.

Rena tried to not look directly at the people, her gaze instead drifting across the tables and structures surrounding her. She noticed that some tents had letters written on them, or signs attached to nearby trees. The one they were standing next to proclaimed itself to be a message delivery service, with various prices listed — depending on which province of the kingdom had to be reached. The tent next to it sold candles and rudimentary oil lamps – a list on its side describing the wax or oil used and their expected longevity when burning.

"Isn't this fascinating?" Rodrick exclaimed, eyes wide with excitement.

Rena only hummed a response, unsure of what she should think of it. She hadn't expected this level of organisation and community when Logan had said they were heading to a camp full of outlaws. She also hadn't expected to see this many children, especially not running around unaccompanied. She still felt like she should be wary of these people – like they were entirely different from her – but looking around at this bustling city centre that seemed so similar to her own town almost made her feel like she belonged, and she didn't know how to wrap her head around that.

Rodrick sniffed the air again, holding his head up high.

"There!" he called out, pointing at a column of smoke rising behind a blue tent.

He hurried forward, but Rena had to force her body to follow him. They reached what could vaguely be described as a bakery. It wasn't much — a small, white dome-shaped oven stood at the back, while two work tables stood in front of it. Red and yellow tarps had been fastened to poles to act as a rudimentary roof.

On the left-most table, three people — two middle-aged women and a boy younger than Rena — were preparing dough. The women were leaning close to the boy and showing him how to use the lower part of his palm to knead the dough, although they seemed to be arguing over the correct technique to use. On the other side, the table was filled with baskets of loafs and rolls and pastries. As people passed, they just plucked food from the baskets – as if it was all free.

"Blue drapes," Rodrick muttered, as he slowly turned to inspect the tents around them. Rena kept glancing at the bakery, at how the women were guiding the boy's hands, at the streak of white flour on his face. The woman to the boy's left – a short woman with almost alabaster skin and thick, curly, copper hair – kept playfully trying to disrupt the boy's efforts, while the other woman – taller, with a serious face and straight, black hair tied into a long braid – had to swat her companion's hands away to let the boy work.

The memories of Rena's parents in their own bakery came flooding back – no matter how much she tried to fight them – and suddenly everything was too much. She wanted to look away, to find the differences in her environment again, to ground herself in the foreignness of the camp, but her eyes wouldn't move. Her vision went blurry along the edges – the bakers the only thing she could still see. She wanted to blink, but she couldn't, wanted to stop her tears, but they rolled down her cheeks without any resistance. Her breaths came in shaky, quicker and quicker, until they were only hitches, and she felt like she was about to collapse if she couldn't get a hold of herself.

Her stomach tightened, her muscles ached, bile tried to claw its way up her throat. She could smell the biting smoke again, the foul smell of melting fat and burning hair. The cacophony of voices around her became a uniform noise in which the crackle and pop of fire arose. And although her fingers were ice cold, she could feel its heat enclose on her.

"Rena!" Rodrick yelled, grabbing her face in his hands.

Her eyes snapped to his, loosing herself in the blue and green streaks in his grey eyes.

"You need to breath," he told her, but she didn't understand what he was saying, because breathing was all she *was* doing.

"Is she all right?" another voice spoke, barely audible over the roaring of the fire.

Her eyes drifted to the ground – dirt peaking out of grass trampled flat by a thousand feet. Something glinted to her left, but it was just the stake of a tent. She was lead away from the crowd that had gathered around her and leaned against a tree.

"You're going to be just fine," Rodrick told her in a quiet, slow voice. "We just need to take longer, steadier breaths."

Rena slid down the trunk of the tree until she was sitting on the ground. She dug her fingers into the ground, feeling the dirt push against the skin underneath her fingernails. She clutched onto it so hard that pain shot through her hands and up her arms, but that was enough to anchor her in the moment. Her breathing calmed down, her hands unclenched, and soon all she could feel was exhaustion.

Slowly, the low hum of Rodrick's reassuring murmurations reached her. He was sitting on the ground close to her – far enough away that he wasn't touching her.

"This is just a momentary feeling," he muttered. "You are not alone, I am here with you. Soon everything will be just as it was before. Nothing can happen to you."

Even though she didn't believe everything he said, hearing the calm monotony of his voice helped her. She took a deep breath and sat back up, leaning hear head against the tree.

"You're right, we should probably go back," Rodrick said in a louder voice, having noticed her change in demeanour. "I shouldn't have pushed us forward. Of course, you're not feeling well after what happened yesterday. Coming here was never a good idea."

She thought about it, about walking all the way back through the forest to find the caravan again, about driving back to Halvint and lying down in the bed again, about having to find a new angle to their investigation.

All of the feelings that had just flooded her would have been for nothing. All the pain and heartache and exhaustion wouldn't even have brought her closer to finding out what had happened to Oceansthrow, to finding out if Maya was still alive.

She swallowed hard and shook her head.

"No," she rasped. "We need to find the informant."

"Are you sure?" Rodrick asked.

She nodded, her throat too dry to answer further. She pushed herself up and wipe down her hands, trying and failing to get the dirt out from under her nails.

"Help an old man up," Rodrick said and reached a hand out to her.

With some effort and the help of the tree they managed to get him back to his feet.

"Right," Rodrick moaned. "Let's find those blue drapes then."

Chapter Ten

—·—

"There it is!" Rodrick exclaimed, pointing towards a small, simple shack – the walls made of wooden boards – with blue drapes hanging behind square holes acting as windows. In its middle, a bigger hole – also covered by a blue fabric – had been cut out to act as a door.

She nodded slowly, hugging her arms tightly around herself. She barely managed to keep her eyes focused, exhaustion having flooded her entire being. Her mind was clouded by a growing headache, and her jaw hurt from the previous tightness.

"It's going to be all right," Rodrick told her. "Even if he can't help us, we can find another way to get to the records. I know it has been a difficult journey for you, but I don't want you to feel bad if we don't get what we need. This is just our first attempt. I'm sure we can come up with different ways to get to the truth."

Rena nodded again, more enthusiastically this time so Rodrick wouldn't think she was scared. She wasn't scared, at least not anymore. She felt drained of all emotions, tired and cold, and she couldn't get her mind to concentrate on what was right in front of them — no matter how much she tried to force herself.

"Thank you," she murmured, "for helping me."

He smiled softly at her.

"Of course."

"I'm sorry if I dragged you into this. I'm sure you had other plans in mind."

"Nonsense." He waved her off.

"I'm serious," she cut him off before he could say anything more. "I don't want you to think I'm not grateful for all of your help. You barely know who I am, but you're okay with spending all of this time with me to find out what happened to my town, and I want you to know that I really appreciate the sacrifices you're making."

"Don't worry, child," he chuckled. "Don't let this weigh on you. My life consists of wandering through the kingdom, there is nowhere I have to be or anyone who is waiting for me. I have gained the liberty of going wherever I feel like going, whenever I feel like leaving. What happened to you and your family, and all of these other towns, cannot simply vanish into obscurity. I know this investigation is going to be a long and difficult one, and I'm very well aware that you do not take my help for granted, so please do not feel bad about not going on this journey alone."

Rena shot him a small smile and nodded lightly.

"Now, let's go find this informant of Logan's," Rodrick said and turned towards the shack.

He knocked on the wall next to the entrance. At first nothing happened. Then they heard shuffling and muttering from behind the drapes. An old, black man pushed the drapes aside and stared at them, first with annoyance, then confusion, then back to annoyance. His face was covered in wrinkles and he still had a full head of thick, white coils. Even though the structure he lived in looked simple and almost crude, the man himself looked elegant – as if he didn't truly fit into this city. Golden and silver jewellery pierced his ears and eyebrows, and he was wearing multiple layers of thick, dark blue fabric that was fastened across his waist with a silver belt to form a tunic.

"Pardon our disruption," Rodrick said, bowing slightly to the stranger. "We are looking for a man named Sayaf. Might that be you?"

The man didn't answer right away, but kept looking them up and down before grunting an affirmation.

"My name is Rodrick Hal'Varika, and this is my companion, Rena," Rodrick continued, gesturing to her. "We have a common acquaintance who told us you might be able to help with our current investigation. His name is Logan. I'm afraid I don't know his family name, or where he is from."

At the mention of Logan, Sayaf's eyes darkened and his lips drew into a thin line.

"What kind of trouble has he gotten into this time?" Sayaf asked dryly.

"None at all, none at all," Rodrick reassured him, though Rena wasn't sure if that was completely accurate. "Would you allow us to enter your home so we could discuss what this is about?"

"Tell me why you're here, first," Sayaf asked, not budging from the entrance.

"We need a specific document to access some official records, and we were told you could help us acquire such documentation," Rodrick murmured, leaning closer.

"I don't do that anymore," Sayaf replied and stepped back, letting the drapes fall shut again. Rodrick's hand shot out to keep the drapes from closing completely.

"Logan told me to mention 'Nura's Pendant' to you," Rodrick said, pulling the drapes open.

The man turned back around and stared at Rodrick's hand before glancing at both of them.

"That boy can mention my wife's jewellery as much as he wants, I still don't do that kind of work anymore," he told them.

Rena didn't know what she had expected from Logan's informant, but it certainly wasn't this. She had thought that maybe he'd want something in exchange, that he would bargain with them, but she wasn't prepared for someone who simply refused their request. Had they found the wrong person? Had they offending him somehow? It didn't make sense to her that Logan would send them to someone who wasn't willing or able to help.

"I'm sorry, sir." Rena forced herself to say something before the man could shoo them away. "I know this might be an inconvenience to you, but it's extremely important that we get access to these records. I promise, we aren't planning on doing anything nefarious with these records."

"You and everyone else in this city," he interrupted her, making her lose her train of thought. She looked at him with an open mouth for a moment before regaining a clear head – an act made increasingly difficult by her exhaustion.

"I-I don't know much about this city. We met Logan in Halvint, and he said he could help us. He actually meant to accompany us to visit you, but when we arrived here he had to attend some other important business. I apologize if this seems strange to you, but you have to believe us."

"Oh, I believe you, I'm just sorry that boy sold you a promise he couldn't keep, because I cannot help you. Now please let go of my curtains."

"I don't know if you've heard of it," Rena continued, rushing forward until she was at the threshold of the door, "but my village burned down and I might be the only survivor. Oceansthrow. It wasn't too far from here. Just south of Halvint. Maybe you've passed through it before. I know this will sound like a made-up story to you, but I've tried talking to the guards, and they refused to tell me about what might be going on, but I know it has to be something strange. It wasn't just an accident, I'm sure of it. But to find out more we would need to get access to these records."

Sayaf looked at her for a moment, his eyebrows drawn together, before he stepped closer to the door again.

"What do you mean the village burned down?" he asked her.

"It's completely gone," she replied, forcing her eyes to focus on the man's. "Like I said, I know it must sound like a fabrication to outsiders, especially me being the only survivor, and I hope that part isn't actually true, but the rest of it is. It happened yesterday. And it just doesn't make sense that it was an accident, I think someone's responsible for it, I just don't know who."

With each word, her muscles wound tighter. A prickling numbness filled her fingers and ran up her arms, her lungs ached with every breath, but she couldn't let Sayaf see it. She dug her nails into the skin of her wrist, letting the tension in her body escape through the pain.

"We also think it is related to other similar incidents that happened throughout the kingdom over the years," Rodrick added.

"And you say the guards didn't want to help?"

"They said they weren't allowed to tell civilians any details about their investigations," Rena replied.

"Of course they did, those leeches of the earth," he grumbled and stepped to the side, waving for them to follow him.

The room was dark, tinged with a blue glow from the drapes, and an orange tint from a lit candle. A tall, muscular woman sat at the table, staring, one leg crossed over a knee, her left arm draped over the back of the chair while the other held a mug. She was older than Rena, maybe in her early thirties. She had the same skin tone as Sayaf, and you could see a resemblance in the shape of their piercing, dark brown eyes. Her head was shaved, and her ears were pierced with golden jewellery similar to Sayaf's, dots of metal and dangling chains. Her clothes resembled those of the old man too, just in a lighter blue mixed with layers of white and gold. Her tunic was tight around her chest, but then wider below the belt, loosely covering a pair of brown trousers. Her upper arms were bare, and leather gauntlets covered her forearms.

"This is Asha, my niece," Sayaf said, groaning as he sat on the chair next to her.

"Nice to meet you," Rena replied, nodding in her direction. Asha nodded back, not taking her eyes from Rena.

"I was serious when I said I don't do that kind of work anymore," Sayaf said, taking a sip from a second mug. "I wouldn't know which names to put on the decree to make it look official. They might even have changed the wording of these documents, who knows. They constantly change something about these things, it's too annoying to keep up. But, I do know someone in the Plains who can make you one. I'll have to bring you to him, though. He doesn't just work for anyone."

"You are not going all the way to the Plains," Asha interjected, her head whipping around to look at her uncle. "You just spent three weeks in bed with a bad lung. I'm not letting you leave this place for some random people you just met."

"I was sick, and now I'm better," Sayaf retorted. "I can make my own decisions on where I go."

"You absolutely cannot. I'm not riding all the way out to the other end of the province to drag your corpse back home."

Sayaf clicked his tongue and waved her off.

"If it is any inconvenience, I'm sure we can figure out another way," Rena stammered.

"I'm not a fragile little bird that just hatched," Sayaf replied. "I can take care of myself."

Asha stood and towered over Sayaf, staring down at him, not saying anything. The air grew heavy as their eyes locked, so much that Rena was about to say something — anything — to alleviate the situation, until Sayaf rolled his eyes and sighed.

"Not even your mother was this stubborn," he muttered, and took another sip from his mug. "So, what are we going to do about their problem?" he asked, gesturing at Rena and Rodrick.

"You could just write a letter for your contact that we can deliver," Rena suggested, hoping that that would quell the argument. "It might convince them to help us, hopefully."

"He's not going to just trust some random letter," Sayaf dismissed her. "You could have forged it, or forced me to write it."

"I will go with them," Asha said.

"What are you talking about?" Sayaf sighed and frowned at her.

"If it guarantees that you stay here, I will accompany them to the Plains. It shouldn't take more than a few days." She said the last part while looking at Rena, who could feel heat rise to her cheeks and nodded out of reflex.

"Cass isn't going to like you just running off with some strangers and abandoning your duties."

"Ocassian doesn't own me," Asha replied, picking up her mug and putting it in a basin on the ground that already held other dishes. "I can go where I want. And if they're breaking into the archives I want in."

Sayaf closed his eyes and ran a hand over his face before slowly shaking his head.

"There's nothing there for you, child," he said calmly.

"You can't know that." She came back to the table and leaned against the table with outstretched arms.

"They aren't keeping records about what happened to the Grey Isles in some archives in Vellashta that anyone can walk in to."

"Isn't that what those decrees are for? To keep random people out? Wasn't that your entire business model? If people can't get access to the important documents, then what were you selling people? What are you promise them?" She pointed towards Rena and Rodrick.

Rena could feel the tension in the room rise again, even though she didn't really understand what Asha and Sayaf were arguing about. She had heard of the Grey Isles before – the group of islands to the south of Vellastha that were veiled in mist – but she didn't know much about them.

"You don't know what these people keep," Asha continued, "or where they keep it. If the takeover was a joint venture, they will have records of those accords in the archives here. You overestimate how much they care about keeping any of this secret."

"You know nothing about how they operate," Sayaf grumbled, turning away from his niece to drink from his mug. "You still think there's anything that can be done against them."

"There is. You've just gotten too old and comfortable at the camp to see it."

Sayaf sighed and took a long drink from his mug.

"You need to let it go," Sayaf said, eyes heavy and tired.

"I won't," Asha replied and turned around. She strode to a bag that lay on the bed in the corner of the room, and pulled something out before returning to the table. She placed a rolled-up piece of parchment and a wooden box in front of Sayaf.

"Write the letter," she told him.

Chapter Eleven

"Do we wait here or go back to the caravan?" Rena asked Rodrick as they stood in front of Logan's tent. She didn't want to stay in the camp longer than necessary, even though her general uneasiness about the place had mostly vanished. She just wanted to be back in the caravan so she could rest and pet Vincent.

"Do you think we could even find our way back?" She added, peaking past Logan's tent and into the forest.

"The sun is still out," Rodrick replied, glancing in the same direction. "It might take us a while, but I don't think we would get completely lost. As long as we can find the road, we should be able to find where we left the caravan."

"Hmmm." Rena glanced both ways down the road, hoping to find Logan.

Asha was standing with them, having pocketed the letter Sayaf had written. She had tied a black scabbard to her waist and was playing with the sword – pushing it out and into its sheath rhythmically, the sun glinting off of its golden blade. Her eyes were fixed on the end of the road they had come from, her face not betraying anything she might be feeling or thinking.

A figure appeared to their right, coming straight at them with determination. Rena tensed before she realised that it was Logan. But the speed with which he approached, and the expression on his face, only heightened her discomfort.

"Aah, there he is," Rodrick said, smiling when he noticed Logan.

"Let's go!" Logan said, walking right past them and clapping his hands.

Before any of them could react, he had already disappeared between two tents into the forest.

Rena's eyes met Rodrick's. She raised a concerned eyebrow but didn't say anything. She quickly glanced to the end of the road where Logan had come from to see if anyone was following him, but no one was there. She didn't have much time to wonder what was going on as Asha slipped past Rodrick and Rena to follow Logan as if nothing was wrong or even out of the ordinary. And so, Rodrick and Rena had to hurry to keep up with the other two, slipping between the tents only to realize Logan wasn't waiting for them, and had already headed into the forest.

It took them half the time to get back to the caravan than it had taken them to get to the camp. Rena had wanted to catch up to Logan to ask him what was going on, but he was walking with such speed that she periodically had to start jogging to just keep up with her group. She didn't even have much time to worry about what might be wrong, too busy focusing on the forest floor so she wouldn't trip.

When they reached the caravan and Rena finally managed to catch up the rest of the group, she had to first lean against the wagon and take in deep breaths before she was able to speak.

"What's going on?" she finally wheezed out.

"We shouldn't stay here for too long," Logan replied, shuffling around, his gaze darting between the spot they had just emerged from and the road.

Vincent jumped down from the driver's seat and strolled up to them, drifting from one person to the next to sniff at them. Rena pushed herself away from the caravan again and crouched to greet the dog. She took his face into both her hands and scratch behind his ears, so happy to see that he was unharmed.

"What did you do this time?" Asha asked, her hand leisurely poised on the pommel of her sword, her eyes fixed on Logan.

"Nothing," Logan blurted out, throwing his arms widely. "None of your business. It's a private affair. Why are you here anyway? I asked for your uncle."

"I wasn't going to let Sayaf go to the Plains with some strangers. Why did you send them to him? You know he's out of the business."

"I was meant to come with them, okay, but then Kalani found us so I sent them off without me. I know he's out of the business, but since when did simply asking ever hurt anyone? Especially since it's such a serious situation they're looking into. I thought your uncle might understand what's at stake. He still has connections, so I knew he could at least point us in the right direction if he genuinely didn't want to help, and since you're here I assume my thought process wasn't that wrong." While talking, he paced around in unpredictable patterns, waving his hands in wild motions. "Can we open the caravan now? We should really be on our way. The Plains are at the other end of the province, it's going to take a while to get there."

Rena didn't like his energy, didn't like what his nervousness might imply. She glanced back at the forest, trying to see if anyone was following them, but it was impossible to see very far. She forced her breathing to remain calm and slowly stood up.

Rodrick stood next to her with his hands on his hips, breathing heavily through his open mouth. Asha's gaze was still fixed on Logan – her jaw clenching, her muscles tight - until her eyes flicked to Rena's, and this time Rena could hold her gaze, and they both understood the unease of the other.

When Rodrick's breathing had calmed, he rummaged in his coat and slipped out the key to the caravan. He walked over to the back door and unlocked it with a loud *thunk*.

"Okay great," Logan said, bounding to the door. "I don't know if we can get to the Plains before nightfall. Maybe we'll have to take a rest somewhere. Rodrick, how far can this thing go? How does it even work? Can it just go on forever or does it need a break? I'm sure we can take a break in some village, not sure what you need to refill it though, but if it's just coal, we can find that anywhere."

"We should be good for the duration of our journey," Rodrick answered as he opened the door and stepped into the wagon. Logan stood right behind him, and had the doorframe been slightly wider he would have surely tried to squeeze his way past Rodrick.

"I have water and coal to refill the tank on my own," Rodrick continued as he turned back around. "We will just have to take a little break on the side of the road somewhere."

"Why are you so nervous?" Asha asked, coming to stand next to Logan.

"I'm not nervous," Logan insisted, avoiding her gaze.

"Don't bullshit me."

"I'm not nervous, I just want to get out of here," he replied, running a hand through his hair, pulling more curls out of his bun. He looked around once more, avoiding all of their stares, before continuing to talk. "Yeah, okay. Maybe things didn't pan out the way I thought they would, and maybe the discussion got heated, and you know me, sometimes I say stuff I probably shouldn't have, but I was in the right so I'm not going to apologise for it. And if Cass can accept that, then Deacon should too. But he's stubborn, and a moron, so I just want to get out of here before he gets it into his head that the discussion isn't over."

"So, we're running away because you couldn't keep your mouth shut? Why am I not surprised?" Asha sighed and motioned for Rodrick to step out of the caravan so she could get in.

"Will you be okay?" Rena asked, finding herself actually concerned for his well-being.

"Yeah, I'll be fine," Logan replied, waving Rena's concerns away. "Anyways, the deal I had with Deacon didn't blow up because of me. I told him it was unlikely to go the way he wanted it to, and lo and behold, his plan didn't work out, and now he's blaming me for selling false hope. But I literally warned him, so absolutely none of this is my fault."

"Excuse me," Rodrick muttered as he slid past them, and Logan didn't miss the opportunity to slip inside the caravan before Asha.

Rena eyed Logan's back wearily and then turned around to glance at the forest one last time to make sure there definitely wasn't anyone chasing after them.

"Do you want to sit in the front with me?" Rodrick asked Rena, leaning down to pet Vincent.

She nodded eagerly, thinking that the long ride would be much more bearable in front, even if the seat wasn't very comfortable.

Rena had rarely travelled this far in one day. She had been at her aunt's house three times in her life, which was beyond Mellahen — the capital of the province which held the archives. But it had been a long time ago, and she had only ever seen Mellahen and the Plains— the accumulation of houses surrounding the fortress that housed the archives —in passing.

Night had fallen long before they reached the capital, so when the road finally widened and they emerged from the woods onto the wide, empty expanse of the Plains, the lights of the makeshift city were clearly visible.

In the far distance, was the outline of the archives, barely discernible against the star-filled night sky. Rena didn't know much about the place, but she knew that no one actually lived inside the fortress – except the administrator and her family. Anyone who worked inside the archives had to live in the Plains. Over the years, so many people from all over the province had travelled here in the hopes of finding a job that the Plains in itself had become a city.

"Do you think we can actually find the truth here?" Rena asked, staring straight ahead at the orange dots of light that slowly drew closer. Rodrick sighed heavily before answering.

"The entire truth? Probably not. But I think we can at least find the beginning of it. Or a few crumbs that will lead us in the right direction."

"I don't even really know what we're looking for," Rena muttered. "Would they already have a file on Oceansthrow? It's still so recent, I'm not even sure they know about it yet."

"I'm sure there will be something," Rodrick reassured her. "If not about Oceansthrow, then about Miller's Knee, or the other towns."

Rena nodded slowly and looked around, her heart heavy, thinking about the journey ahead. She was still exhausted from their visit to the city of Rancor, and her eyes burned as she forced them to stay open. Her mind felt like she was under water, preventing her from forming any coherent thoughts. All she knew, was that she needed to find out what happened to her village so she could save her sister.

As they came closer to the Plains she started recognising buildings. Large structures stood close to the road that led into the city, sparse and far apart. They looked fragile and decrepit, as if they had been built quickly without any regard for comfort or longevity. Past those, speckled across the grassy field to their left and right, were smaller houses – shacks that had been built in only a few hours and that could easily be dismantled. No road led to these buildings, and no lights glowed inside. Rena couldn't even see what was beyond, but she imagined tents like those she had seen in the city of Rancor, something that could be moved at any moment, inhabited by people who barely owned anything but still wanted to try their luck in Mellahen.

Even though night had already fallen, the streets were still alive. People were standing around talking and laughing, and Rena even saw a man get thrown out of a pub – the assailant stomping out after the man to continue their fight. Rena's body tensed and she quickly looked away, feeling grateful she was in a moving vehicle and not walking past on foot.

The further they got, the closer together the buildings were, and the more they looked like they could withstand a strong gust of wind. Side-streets had formed naturally through foot traffic, and dark shapes darted in the shadows between houses – feral dogs and rats and other creatures. On a crate between two houses, Rena even saw a fox. It didn't scamper away like the rest of the animals. It just sat there, facing the street, looking right at her. It took her a while to register this oddity, but when she turned around to look at it, the crate had already disappeared behind the edge of a house. She had heard that animals behaved differently in cities – that they lost their fear of humans – but she had never felt so acknowledged, so seen, by a wild animal before.

Rodrick drove them further into the city, and the actual street – which was now paved with cobblestones – started to branched out to the left and right. By now, the structures facing the road were mostly shops and other businesses, although most were closed at this time of day. More and more stone houses appeared, as if people had committed to remaining in the Plains. At first, it seemed like daily life had died down this far into the city, but Rena quickly realised that people had just wandered away from the main road and were now socialising on the side streets.

Apparently, Rodrick knew where he was taking them, because he took a right turn and then a left and another right, leading them to an open square between a tall building and a lower, wooden stable.

"Have you been here before?" Rena asked, glancing up at the high building rising next to them. She counted four stories, maybe five seeing as the windows weren't all in neat rows. The wall was different shades of white and beige, as if the upper floors had been added over the years.

"A long time ago," Rodrick answered, driving the caravan up to the other end of the square. He pulled a lever, and the caravan sputtered to a stop. "They only had two stories back then, and the Plains definitely didn't reach as close to the forest as they do now, but I remember the inn having very comfortable beds back then, so I hope that has remained a constant over the years."

She hummed at the thought of a comfortable bed – or any bed for that matter.

Rodrick climbed down and walked over to her side, reaching out a hand to help her down, pulling Rena out of her reverie.

"Finally! Freedom!" Logan cried out as he threw the door open and burst out of the caravan. "I couldn't even hear my own thoughts with all that noise."

He stretched his arms out towards the sky and then bent to the ground, swinging his arms back and forth.

Asha climbed out behind him and strode right up to Rena and Rodrick, craning her neck from side to side.

"Why does your vehicle have to be this loud?" Logan whined, joining the rest of the group. "What's wrong with the normal kind with horses? Why can't you just have one of those? This is torture. I can't believe I was intrigued by it this morning. Are you so old that you don't hear the noise anymore, is that it? And the vibration is good for your aching bones? I'm too young to get shaken around like this."

"For once, I have to agree with him," Asha replied.

"Because it is a marvel of technology and it reminds me of home," Rodrick said fondly, patting the side of the caravan.

Rena stepped past her companions and looked up at the mismatched windows on the façade of the inn. Even though they all had different shapes and sizes, similar elements could be found again and again – a rounded arch at the top, an ochre-coloured border, and metal grates encasing them. The double doors to the inn stood wide open, letting the chatter of its guests escape to the street.

Vincent strolled past her, furiously sniffing the ground, before turning back to the group – examining the street around them but never straying too far.

"I suppose it is too late to go looking for your uncle's contact this late at night," Rodrick mentioned.

"We can go first thing in the morning," Asha replied. "He should be able to tell us what exactly we need. It has been almost a decade since I last met him, but if my uncle recommends him, then I don't think he'll rip us off. I'd still only trust a stranger in this profession as far than I can throw them. He'll try to sell us more than we actually need, so just keep that in mind when we visit him."

"What do you think Emmson will want in return?" Rena asked, stepping back to her companions. It slowly dawned on her that he very likely wouldn't just give them the decrees for free and that she had nothing she could bargain with.

"Money?" Asha replied, side-eyeing her as if Rena might have been asking them a trick question.

"I don't have any," Rena muttered.

"Don't worry about it, we'll figure something out," Rodrick told her. "We can always try to sell one of my knickknacks. I have too many things in the back of the caravan anyway."

"You don't have to sell your possessions because of me!" Rena exclaimed, terrified at the idea that someone might even consider that.

"We can always try to bargain with him," Logan said with a shrug. "He gives us the decrees, we do something else for him."

"I suppose," Rena replied, unsure of what someone who sold forged decrees would ask as a favour in return.

Chapter Twelve

Rena looked around at the room she shared with Asha that night, bewildered by the choices the innkeepers had taken for the decoration. Five paintings of marbled ducks hung on the walls, all drawn in different styles. The nightstand between the two beds held a row of wooden marbled duck figurines, arranged in a circle from smallest to biggest. In the middle of the circle was a bouquet of red carnations – although Rena had already touched them and figured out they weren't real flowers, but made of tissue instead. The drapes in front of the window were black with red dots that she supposed were meant to also represent red carnations. The wooden window and door frames had more marbled ducks in various stages of flight carved into them – although whoever had been responsible for them had clearly not been a professional. The room was illuminated by two candles, each placed on a simple, floor-length candle holder.

If this much effort had been put into just one regular room of this inn, then Rena couldn't even imagine how much money and time had been invested into the entirety of the building.

She finally sat down on her bed, her bones aching for rest. She ran her hands over the fresh linen, marvelling at its softness. She had had the privilege of getting into a bath first, and was now wearing one of the thick cotton robes Rodrick had given each of them. It was much too wide and long for her, which was perfect for sleeping. Her own dress had been washed and hung up to dry overnight. The few possessions she had on her had simply been placed on the nightstand in between the ducks and fake flowers – careful not to touch either of them.

Her body wanted to lean back and drift off into sleep, but at the same time, something in her stomach tightened and her blood ran cold. Flashes of a dream she had had the previous night came back, quickly followed by the echo of how she had woken up.

She stood back up and walked over to the window. Even from her viewpoint on the fourth floor, she couldn't see much of the city. She could only really see the buildings surrounding them, anything beyond were just spots of dim lights in the darkness. She opened the window and leaned out, looking to her right to see the lights outlining the shape of the fortress.

"Careful with that," Asha warned as she walked into the room.

Rena turned around to lean against the windowsill, observing as Asha rolled her shoulders and moved her arms, frowning at the straining fabric of her own cotton robe that was much too tight on her arms and chest. She folded her other clothes together on the bed before placing them in a neat pile on one of the two chairs on the opposite side of the room.

"I'm sorry we had to drag you into this," Rena told her, her eyes drifting off to stare at the floorboards in front of her, too exhausted to stay focused.

"I'm using you just as much as you're using me," Asha replied. "There's nothing to apologize for."

"Still, I'm sure you had other things planned for this week." Rena forced herself to look up at Asha and gave her a small smile.

"You don't have to worry about how I plan my time," Asha replied, too busy tugging at the fabric of her tunic to reciprocate Rena's smile. "If you worry about everyone else's decisions all the time, you won't get anywhere in life."

Rena nodded slowly, unsure how to respond. The exhaustion was spreading through her body – the tips of her fingers were ice cold and prickling while her eyes burned each time she blinked – and the thoughts in her head entangled themselves into one big ball of noise.

Asha sighed before turning to look at her.

"Listen, I'm sorry. I don't know what exactly happened to you or your hometown, but I know how these things can weigh on someone. I know I shouldn't be too harsh on you, but this life we live, it doesn't blend well with being selfless and generous."

Rena looked up at Asha and nodded again.

"I know," she murmured, although she really didn't. She couldn't imagine having to live a life where being polite and acknowledging other people's feelings and needs was seen as counter productive to your own growth.

"Your uncle mentioned you were from the Grey Isles, right?" Rena tried again, hoping to finally lead them towards an actual conversation.

Asha turned and wandered over to the nightstand. She picked up one of the duck figurines and turned it around in her hand. Rena waited for her to say anything, but nothing came.

"How did you and your uncle arrive in the city of Rancor?" Rena continued, desperate to fill the silence.

Asha took a long breath and sighed.

"We don't have to talk about this. You can concentrate on what you want to get out of the archives, and I will concentrate on what *I* want to get out of them. There is no reason for us to discuss our backstories."

Rena pressed her lips together and glanced back at the floor, feeling the heat rise in her cheeks.

"Okay," she murmured. Her hand reached up to idly play with the ring hanging from her necklace.

She should have known better to pry into someone's past like this, should have known that people who lived in the city of Rancor might not have had the most pleasant of lives. Certainly, on a better day, Rena would have remembered her manners. But she felt so alone and lost and craving connections, that she was desperate to know even the tiniest details about her companions.

She pressed the ring against her lips, her eyes wandering lazily up, snapping to meet Asha's when she noticed the other woman was looking at her. Rena froze, unable to read her new companion's mind, a feeling sinking deep into her stomach that she had offended Asha more than initially thought.

Asha cleared her throat before looking down at Rena's necklace and nodding towards it.

"What's that?" she asked.

"Uhm," Rena started, even though her mouth was bone dry. "It's my sister's ring."

"You have a sister," Asha repeated, her voice monotone.

"Yes, and three brothers," Rena said, looking down at the ring and pendant around her neck.

"Hmm," Asha hummed, then let silence linger for an awkward moment, before continuing. "I also had siblings once. Two brothers."

"I'm sorry for your loss," Rena said in a small voice.

Asha simply nodded, her eyes still fixed on Rena's necklace, as if she was thinking of something else.

"I'm sorry for yours," she added hastily after a few seconds.

"Thank you," Rena replied, and then the silence encroached on the room again, heavier than it had been before.

"I found the ring on the ground near our house," Rena burst out, "when I was walking through the ruins of our town. Before I left she had been cleaning my grandmother's old jewellery, so actually the ring belonged to my grandmother, but Maya said she wanted to keep it, so in my mind it's actually hers now." Rena paused for a moment, waiting for Asha to say anything, but she remained silent. "I can't figure out why it was outside of the house. I keep wondering, what if she's still alive? What if she somehow managed to escape? What if the ones who set the fire took her for some reason?"

At that Asha looked up at her and her face grew weary, before she turned around and walked over to her pile of clothes. She slid the arm guards out from under her tunic and handed them to Rena. Confused, Rena took them, and looked up at Asha to figure out what she wanted Rena to do with them.

"These belonged to one of my brothers," Asha finally said and sat down on the bed opposite Rena. "He died a few years ago. I don't like talking about it, but every day when I put these on, I think of him."

Rena glanced down at the braces and ran her thumb over the worn leather.

"You must miss him terribly," Rena murmured.

"And it never gets easier," Asha told her. "You can only accept that your life is different now and there's no going back. I also spent months after his death bargaining and trying to figure out all the possibilities for how he could have survived, but it was all just a waste of time."

Rena looked up at her and opened her mouth to protest – to tell her that there really was a chance that Maya might still be alive – but before she could say anything Asha continued talking.

"I'm telling you this because those months were agony for me. Even now I still catch myself thinking that he might be out there somewhere. He isn't. He died that day and I have to live with that knowledge. There is nothing to be done about it. I don't want you to go through the same pain."

Rena stared at her, mouth agape, until the tears started running down her face. Her left hand came to cover her mouth while she sobbed, her right clutching the arm guards tightly to her chest as if they meant something to her.

"I don't expect you to believe me right away," Asha told her. "And I'm not telling you to abandon your quest. Whoever did this has to be punished. But I don't want you to keep going on this journey expecting to get your sister back in the end. Not if the only evidence you have is a ring you found in a muddy street."

Rena bit down on her lips to get her breathing back under control. She shut her eyes tightly and willed the tears to stop flowing. Maya had to be alive. What had been the point of her finding the ring if it didn't mean anything?

"This is going to sting for a while," Asha said and got up. "Don't pretend like you're doing better than you actually are."

She stepped past Rena and towards her own bed.

"We should go to bed," she said and blew out the candle on her side of the room.

Rena took in long shaky breaths until she had calmed down again. She pushed herself away from the windowsill and closed the window behind her. She carefully placed the arm guards on top of the pile of Asha's clothes, blew out the second candle, and slipped into her own bed.

She let the events of the morning she last saw her family pass before her eyes, holding her necklace tightly in her fist. She saw her grandmother's ring so clearly in Maya's hand, saw it so clearly in the mud and ash outside of her house. It had to mean something, no matter what Asha had said. It couldn't have simply been a coincidence.

Chapter Thirteen

The next morning, Asha led them further into the city, closer to the archives. They weaved their way through side streets, past large, opulent houses. They had been painted in white with brightly coloured window trims, with the windows being barricaded by cast-iron bars. The cornices atop the houses had been carved from stone – delicate, repeating patterns depicting plants, flowers, and sometimes animals. The road was large enough for two carriages to pass, and had been paved with cobble stones. It was as if they had stepped into an entirely different city, one where the inhabitants didn't have to fight for their survival each day. Walking through these streets was an even stranger feeling for Rena than being in the city of Rancor had been. It didn't even feel like her province anymore, as if they had been transported to the capital – or what she imagined the capital to look like. Some of the houses had been built in styles she had never seen before, with dark stones and pointed roofs. The people around them wore equally opulent and strange clothes – more elegant than the few dresses she had owned for special occasions.

Asha entered a store, and Rena frowned up at the sign over the door that read *antique books*. Her confusion only grew when she entered the building and the room was, in fact, packed with bookshelf upon bookshelf of aged books, with tables in between that held other knick-knacks – reading glasses, candle holders, leather covers for notebooks, the occasional map or two. The air smelled stale, as if the mere presence of humans stirred up the dust ingrained in the objects.

While Rena and Rodrick were busy marvelling about the place they had just stepped into, Asha strolled right past all of it and towards a man standing behind a counter at the other end of the room.

"Good morning, how can I help you?" The man asked politely, his hands clasped behind his back.

"I've got a letter from my uncle for you," Asha replied and dug the letter out of her tunic.

Emmson's smile didn't falter, but he tilted his head slightly to the right and looked at the letter Asha was holding out to him for a while.

"You are Sayaf's niece, if I'm not mistaken," he said, looking back up at Asha, still not taking the letter. "Yes, we've met before. Excuse me, I should have recognised you quicker."

"The letter," Asha repeated, pushing it out towards Emmson.

He looked back at it and finally unclasped his hands. He opened the letter and held it up to the gas lamp behind him, humming slightly as he read it.

He didn't look like Rena had imagined. For starters, he didn't actually seem that much younger than Sayaf. He was a thin man, not very tall, with sharp features and protruding ears. His skin was a warm light brown, with freckles running over his nose and cheeks. His clothes were as fine as any of the passers-by outside – a layered tunic made of different shades of brown with red seams, similar to what Asha and her uncle wore – and he had round, wire-frame glasses on. He also sported similar jewellery as Asha and her uncle – several golden rings pierced into the upper cartilage of his right ear, and a dangling pendant on his left.

"Ah, I see," he said, and folded the letter back up. "Please follow me."

He turned around and walked to a door to his left. As they passed through the backroom that was filled with more bookshelves, he instructed a young woman who was reorganising books to go to the storefront and remain there until he got back. The woman hurried away without a comment and Emmson led them further into the building until they reached a small room behind a locked door. After they had all stepped inside, Emmson locked the room behind them.

Rena looked at the door in panic, then at her companions, but Logan and Asha didn't seem perturbed, and Rodrick shot her a reassuring smile. She glanced around to see if there was anything Emmson could use to overwhelm them, or if there were any hidden doors through which goons could burst in, but the room was sparsely filled. At the back, opposite the door, stood a sturdy wooden desk, with a lavish, cushioned seat to one side, and two smaller chairs to the other. Behind the desk was a row of bookshelves, filled with various boxes and ledgers.

Emmson walked around the desk and sat down in the cushioned chair. He unfolded the letter in front of him, smoothing it down on the desk. Without looking up, he gestured towards the two chairs opposite him.

"Please, take a seat," he told them, his attention fixed on the letter.

Asha sat down on the right-most chair, while Logan stepped aside to let Rena take the other.

"I haven't heard much from Sayaf in a long while," Emmson said, looking up at Asha with a polite smile and interlocking his hands in front of him. "I hope he's doing fine."

"He is," Asha replied, leaning forward in her chair, resting her elbows against her knees. "But we're not here to chitchat."

"Of course not." Emmson turned around in his chair and pulled a heavy leather-bound ledger from the shelf behind him. He gently placed it on the desk next to the letter, intertwined his hands again. "So, you require access to the archives. What exactly will you need?"

Asha looked over at Rena, and Rena realised with surprise that Asha expected her to talk. She had no idea how these kinds of interactions worked, or how much she was allowed to tell this man.

"Uhm." Rena glanced over at her companions, hoping one of them would help her out. "I'm not exactly sure. We were told you could get us a decree that would grant us entry into the archives."

"There are many different kinds of decrees." Emmson smiled at her.

"Would you potentially have a list for us?" Rodrick asked, saving Rena from her unease.

"Not a list per se, but if you tell me what you are looking for, I can tell you which decree you need. But it will cost you."

"Yes, of course," Rena said slowly, apprehending to hear that she wouldn't be able to afford any of the decrees.

"I will need an exchange of documents from you."

"An exchange of documents?" Rena repeated dumbfounded.

"Sayaf didn't explain how I conduct my business, did he?" Emmson said and squinted at her.

"He didn't exactly tell us much about you," Asha replied.

"Very well," Emmson said, glancing down while running his hands over the cover of the ledger, before looking back up at them. "Depending on which section of the archives you visit, you will either bring me back some information, or bring something *to* the archives. If you were to be tasked with bringing back information, I will need the original documents."

"The originals?" Rena asked in bewilderment, not having expected to be tasked with theft.

"Yes." He smiled politely at Rena. "Copying the information just won't do. It would take too long for you to copy everything that I need, and it would be difficult for me to trust the accuracy of the information."

"If you can make your own decrees, why don't you just go into the archives yourself?" Logan asked.

"If I went in myself multiple times a week with a variety of different decrees, they would instantly get suspicious. It's much safer if strangers do this work for me. And I am also much too busy to search for the documents myself. Like this, we both gain something from this interaction."

"Fair enough," Logan said with a shrug then stepped forward. He crouched down next to Rena and placed his arms on the desk. "So, I need anything that relates to the train."

"Certainly," Emmson replied and turned his attention to the ledger in front of him.

"The train?" Rena asked in a hushed voice while Emmson was busy leafing through the pages.

Logan simply put his fingers in front of his lips and winked at her.

She squinted at him in confusion. She had heard that a new machine was being built in the north, something massive, that could transport hundreds, if not thousands of people, from city to city at a much faster rate than a caravan. It was supposed to be able to run at any hours of the day or night, and would even be able to opperate under water to reach the peninsulas to the north-west.

"What's the most restricted area you can get us into?" Asha asked.

"I can get you a decree for any of them," Emmson replied, looking at her from over the rim of his glasses, then turned his attention back to the ledger. "But they require that a clerk accompany you to the more restricted areas. The stronger the restriction, the more difficult it is to forge a decree. The clerks will question who you are and why they hadn't been informed of your arrival before. So, it all depends on how well you can lie."

"I don't know if I would risk that, Asha," Logan told her. "Would be hard for you to pretend to be someone else, with your one facial expression."

"Don't pretend like you would be able to fool them either," Asha shot back.

"How dare you? I am a professional," Logan opposed in mock offense.

"I need to get to the section where they talk about other provinces," Asha said, ignoring Logan's protest.

Emmson stopped leafing through the ledger and smoothed the pages out with both hands, going from the centre to the outer edges.

"Which provinces?" he asked.

"The Grey Isles."

The corner of Emmson's mouth twitched and he looked down as he interlinked his fingers again, before looking back up at Asha.

"I doubt you would find much of what you're looking for, and it would cost you more than you could realistically procure me."

"I can take my own decisions," Asha replied dryly.

Emmson raised his hands in surrender.

"As you wish, but I cannot guarantee that you will find what you seek. That applies to all of the decrees I can give you. I simply give you access to the archives and advise you on where you *might* find certain information, nothing more."

"Yes, of course," Rodrick answered.

"Now," Emmson continued, turning to Logan. "There are a few sections you could visit if you wanted to know more about the railway system."

Chapter Fourteen

By mid-day, they were travelling up the main road that led to the archives. Rena had opted to only get decrees in the lesser restricted sections, not knowing what she was really looking for, and afraid of what Emmson might have asked of her for the higher restricted ones. To her relief, he had only demanded she bring documents back into the archives. As he explained it, if he were to only ever request documents be taken out of the archives, the clerks would soon be wary of the massive number of absent files. If, however, periodically, people brought the documents back, the clerks would simply think they had been declared absent by accident. Emmson had given her three tightly wound rolls of parchment, and asked that she damage or flatten them as little as possible.

Before leaving for the archives, they had tied the rolls to Rena's biceps, hiding them underneath her sleeve. She had to hold her arm slightly away from her body so as not to crush the documents. Their presence felt like a burning mark to her, as if the constant contact hurt her skin. She was certain that anyone could see that she was hiding something, that the second she attracted any kind of attention, she would be found out. But people surrounding them were too busy with their own affairs, and if they ever thought of glancing their way, it was to stare at Rodrick's caravan.

The road to the archives was divided into two lanes, one for carriages to the left, and one for those on foot to the right. On each side of the road, four tall poles with milky white bulbs guided the way. The lights were still on, colouring the clouded glass in a dim orange hue, even though they were travelling underneath an blue sky and the sun was out. Rodrick slowed the caravan, trying to leave enough room between them and the carriage in front. They were coming up to the entrance, the giant metal gates having opened outward. Etched into each side of the gates was a tableau of scholars and record keepers entangled with long rolls of parchment.

Rena kept her gaze low as they were led through the gates and towards a covered space near the rest of the horse-drawn carriage. She thought that if she let Rodrick talk to anyone approaching them, then she could go unnoticed. She was simply his humble assistant, fated to remain in his shadow until he called for her.

They exited the caravan, and a clerk instructed them to leave the dog and any weapon inside the vehicle, which Asha only reluctantly agreed to. They were then led to the main entrance, and they stepped into a wide room with a high, domed ceiling. White, blue, and green-patterned tiles covered the floors and the lower parts of the walls, while delicate swirls had been carved into the white stone of the upper half. To their right, a row of desks housed clerks who wore long, yellow and green robes. Two hallways to their left and at the far end of the room lead inside the fortress, next to which large signs listed which departments lay beyond.

Rena gazed at the room in wonder, eyes wide, lips parted, and only remembered belatedly that she had planned on not drawing any attention. She slowly closed her mouth and glanced at the people around them, but no one was looking in their direction. She straightened her back and clasped her hands in front of her, awkwardly pushing her arm out just the slightest to not flatten the documents. The constant tension in her arm was starting to make her muscles ache, but she couldn't let the discomfort show on her face.

"Guess this is where we split up," Logan said.

"Rena and I will be in the department of topographical works," Rodrick told the group. "If you run into any trouble, or can't find where you have to go, come and find us there. I'm not sure how long we'll be there, however."

"We'll be fine," Asha said dryly, craning her neck to read the signs next to the hallways.

Logan leaned forward and patted Rodrick on the arm twice, flashing a grin.

"Don't worry, old man. We know how to get out of tricky situations on our own."

He leaned over to ruffle Rena's hair and winked.

"Let's go."

He turned around before Rena could protest, her free hand frantically trying to smooth her hair out while her other arm remained stiffly at her side. Asha followed him without any further comment, and they weaved their way through the crowd to the end of the room. Rodrick shook his head at their retreating figures before turning to Rena and smiling.

A SEARING FAITH

"Shall we?"

It took them some time to find their way to the correct room, having opted to deliver Emmson's documents first. Even though all the rooms were neatly numbered, the hallways branched out in such weird and unexpected ways that they had to backtrack a few times before finding where they were actually meant to go. Rena had expected guards to stand in front of each room to make sure people couldn't just enter wherever they wanted, but they only saw a handful of them leisurely strolling through the hallways in groups of two, talking to each other and barely regarding the people hurrying from one place to the next. Each time Rena passed them, she made sure to keep her head bowed and her eyes fixed on the ground, too afraid of making eye contact with one of them.

For most of their journey, however, Rena couldn't keep herself from at least glancing at the people surrounding them. Some stood to the sides in deep conversation, some rushed past them. Some wore long, embroidered robes in a multitude of colours, some paraded in tight-fitting leather trousers that had to be laced at the sides. Some had wide-brimmed hats, some wore veils covering their faces, and some even wore the clothes Rena was used to seeing in her small village. She tried not to stare, to pretend like she belonged there, but some of the clothing was so unusual, so fascinating, that she had to hold on to Rodrick's sleeve to not lose him in the crowd.

But now, as they neared their destination, they barely met anyone. Rodrick pushed open the simple, dark brown door and they entered into a room that was only dimply illuminated by the same milky white bulbs they had seen outside, fixed high on the ceiling. The floor tiles were a continuation of the intricate, symmetrical blue, white and green star pattern that had stretched throughout the entire building. In front of them stood rows of dark brown bookcases, made of the same wood as the door and the rest of the furniture in the building. They were filled not just with books, but also rolls of parchment in stacked boxes.

"Permit, please." A boy not much older than Rena sat behind a table to their right. He looked at them with the greatest disinterest, as if sitting there had been a punishment imposed upon him by his parents.

When Rodrick handed him the appropriate decree, he barely looked at it before giving it back, not asking for any verification or explanation of what they were looking for. Rodrick simply turned around and walked away as if he hadn't expected to be questioned. But as Rena followed him, she couldn't stop herself from glancing back at the boy, making sure he hadn't changed his mind. The documents tied to her arm felt heavy, as if they could slip out at any moment and reveal their plan. The boy, however, had slumped back into his chair, shoulders drooping, and stared off into the distance.

Rena turned back to Rodrick, leaning in so no one else would hear her.

"Doesn't he want to know why we're here?" she whispered.

Rodrick had stopped in front of one of the bookcases, reading the sign hanging on its side. He frowned before looking from side to side, glancing back at the sign, and only then looked over at Rena.

"Hmm? Ah, I don't think these records are that important, so they probably don't care too much about who gets access to them. It is more like a formality. And I don't think that boy cares about it either."

"Then why not just make them available to the public if they barely look at the decrees anyway?"

Rodrick chuckled softly.

"Well, they can't just let anyone look at their records, now, can they? There needs to be some weeding out or who knows where we'd get. Ah, this way I believe."

He turned to the right and strode past a dozen bookshelves, keeping track of the signs before abruptly turning left and hurrying down one of the rows. Rena stared after him, frowning at what he had just told her. She tried to wrap her mind around it, tried to figure out how it could make sense, but all she ever came back to was the question of why make people go through the process of getting a decree if they didn't look at them. Surely, it would be less work for everyone if this section of the archives was simply open to the general public.

With a sigh she followed Rodrick and finally realized how deep the room went. Even just one of these bookshelves barely would have fit into any of the rooms in her parents' house, and if she counted correctly, there were five in one row, with space for a passageway between each. Rodrick only led them to the second bookshelf though, to a part that seemed quite empty in comparison to the one they had just passed. No books were present in this section, only rolls of parchment at the top, and wooden boxes at the bottom. Each shelf was labelled with letters and numbers, abbreviations that Rena couldn't decipher, and each box was fitted with a longer label that seemed an even greater mystery to her. But not to Rodrick, who after only a few seconds of careful consideration reached to pull one of the boxes out, and crouched to place it on the ground. Without hesitation, he opened the lid, and revealed rolls of paper, bound shut by differently coloured ribbons.

He looked up at Rena, and furtively glanced at her arm. A cold shudder ran over her body, making it almost impossible for her to move. She carefully glanced to both sides of the corridor, making sure no one was near them. Now and then, people passed between rows, but no one stopped long enough to look at them.

Rena took a deep breath, then slowly reached her hand down her sleeve, and pulled the first roll out. She had wanted to drag it out in one, smooth motion, but it got stuck, and she had to pull on it. The other two rolls tumbled out of her sleeve, having yanked the string holding them to her arm out of place.

Out of reflex, Rena dropped down to pick them up and turned to look both sides, before realising how suspicious that looked. She froze, and slowly turned back to Rodrick, clutching the documents to her chest. Her heart was hammering in her ears, and yet, she tried to hear if anyone was running up to them to confront them.

"It's fine," Rodrick whispered, holding his hand out to her. "No one's looking at us."

She gently handed him the documents, then clasped her trembling hands in front of her. Rodrick loosened the ties binding the parchment rolls, and retied them once they had the same diameter as the rolls in the box. He buried their documents underneath the rest of parchment rolls, then pushed the box back in its place.

"Let's go find our information," he said and got up with a groan.

Rena kept her eyes decidedly on the ground as they exited the room, not even daring to glance at anyone they passed. She stayed behind Rodrick as he led them through the hallways, following him like a shadow. It took them longer than it should have to find the next room, one labelled "R1TG3" in big letters with a barely legible subtitle reading "Topographical Works".

This time around, the young girl behind the desk read their decree very carefully, nodding along a bit too enthusiastically. She handed it back to them with a wide smile and wished them a pleasant visit. Rena forced herself to smile back, telling herself that if no one had caught up to them until then, they had gotten away with their reversed robbery.

Rodrick hurried from bookshelf to bookshelf, picking out box after box. Rena tried to follow his thought process, but the labels on the ledgers and boxes just looked like a jumble of letters and numbers to her. By the end of it, all she had gathered was that the number at the end had to be the year the documents had been written.

Rodrick led them to a section in the middle of the room and pulled out another box. He sat it down on the ground, and together they unrolled a few of the documents. Most of the rolls contained a few pieces of loose paper. The first page was always the same, with small boxes at the top indicating the location, date, and who had been responsible for the project. The rest of the text was usually a detailed description of what exactly had been done, and why.

They went through five rolls before they stumbled upon one that mention Miller's Knee. Instantly, the paper looked different than the previous documents. At the bottom of the first page, a line had been cut out and a note had been scribbled in the margins next to it. The further they got into the report, more pieces of the pages were missing, or had simply been crossed out to make the text impossible to read.

"What do the margins say?" Rena asked.

She leaned closer, trying to read the tiny font, but it looked like more of the abbreviations she didn't understand.

"It appears it's sending us to a more restricted area," Rodrick said, holding the page at arm's length before bringing it closer to his face.

He rummaged around in his coat before pulling out a little tin box that held a piece of charcoal. He took the decree they had used to get into the room, turned it around, and noted down the abbreviations from the margins.

"Should we be writing on that?" Rena asked, side-eyeing him.

"Such a little note will hardly invalidate the legitimacy of this decree," he replied.

"Especially since it doesn't have any," she murmured, and turned her attention back to the strange document.

The longer she looked at the cut-up pages, the more her confusion grew. The fact that these documents had been censored was proof enough that something strange was going on, but why keep the records at all then? Why not simply keep them in the most restricted areas that regular people could not access?

She turned to Rodrick with a sigh.

"Where should we start?"

The notes led from one room to another, until Rena felt like she had seen the entirety of the archives. And still, none of the documents they found answered any of their questions. They all had holes in them, referring to yet another room, and Rena and Rodrick spiralled deeper and deeper into the fortress, getting closer to the areas they did not have a decree for.

Rena's unease grew with each time they had to show anyone a decree. She could still feel the phantom of the documents she had tied to her arm earlier. Her skin itched, as if her body demanded to get out of the building, and as far away from anyone who could arrest her as possible. It didn't feel like they were making any progress anyway. She had barely learned anything about the fire that destroyed Miller's Knee, and why it had to be kept such a secret. She had, however, learned a lot about the guard corps' process for clearing an area after such events.

But Rodrick insisted on continuing their investigation, even knowing full well that the decrees Emmson had given them would only get them so far.

The sound of their footsteps echoed around them as they went down the spiral staircase to the second basement, the smell of humidity heavy in the air. No one else was around this deep in the archives, and it was quiet enough that she heard the hiss of the gas lamps. They weren't nearly as bright as the lamps that had illuminated the hallways above them, as if it didn't matter as much if people down here could see where they were going.

She nervously looked around, hoping to spot anyone else, afraid they had strayed too far from where visitors were allowed to go, but the hallway was long and empty, and only then did she notice that there weren't any doors or signs around them.

"Are we going in the right direction?" Rena whispered.

"We should be," Rodrick whispered back. "At least that's what the signs upstairs were saying."

They suddenly stopped when a door creaked shut and they could hear faint whispers in the distance, slowly coming closer from a bend in the hallway in front of them.

"Quick, show me your list," Rena hissed.

She motioned for Rodrick to hurry up, turning him around to face the wall and huddling close so they could both look down at the list.

The voices got louder as they got closer, and soon Rena was able to understand what they were saying.

"I could arrange for one of the records keepers to accompany you next time if you have more specific questions," an older voice with a haughty undertone said. "I'm sorry I couldn't be of much service to you, that area isn't my expertise. I do know a lot about the inner workings of the military academy, if that is another area you would be interested in."

"Not really, no," a clearly disinterested voice answered, as if the person wished they didn't have to answer at all.

"Tragic. I find it quite fascinating. Maybe for a later book of yours. Oh, but I have heard that Aminah Burhan was appointed Chief Court Historian in Dam'vala. Is that right?"

"Sadly, yes."

"What a dreadful woman. The last time she was here she insisted on staying in one of the rooms for hours, completely disregarding that I still had other work to get to that day. I've decided that the next time I hear she's about to arriving I'll assign one of the younger clerks to her. I've earned at least that from all my years working here. You know we've been asking for a raise in our pay for years, but it's as if we're trying to negotiate with the ocean. Back and forth and back and forth—"

When the two had passed, Rena finally dared glance back at them. One was an older black man with short, tight, greying curls, who wore the same uniform the clerks had worn in the entrance hall. The other was a middle-aged woman with slightly darker skin than Rena, wearing a wide, dark-blue robe with golden inscriptions rising up from the bottom. She had braided her long, black hair into one thick braid and had slung it over her shoulder like a scarf.

The man kept prattling off his worries as the two walked down the hallway towards the staircase. Rena listened until she was sure she couldn't hear the voices anymore, then took a step away from Rodrick and his list.

"Let's be careful," Rodrick whispered, folding the document back up and sliding it into his jacket.

The two strangers had barely noticed them and were well on their way to the staircase. Rena took her eyes off them and turned around to face the way they had come from.

"Wait here," she told him in a hushed voice.

She pulled the skirt of her dress up so it wouldn't rustle and inched closer to the corner of the hallway. She dared glance past it, keeping herself close to the wall. What she saw could barely be called a hallway, more like an alcove. Two doors stood opposite each other, each flanked by two guards. They were facing ahead, unmoving, a curved sword hanging from their belts. She glanced up at the signs next to the doors before turning around and walking back to Rodrick.

"We've found the room," she murmured. "But there are guards in front of the door."

"Yes, I thought there might be." Rodrick looked pensively at the end of the hallway. "We will need to find a way past them."

"I don't think we can just convince them to let us pass."

"Very unlikely. And as Emmson mentioned, a clerk has to accompany any visitors to these areas."

"We don't have the right decree for the room anyway," Rena sighed, her right hand idly playing with her necklace. "I wish Logan was here."

Chapter Fifteen

Rena grabbed Rodrick's upper arm and led him back to the stairs until she felt confident that the guards wouldn't be able to hear them talk.

"Maybe if we pretended like we lost our decree the clerks might still accompany us," Rena suggested. "We can show them the other ones, and say that we're in a hurry."

"No, they would simply tell us to come back another day with a new one," Rodrick answered. "But we could steal someone else's."

"Steal?" Rena repeated, taken aback by his suggestion. "Are we really that desperate?"

"As you have seen," Rodrick continued calmly, "all the documents in the less restricted rooms have been censored, and it would just be a waste of time to search through more of them. There is no other method of getting into these rooms. We wouldn't be able to fight the guards, and any ventilation shafts would be too small for us to fit through, or at least for me. No, getting our hands on an actual decree is the only way."

"But what if the documents in this room are like all the others and we might be putting ourselves in danger for nothing?"

"That is simply a risk we might have to take."

Rena frowned down at the ground, crossing her arms tightly in front of her. They had lied and snuck around and obtained false documents to get to this point, so was stealing really that much worse? Logan and Asha were probably in the middle of stealing the documents for Emmson, and she hadn't objected to that either. She tried to rationalise the decision in her mind, to tell herself that they weren't stealing anything important that people needed to survive, but no matter how she turned it around in her head it kept leaving a sour taste in her mouth.

"It is the only option we have," Rodrick insisted. "Whomever we steal the decree from can simply get a new one reissued. You would be astonished how often scholars lose important documents, or don't remember where they put them. Take the scholar who just passed us. She might have simply dropped the document while exiting the room. The clerk has already seen it, so it would be easy for her to get a new one. And, in any case, she seemed finished with her research."

Rena sighed and looked out over the hallway, absent-mindedly running her tongue over her teeth.

"I suppose," she answered reluctantly.

She had to admit that his reasoning made sense. It wouldn't be the end of the world for the scholar if she lost her decree, and theft truly seemed like their only option, no matter how much the thought of it made Rena's skin crawl.

"She might not have left the building yet," Rodrick continued. "If we hurry, we could catch up to her."

When they reached the entrance hall, the room was more packed than when they had first arrived, as if all the people who had been standing around in the corridors earlier had shifted towards the exit. They stepped aside from the entryway and craned their necks to look over the crowd, hoping to find the scholar. Rena hadn't exactly gotten a good look at the woman's face, but as luck would have it, her dress was instantly recognisable even from across the room, and the way she carried her hair convinced Rena she had found the right person.

"Over there!" Rena whispered, leaning closer to Rodrick before nodding towards their target.

The scholar still stood next to the clerk who had been talking to her earlier, or more accurately, who had been talking *at* her — which, he seemingly hadn't stopped doing. The scholar, on the other hand, kept looking away, glancing around and behind, scanning the room as if searching for someone or something.

"Do we approach her here?" Rena asked. "What do we say? What should we do? Or do we follow her outside?"

"We don't know where she'll go next," Rodrick explained. "I want to avoid her going somewhere we can't follow. I know her dress. That's the uniform of the historical academy in Dam'Vala. I think I could distract her with some questions, but you will need to figure out where she's keeping her decree and get it from her."

"Okay," Rena answered hesitantly.

"She doesn't have a backpack or other bag with her, so she has to have the decree on her person. In a pocket or inside her shirt sleeve. You will have to circle around her and find out where it is."

"I don't know if I can do that," Rena told him, having to crane her neck to keep her eyes on the scholar. "I've never pickpocketed anything. She will definitely notice something's up. I don't even know how deep her pockets go."

Rena quickly averted her gaze when the scholar turned around. Her heart started racing as heat rose to her cheeks. She held her breath for a moment, hoping that she was small enough to disappear inside the crowd. She instantly realised that no matter how Rodrick had imagined this to play out, she wouldn't be able to accomplish it.

"I doubt she's going to stay here for much longer," Rodrick whispered.

"I don't think this is a good idea," Rena murmured, slowly lifting her eyes to look at Rodrick.

"I should be able to maker her show me her decree," he continued, ignoring her concerns, "if you bump into her, you could exchange it for another document."

He rummaged around in the inside pockets of his coat until he pulled out a folded piece of paper and handed it to her. She took it with both hands, staring down at it with wide eyes.

"Try to fold it the way she has so she won't notice it isn't the same," Rodrick said before Rena could protest. "You're a smart kid, you can figure it out."

He smiled at her then turned his attention to the crowd.

Rena stared at him for a moment, unable to truly process what he expected of her.

"This is–," Rena started but before she could voice any of her concerns, Rodrick stepped forwards and slipped between two groups of visitors.

"Wait!" Rena hissed, her heart hammering wildly in her chest.

She lost sight of Rodrick instantly as a group of chattering students passed in front of her and cut off her path.

She stood there with unfocused eyes, mouth agape, and crumpled Rodrick's document between her hands. She quickly snapped out of it and tried to smooth the wrinkles out of the paper again. With trembling hands, she slid the letter into the pocket of her dress. She closed her eyes and took a few deep breaths, hoping they would calm her, but it only made her realise how the fear was twisting and squeezing her stomach, and she had to open her eyes again or she would have vomited.

Rodrick trusted her to do this, and the longer she waited the higher the chance was that the scholar would leave. She didn't want their plan to fail because she couldn't calm herself down – especially since they had only come to the archives because of her. She just had to believe in herself, even if she had never done anything similar before. Even if her body revolted at the idea of it.

She wiped the sweat from her palms and looked back up at the crowd. She took a few careful steps forward to where she remembered the scholar to be. She slid from behind one group of people to the next, her eyes constantly darting between the floor, the people surrounding her, and the far side of the room – making sure the scholar wasn't escaping the archives. She was painfully aware of the fact that she had to look highly suspicious, but she hoped that the other visitors were too busy with their conversations to notice her. She made a wide birth around the scholar – always making sure to have the scholar's back turned to her so she couldn't see her – while the clerk seemed too engrossed in his own recital to notice much of what was going on around him.

As Rena got closer she finally spotted Rodrick's mop of white hair. He had decided to walk past their target and go chat with one of the clerks behind the desks. She hid behind a group of older women who all wore the same kind of clothing – what appeared to be a white and brown uniform. One of the women gave her a puzzled look so Rena shot her a faint, apologetic smile and soon the woman was engrossed in her groups' discussion again.

The scholar and her companion stood only a few meters away. Rena tried to figure out from the corner of her eyes where the scholar could be hiding her decree, but every time she turned her head even slightly, Rena instantly looked at the floor, too afraid their eyes might meet. Her fingers felt ice cold, and she tried to rub them warm, but it didn't seem to work.

She had to just believe in herself, no matter how her body felt. Once Rodrick was in position and she willed her body to move forward, her movements would be unconscious. She didn't have the luxury of letting her mind dictate how to approach the scholar.

She took a few steps back and snuck past the group of women so she could put a greater distance between her and the scholar. She approached the reception desks at a spot between two clerks, hoping neither of them would notice her, and turned her back to them, looking over the crowd as if searching for someone. Her eyes lingered a second longer on Rodrick and the scholar before wandering over the rest of the room. When she was sure no one was looking in her direction, she slowly slid closer to her target, anticipating the moment Rodrick would move.

She hated this waiting game. It gave her too much time to think of all that could happen if she got caught. She kept picturing herself running away from the guards, or being thrown in a holding cell, or getting away but having to live the rest of her life in hiding to avoid persecution. Was the information they might gather in that room really so important to potentially risk her life for it? She was sure they would be able to find another way that would lead them to whomever had set the fire. This had been a terrible mistake. She should have never come to the archives. Why hadn't she just gone to live with her aunt instead? Asha had been right, she was foolish for believing that Maya was still alive. There wasn't anything she could do about her family's fate anyway. She was simply destroying her own life over nothing.

In the corner of her eye, she caught Rodrick move away from the desk, turn around and walk towards their target. Her body froze immediately. She kept her gaze steady, keeping track of Rodrick's movement in her peripheral vision. He looked down at a piece of paper in his hands, slowly drifted away from the desk, and almost ran into the scholar. His head whipped up as if shocked to see anyone in front of him, but then his face brightened, and he hurried to fold his document before sliding it into his jacket and shaking the woman's hand. He didn't let go of her while talking to her, even though the scholar stared at him in confusion. Rena couldn't hear what they were saying, just more murmuring drowned out by the general cacophony of the room. She could, however, see how the woman turned away from her previous companion and engage fully in Rodrick's conversation, the confusion quickly fading from her face. The clerk, who stood perplexed and somewhat annoyed next to them, pressed his lips together tightly, waiting impatiently for the conversation to shift back to him.

Rena pretended to look through the room and scooted closer to them, making sure no one was observing her as she forced herself to take a few steps to her left. She clasped her trembling hands in front of her, squeezing one with the other so tightly that the pain forced her to stay still. She wanted to scream, to move, to run away. She wanted to do something, anything, and not just stand around waiting for a moment she didn't even know would come. She glanced at the sliver of blue sky she saw past the entrance doors and thought that she could simply run away. Nothing would happen to Rodrick if she abandoned him. The scholar might simply think he was odd, but he would have committed no crime. No guard would be able to arrest him.

But then, suddenly, out of the corner of her eyes, Rena saw how the woman reached down, fumbling around in the right pocket of her robe until she pulled a piece of paper out and handed it over to Rodrick. He took the document and turned it around in one hand, inspecting the back of it before opening it up.

Without thinking Rena rushed forward, straight towards the empty space between Rodrick and the scholar. She didn't plan her movement, didn't plan how she would exchange the two documents, she simply dashed towards Rodrick and ran into him.

"Oh!" Rodrick exclaimed as she collided with him.

Rena positioned herself between Rodrick and the scholar, fumbling her document out of her pocket and pressing it into Rodrick's chest.

She tried to grab the scholar's decree but it slipped out of her hands and floated to the ground.

"I'm sorry!" Rena blurted out, reaching down to pick the paper back up.

"Are you all right?" Rodrick tried to ask as Rena shot back up.

"Yes! I'm truly sorry," Rena exclaimed, interrupting Rodrick's question. "I need to leave. I'm so sorry."

"Wait," the scholar called, but Rena had already turned around.

"I'm late, I have to go," Rena repeated, half turned around as she hurried away. "I am so sorry."

"It's fine," Rodrick called after her. "Nothing happened."

She slipped behind a group of people as she rushed into the crowd.

"Did she take the wrong document?" she faintly heard the scholar ask, and her blood ran ice cold. Her body led her forward, moving on its own, while her mind screamed. Screamed for her to leave the building, to escape before any of the guards could find her again, to hide until they had forgotten about her.

She realised then that she had forgotten to refold their decree. Any second now the scholar would call after her. Rodrick wouldn't be able to convince her that he still held her original document. The scholar would see right through their scheme and have Rodrick arrested right away. She had doomed him by her inability to remember a simple instruction, even though it had been the only one he had given her.

She clutched the new decree tightly to her chest, terrified she might drop it. She managed to weave her way through the crowd even though her vision was blurry and all she could hear was the blood rushing through her ears. Out of habit she apologized to the people she bumped into, but it was almost as if her being had shrunk into a tiny ball and was looking up at her body react on its own.

She reached the end of the foyer and slipped into the hallway that would lead her back down into the belly of the archives, too afraid to look back and make sure she wasn't being followed.

Chapter Sixteen

Rena rushed through the corridors, forcing herself not to run so she wouldn't look suspicious. She kept her eyes fixed on the ground, even though she barely registered her surroundings. She pressed her nails into the palms of her hands, concentrating only on that pain. She matched her breathing to her footsteps and her footsteps to her breathing until she was walking at a normal pace.

She hadn't looked at the document in her hand yet, hadn't checked if it was really the decree they needed. She was gripping it so tightly that it was crumpled and damp from her sweat, and she knew she had to unfold it and smooth it out if they wanted to not raise any suspicions while entering the restricted area, but she couldn't get her hand to relax.

Her mind ran in a million different directions. She was convinced that Rodrick had been arrested and was probably on his way to the holding cells and it was all her fault. Because she couldn't get her hands to stop trembling and had fumbled the transfer. And now the guards were on their way to arrest her and punish her and maybe exile her or even worse.

She reached the hallway to the restricted rooms and stopped. She was in luck. No one else was currently in the hall. She stepped up to the wall opposite the stairs and leaned her forehead against the cold stone, gripping the decree tightly to her chest. She felt like she was about to throw up. Instead, she concentrated all of her mind on the chill of the wall, letting it wash over her.

What was she supposed to do? If Rodrick truly had been arrested, was she to enter the restricted area on her own and try to continue their quest with only Asha and Logan? Was she supposed to run out of the archives as fast as possible and try to get away? What would happen to Vincent if Rodrick had been arrested? If it was truly that difficult to break into Rodrick's caravan, she wouldn't be able to get the dog out to take care of him.

She took in a few shaky breaths through trembling lips and pushed herself away from the wall. Her heart had calmed down again, but it was still impossible for her to keep her eyes focused. All she could hear was her own heartbeat, which reassured her, because that meant no one was following her. She took the decree and flattened it against the wall – pressing hard with the palm of her hand to get the creases out.

She delicately unfolded the document, as if it would crumble in her hands if she wasn't careful enough. She had to scoot closer to one of the lamps to be able to read it, but there it was, their access to what they were looking for. Issued by the magistrate at the military academy, full access to restricted sections for the delegation of the historical academy of Dam'Vala. She folded the page carefully along the initial crease lines and placed it in the front pocket of her dress. She turned around to lean back against the wall and rested her face in her hands.

What had Rodrick imagined would happen? She had no experience in pickpocketing or sleight-of-hand or any other such activity. They had barely even formulated a plan before he had rushed into the crowd. She didn't know where he had gotten the confidence from that she would be able to figure it out on her own. Of course she had failed. How could she ever not have?

Anger bubbled in the pit of her stomach and mixed with her fear and anxiety. She started pacing, until she realised how loud her footsteps must be in this empty hallway. She had to remember that she wasn't actually alone, that only a few metres away there were four guards who were probably already very aware of her presence.

She pressed her back against the cold wall and crossed her arms, starring at the ground in front of her. She started counting the irregularities in the stone to keep her mind occupied. She wasn't sure how long she was supposed to wait, had lost any sense of time. Occasionally, she would hear motion from the floor above, and one time a group even walked down the stairs, but as luck would have it, they didn't stop at her floor and continued on below. She had held her breath and remained as still as possible, hoping that if she didn't move, no one would notice her being there. With every passing second, her worry grew and her anger transformed into guilt, thinking that if Rodrick hadn't met up with her yet, he had certainly been taken away by the guards. And it was all her fault.

From far away, another set of footsteps came closer. She leaned back, eyes fixed on the bottom of the stairs, waiting for whoever it was to emerge. The footsteps were slow, sluggish, not like a person who was looking for someone. She didn't dare blink, didn't dare move, as if she was prey hiding in tall grass.

"Oh, thank the stars," Rena exhaled as Rodrick appeared.

She rushed forward and met him at the foot of the stairs.

"Are you all right?" she asked in a hushed voice. "Did anything happen?"

"No, no, everything's fine," Rodrick said, placing his hands on her shoulders to calm her down.

"But the scholar noticed I took the decree, didn't she? I heard her mention it when I ran away."

He shook his head solemnly at her.

"She did, but it is of no importance."

"How can it not be of importance?" Rena burst out, her head whipping to the side an instant later to make sure the guards hadn't heard.

"She didn't see your face, she doesn't know it was you," he whispered.

"But they're going to be looking for a thief!" Panic started rising in Rena, her breath coming in fast and shallow. "How could they not notice it was us?"

"Not if we remain calm. We should just proceed as if nothing was wrong, as if we were always meant to have this decree and get access to the room. I already talked to the guards and gave them a false description of you. It is highly unlikely that they would be suspicious of me."

"But they might," Rena hissed.

Rodrick closed his eyes and frowned, shaking his head at her.

"Why did you just run out?" Rena asked before Rodrick had the chance to say anything.

He opened his mouth and looked at her, as if he hadn't understood her question.

"When we were in the foyer," Rena continued, "why did you just run out? You know I've never done anything like this. Why would you put all your faith in me if you know how badly it could go? And look what happened!"

He slowly closed his mouth, not responding for a while. Rena tried to find an answer in his eyes but she couldn't discern what he was thinking. She waited for him to respond, to tell her that it had all been part of his plan, or that she should just have known what needed to be done, that anyone would have been able to not mess it up. That she was the only one who wasn't good enough.

"You said that I would figure it out," Rena muttered when the silence started to weigh too heavy. "That it shouldn't be difficult for me, but how would something like this be easy? I told you I didn't think it was a good idea, but you didn't listen to me. You didn't even tell me what your plan was. You just left."

"I know, I know," Rodrick murmured. "I'm sorry. I truly am. I shouldn't have acted so hastily. I was scared our target would leave the archives and we would miss our only opportunity of getting this decree. But I know that isn't an excuse for not communicating well."

Rena opened her mouth to answer but froze instead when she heard the faint sound of footsteps.

"Someone's coming," she hissed, and pushed Rodrick away from the stairs and towards the wall.

Two people came up the stairs, one man in black trousers and a floor-length brown coat, and a young woman in the archives' uniform. She was plump with fair skin and rosy cheeks, with light brown hair in two long braids running down her chest. Before Rena even realised what she was doing, she was rushing towards the clerk.

"Excuse me," she said as she approached the two strangers.

The clerk turned around with a little jolt, as if Rena had startled her.

"I'm terribly sorry," Rena continued in a hurry. "We are looking for someone to accompany us to one of the rooms on this floor. Would you be free to accompany us? I'm truly sorry, we're in a bit of a hurry, or we would have gone upstairs again."

Rena wanted to avoid having to go back upstairs at all costs, and if the clerk had stayed on the lower floors for the last hour or so, she might not have heard of the theft yet. Rena clasped her hands tightly in front of her to mask how much they trembled. She had to keep her face in a polite smile, convince the woman that nothing was wrong. That her fear and worry weren't tearing at her body as if they were about to rip her to shreds.

"Oh, umm, I-I think I'm available?" the young Clerk replied, flashing Rena a quick smile before turning to her companion. "If that would be okay with you, sir?"

"Yeah, I'm good. I know the way out," the man replied with a small, amused smirk.

"Thank you so much!" Rena told him, and instinctively bowed to him.

"Sure." He chuckled, before nodding to the clerk, and walking back up the stairs alone.

"G-goodbye, sir," the clerk called after him.

"Thank you so much for your help," Rena told her, grabbing her hands in her own, hoping she wouldn't notice how sweaty Rena's hands were. "We're with the delegation from the historical academy in Dam'Vala. This is my master Samerec Cenred." She turned to gesture towards Rodrick, who stepped forward and nodded at the clerk.

"I'm honoured to meet you, sir," the clerk told Rodrick with a polite nod of her head.

"I've got our decree right here," Rena told her, letting go of the clerk's hands so she could grab the paper. "We only need to go to one of the rooms right here."

Rena handed the decree to the clerk, but barely gave her enough time to open it and glance at it before looping her arm around the clerk's elbow, and guiding her towards the stairs.

"I'm sorry to rush you like this, but we really are in a bit of a hurry."

"No problem at all," the clerk said, looking down at the floor so she wouldn't trip. "I know that the envoys from the historical academy are always very busy. I wouldn't want to delay your research."

"I'm sorry if this is too forward, but I adore how you braided your hair," Rena added hastily, hoping the change in subject would distract the clerk.

"Oh, thank you." The clerk smiled shyly, a blush spreading across her cheeks and ears. "I wanted to add some ribbons to them, but then I thought it might look too childish."

"No, no, no, I think it would look fantastic on you," Rena answered, and patted the clerk's arm reassuringly.

She felt bad for dragging such a sweet girl down with them, guilt twisting in her stomach when she realised she might lose her job over this. But she couldn't go back on her decision now. The quicker they got into the room, the quicker they could get out of the archives, and then maybe, if luck was kind to them, no one would notice that it was them who had stolen the decree.

They hurried down the hallway, Rodrick following close behind both girls. The clerk didn't ask to see their decree again before opening the door to their room, nor did she acknowledge the guards. Rena's heart hammered in her chest with fear and apprehension, but she was determined not to show it. The scholar hadn't seen her face, and the guards didn't suspect Rodrick to be part of the theft. They wouldn't expect the thief to enter the room accompanied by one of the clerks. As long as they didn't stay longer than necessary everything would be all right. She had to believe in it.

Chapter Seventeen

The clerk lead Rena and Rodrick into another deep, dimply lit room. It was filled from floor to ceiling with bookshelves that were packed with the same type of bound book over and over again.

Rodrick leaned towards Rena to whisper into her ear.

"Go find the documents. Look for 'ARC'."

He leaned away again and turned towards the clerk.

"Could I ask for your assistance?" he asked with a wide smile. "A member of our delegation is currently looking into a rather confidential subject, and she has asked me to look at some documents while I'm here. She is investigating the disappearance of High Lady Silvid's daughter, the princess Amirid. I know it is a delicate subject, but would you know where to find any information about this subject?"

"Yes, of course," the clerk added, baffled for an instant before her face remembered it had to stay professional.

"My apprentice can go find the documents I need for my own research in the meantime," he added offhandedly and turned to Rena, nodding at her with a polite smile. "Since we have an appointment soon and shouldn't dawdle."

Rena was momentarily confused, having heard that princess Amirid died at birth. She managed to snap out of her stupor quickly enough that the clerk didn't grow suspicious, but as she turned around and walked further into the room she couldn't stop wondering if she had remembered the name of the princess wrong or if Rodrick was trying to confuse the clerk.

She forced herself not to walk too briskly until she was sure the clerk couldn't see her anymore – and even after, she couldn't run as each footstep echoed through the room. She slipped between two bookcases and hurried down the passage. She only briefly stopped to look at the signs hanging on the side of the shelves, to figure out where the documents they were looking for could be. But since she wasn't sure how to interpret the abbreviations, it took her several minutes to figure out where she was supposed to go, seeing as the bookcases weren't simply ordered alphabetically. She repeated the name of the category she was looking for over and over in her mind, trying to keep herself from thinking about the guards that must be looking for her.

When she had finally found the correct bookshelf, she was faced with the boundless amount of information she would have to wade through. Rows and rows of identical books stretched out to either side of her. The sheer number of them felt like the books extended above her, pushing the ceiling of the room further and further and further away from her – the ends of the shelves curling in and enclosing her in a cage of books. She shook her head to stay focused and looked at the dates of the books, searching for the year of the fire.

She suddenly felt a presence next to her, and turned around in terror, believing that the guards had caught up to her without her hearing it, but it was only Logan.

"Hey," he whispered, standing only an arm's length away from her. "You okay?" he added, looking at her with concern.

"What are you doing here?" she hissed, deliberately ignoring his question. "How did you even get in here?"

"I have my ways," he replied casually, looking at the bookshelf instead of her.

He nodded at the books in front of her.

"What are you looking for?"

"Well, umm," she started, not really knowing the answer to the question herself. "I think I need to locate the books from the year of the fire, but even if I find those, it's going to take forever to find the information we need, because, just look at how many there are! And what if this isn't even the correction section? It's going to take forever to read through all of them, and we really, really shouldn't be wasting that much time!"

"Why are you so nervous?" Logan asked, side-eyeing her.

"Coming here was a mistake! Everything's gone wrong. I never wanted to get this deep into the archives, but the other rooms only had censored documents and they kept sending us from one area to another with their stupid notes in the margins, so we either had to leave with no information at all, or find a way in here." She stopped and sighed, keeping her eyes fixed on the books in front of them so she wouldn't have to look Logan in the eyes. "So Rodrick and I stole someone's decree, but I screwed up and the person noticed and even if Rodrick assures me that she didn't see my face it still means that the guards are looking for *someone*."

"Yeah, that's not ideal," Logan chuckled, and turned his attention back to the bookshelf.

She glanced over at him, waiting for him to reprimand her, to get angry with her, or at least to ask for more detail, but nothing came. Instead, he ran his fingers over the spines of the books, concentration on finding something specific.

"How can you be so calm about this?" she asked him, bewildered.

"Comes with the profession," he said and ripped three books out of the shelf. "Just act like you're supposed to be here and they won't suspect you."

"That's easy for you to say," she mumbled.

Logan spread the books out on the ground and knelt in front of them.

"What are we looking for?" he asked.

"I don't know," she sighed and sat down next to him. "Any mentions of the fire, I guess. Any mentions of Miller's Knee, maybe. Or even just orders to change the road signs. Anything like that. I'm honestly not sure. We've just been following this trail of abbreviations, it's difficult to say what they really mean."

Logan pushed one of the books towards her and opened up another one.

"Yeah, I had that too. It was like going down a spiral of clues. Fun to follow, but I'm not sure I got anything useful out of it either."

Rena opened up the book to pages and pages of hastily written text. They appeared to be letters written from and to the administrator, bound together into large tomes. She closed her eyes and took in a deep breath, wishing she was back in the other rooms where the documents had had a clear structure. She leafed through a few of them, feeling the rising dread with every second that passed. The room was completely silent, safe for the occasional rustling of paper. She was starting to wonder if they should just try to steal the books to be able to leave the archives quickly, but was instantly taken aback by her own thoughts. Just because she had stolen one document, didn't mean she had to stoop so low as to steal entire books. That was definitely not how her parents had raised her.

"Wait, here," Logan said and pushed his book towards her so she could read the text. "I think this is what you're looking for."

Rena scooted closer and craned her neck to read. The pages contained letters between the administrator and a member of the Royal Council, High Lord Armanid Harkid. Logan leaned over the book and pointed to a section in one of the letters that mentioned Miller's Knee. Rena's eyes grew wide, turning immediately to a frown as she skimmed the letter.

"How dare she say the town had no great importance, and then mention right after that thirty-seven people died?"

"Yeah, these people are assholes. Don't expect compassion from them," Logan said, seemingly unphased by the horrors inscribed in the letters.

Rena stared at him, mouth agape, ready to argue, but then thought better of it and focused on the letter again. They would have time to discuss ethics once they were out of the archives.

"Wait, she mentions the crow effigy," Rena blurted out, her eyes moving frantically over the text. "Wait... "as per protocol, the complete elimination of the town's memory has commenced"? What does that mean? How can they eliminate a town's memory?"

"What? Show me!" Logan grabbed the book out of her hands. "What the — They just *admit* to that?"

"But what does it mean?" she asked, eyes wild as she looked up at Logan.

"I don't know. Maybe they try to pretend the town never existed. You know, like, if they never talk about it, then the town's destruction never happened, and everyone who says otherwise is silenced. Like, there's no problem if no one remembers the tow– Wait."

Logan shot up, holding out a hand to stop her from moving. He looked up, his gaze scanning the room. From far away, they could hear someone come closer. Rena froze, eyes wide, hearing nothing but the rapidly approaching footsteps. She didn't know if it was best to stay quiet and hope the person didn't see them, or if they should run away. But where could they run to? The room only had one exit, and there were guards outside. Could they hide from the person by sneaking between rows? But Logan wasn't moving, and the footsteps were getting closer, and panic started to rise in her. Her eyes darted between both ends of the corridor, her hands clutching the skirt of her dress tightly. She held her breath, hoping that no one had heard them speak, that no one had noticed their presence.

"It can't be one of the guards," Logan whispered.

"How do you know?" Rena asked, her voice barely audible.

"The guards wear heavier armour and a sword. You'd hear that immediately when they're walking. It's gonna be fine, let's just keep reading. No one knows we shouldn't be here."

Rena stared down at the page in front of her as the footsteps got louder, letters melting together in front of her eyes. She forced herself to blink, but the motion felt unfamiliar, as if she had never done it before. The rhythm of the footsteps and her heartbeat blended together into one and soon it felt like whoever was approaching was walking inside her chest.

"Thank the stars, it's only you," Logan exhaled and got up, ripping Rena out of her trance. She looked back at the approaching figure and realised, with relief, that it was Asha.

"Where's the old man?" she asked, turning towards one of the bookshelves a few metres to their left.

"He's distracting the clerk," Rena managed to say even though the muscles in her throat were so tight that it was difficult to breath.

Logan handed the book back to Rena and stood up to join Asha. Rena closed her eyes and unclenched her hands. She was starting to feel like she was back in the city of Rancor, exhaustion washing over her as the panic receded. She opened her eyes again and looked up at her companions, her tongue heavy and dry in her mouth.

Asha reached out and pulled one of the books off the shelf, leafing through it 'til the very end. She stopped at a certain passage and ripped out the page.

"What are you doing?" Rena exclaimed and shot up, the book sliding from her lap.

She rushed over to where Asha stood, who placed the book back onto the shelf. Asha folded the ripped-out pages in four before sliding them into the inside pocket of her tunic.

"You know what, you're right," Logan said and walked back to where Rena's book had landed on the floor.

Rena hurried back to him, but he had already found the correct page and torn it out.

"We can't just steal these things," Rena hissed, dread rising up in her.

"I kinda already did it earlier with my stuff," Logan said sheepishly, and folded the ripped page in four.

A claw wrapped around her stomach and twisted, pulled, crushed, until she felt numb, the heat receding from her body and collecting at her core.

"But they'll notice!" Rena exclaimed, then instantly pressed her lips together and looked around in panic, scared she had been too loud.

"They won't notice anything," Asha deadpanned. "They're too self-absorbed and ignorant."

"Yep, definitely agree with that," Logan said as he slid the book back onto the shelf.

Rena stared at Asha, unable to say anything, unable to even form thoughts.

Asha sighed heavily.

"I would agree with you if these were upstanding citizen, but if they were, we wouldn't be here in the first place. I'm sure what you found in that book showed you what kind of morals these people have."

Asha looked at Rena, waiting for her to confirm her statement, but all Rena could think of was how she was certain she had doomed them all. She had brought them here, she had messed up the theft, she hadn't stopped them from ripping out the pages, she would lead them to ruin.

Seconds passed, maybe even minutes, she couldn't tell anymore, but she knew she had to react. She nodded slowly, the movement jerky, hoping that was all Asha was waiting for.

"So, there is no need to feel bad for them," Asha said, and turned back to her bookcase.

"And if you're afraid of what might happen to us if they catch us," Logan added, "we just won't let them catch us."

He winked at her with a smirk, but a second later his face grew serious, eyes wide as he looked up. Rena already knew what he was about to say.

"Wait, shut up," he hissed, his eyes scanning the room around them.

Faint footsteps approached. Heavy boots strode towards them with a purpose. The dull, rhythmic sound of metal hitting against metal.

"Shit, we need to leave!" Logan hissed and shot upright.

"Over here," Asha said as she rushed past.

Before Rena had regained her composure, Logan had grabbed her by the wrist and was pulling her towards the back wall of the room. They turned left, but just as they emerged from behind the bookshelf, they almost ran into someone. Someone in thick leather armour with glinting plates of metal on their arms, legs and chest, and a curved sword in their right hand. Immediately, Logan swivelled around and pulled her back so they could run in the opposite direction. They ran along the backwall of the room for a few metres, before another guard emerged in front of them, blocking their path and forcing them to turn right, back towards the centre of the room.

As they reached the end of the row, Logan stopped abruptly, letting go of Rena's wrist as his arm shot up in front of her. Asha had to pivot to the left so she wouldn't crash into him, her back instead hitting the bookshelf. Rena lost her balance and fell backwards. It was only after she hit the ground that she saw the rapier blade pressed against Logan's throat, and the man the sword belonged to. He didn't look like one of the guards. He wore a long, blue coat with gold details that told Rena he was the one giving orders, even if he barely looked to be Logan's age.

She scrambled to her feet and tried to run back to where they had come from, but one of the guards had caught up with them and was now barrelling towards her. Rena stepped backwards until she hit Logan's back, keeping her eyes fixed on the approaching guard.

"Who are you?" the blue-robed man growled.

"Hey man, I could ask you the same." Logan chuckled nervously, holding his hands up in defence. "This all seems a bit abrupt. We weren't doing anything wrong, just looking at some documents like we're allowed to. You're coming on a bit strong here."

"Then why did you run away, smartass?"

Chapter Eighteen

Rena felt Logan shift behind her so their backs were flush against each other. She kept her eyes on the approaching guards. One was already halfway down the passageway, while the other was just rounding the corner of the bookshelf near the back wall. She momentarily glanced away, remembering in panic that Rodrick was still in the room somewhere. Her eyes darted back to the guards, widening in fear, as her mind filled with a million different possibilities of what these people could have done to her friend.

Next to Rena, Asha pushed herself away from the bookshelf and came to stand in front of her. Rena wanted to tell her that they needed to find Rodrick, that he would not be able to fight them on his own, but her jaw was frozen shut.

"Listen, we don't want any trouble," Logan told the man holding the blade to his throat. "We're simply here to read some documents. This is a public archive after all, right? You didn't even ask us for our paperwork, I think that's a bit rude, considering who we are. But I'll be gracious. If you back off now, and let us be, I won't complain to anyone about you. You know, I could go to your superiors with this kind of behaviour."

"Yeah, I don't think so," the captain said, an air of menace in his voice.

Rena heard him step closer, although she couldn't tell what exactly was going on. She was too afraid of taking her eyes off the approaching guards, or even to blink, as if they might disappear and reappear much closer if she couldn't see them.

Logan's hand grabbed Rena's arm at their side, his fingers wrapping tightly around her wrist. Asha stepped closer to Rena and blocked her view of the guards, forcing Rena to anxiously shift to the side to at least keep an eye on parts of their bodies. Asha's hand slipped beneath her tunic and slid around her back, her fingers wrapping around something Rena couldn't see.

"You can drop this foolish act," the captain said in a low voice. "I don't know who you are, but I don't think I really care either. I don't believe you're just some innocent researchers. Not with the whole archives in uproar over some stolen decree."

"And you're just assuming that was us?" Logan replied.

"You're not as subtle as you think you are," the captain whispered and shifted closer.

Rena's mind screamed. She had doomed them. Because of her, Asha would never see her uncle again. Vincent would never be able to get out of the caravan. No one would find and save Maya. The guards would take them away, lock them up, and forget about them, until they were only dust.

"As much as I am weirdly enjoying this," Logan said, his smile apparent in his voice. "I have no idea what you're talking about."

Rena's head momentarily darted towards Logan, questioning how Logan could find any of this enjoyable. This whole week had been one nightmare after another for her, and she didn't know if her heart could take it much longer.

"Of course, you don't. You know, you're not as good at sneaking around as you think you are. Sure, the surveillance in this place is — quite frankly — abysmal, but I notice. I always notice."

Logan chuckled softly.

"Well, good for you. You seem to be a very valuable member of this establishment. Like a well-behaved, loyal dog."

Rena's stomach instantly tightened into a tight knot. How could Logan even consider antagonising this man? She thought he was smarter than this, that he realised what kind of danger they were in.

"You think you're so clever, but look at where you are now," the captain replied slowly.

"Being threatened by an asshole with a great jawline and delusions of grandeur who thinks he's just uncovered a conspiracy in his basement?"

"Logan," Asha exclaimed. "Shut your mouth or I swear I will shut it for you once I'm done with the rest of these fools."

The first guard was almost upon them, and Asha finally pulled out what she had been hiding. At first, it looked like a thin, black handle until she flicked her wrist and it expanded into a rod the length of her forearm.

Rena didn't know what to do, didn't know what she could add to the conversation to help them out. She knew she wouldn't be able to fight. Asha and Logan probably, but definitely not her. She couldn't just stand there and wait for Logan to make the situation worse than it already was. No matter how much she wanted to, she couldn't stay still and hope for everyone to forget she existed. She owed her companions more than that. She owed her sister more than that.

With great effort, she turned and opened her mouth to say something, determined to rectify the course of this interaction. The second the captain's eyes shifted to look at her, however, Logan lifted his free hand to push the blade up and away from his throat, making the captain stumble back. Logan ran forward, his grip tightening on Rena's wrist as he dragged her behind him.

Rena almost fell, not expecting the sudden shift in movement, but somehow managed to keep her balance. Her dress wasn't made for running. Her legs kept getting tangled in the fabric and even though she tried bunching the skirt up with her free hand, she barely managed to hold on to it.

She looked back and realised Asha wasn't behind them. She still stood between the bookshelves, the captain at her feet while she held onto his coat, his blade on the ground next to him. With her other hand, she swung the rod towards the first guard, hitting him on the side of the head before he had finished lifting his sword. He slumped to the side and crashed into the bookcase. The captain tried pushing himself up to his feet, but before he regained his footing, Asha swung him and threw him at the second guard.

"Wait!" Rena shouted, as the echoes of their footsteps resonated through the room.

"There's no time!" Logan called back to her.

"But Asha!"

"She can manage on her own!"

"What about Rodrick?"

She looked around at the aisles they were passing, but Logan dragged her along too quickly for her to really see if Rodrick was anywhere near them. She spotted the entrance to her left, but it seemed deserted.

When she realised Logan wasn't going to answer her, she tried to pull her wrist out of his grip. His hand clamped shut, blocking the flow of blood to her hand.

"No. Wait!" She called out again.

She almost lost her footing trying to get him to stop, but he just kept going — kept running down the endless hallway between row after row of bookshelves. She turned one more time, glancing back at Asha while Logan led them to the other end of the room. She had picked up the captain's rapier and swung it with the same form and force like you would a heavier sword.

Before Rena could see any more of the fight, Logan pulled them to the right, down the passage between bookshelves that ran along the wall of the room.

"Wait! Where are we going?" Rena asked.

"Out of here."

"But the door is the other way."

He didn't reply, just ran to the end of the passage. He stopped abruptly and turned towards her, dropping down to one knee in the same motion. He held his hands out to her, interlinking them, palms-up at knee height.

"What about the others?" she said, turning around as if she could see her companions through the bookshelves. She could still faintly hear Asha fight at the other end of the room.

"Climb up," Logan told her, not looking up at her.

"What?" She looked back at him, not understanding what he wanted from her. "Where?"

Rena glanced up at the bookshelf in front of them and then looked around, trying to figure out what he wanted from her, but the shelves looked exactly the same, like any other in this room.

"On top of the bookshelf," he said, finally looking up at her. "There's some tunnels in the wall that connect the rooms together. Now climb, we don't have all day."

"Ventilation shafts?" she asked, dumbfounded.

"Yes! Maybe. I don't know, it doesn't matter."

"We can't just leave?" she almost yelled, horrified at his plan.

"Rena, we either all get caught or some of us escape. They're old enough to figure out how to save themselves. So, get up, and get out!"

"But, what if they need help?"

"Now!"

"Okay, okay."

Reluctantly, she turned towards the bookshelf and grabbed onto its boards with her left hand – testing whether they would hold or not – and placed her other hand on Logan's shoulder. She stepped on his intertwined hands and he hoisted her up with such force that she almost hit her head on the ceiling. Somehow, she managed to hold on to the bookshelf and slide on top of it. There was barely any space between the bookshelf and the ceiling, and she had to lie flat on her stomach to fit into the space.

Like Logan had mentioned, there was a rectangular opening in the wall covered with an ornate, cast-iron grate. While Logan was climbing up the bookshelf in front of her, Rena tugged at the grate with all of her force, which wasn't exactly much, considering the awkward position she was in. It slid out with a groan and a thud that reverberated much too loudly for her liking.

"Go in first," Logan told her. "I'll close the grate behind us."

Rena took one last glance at the room before sliding forward, contorting her body to fit into the opening. She wanted to cry, to run back and save her companions, to not just selfishly run away. But the worst part was, that deep down, a growing part of her was relieved that they were getting away.

The cast-iron grate dug into her hip on one side while the ceiling dug into the other. Somehow, after a lot of back and forth and almost falling off the bookshelf, she managed to squeeze her body into the opening. She crawled forward, realising that the stone under her was covered in dust. She could smell it in the air, feel it tickle her nose as she stirred it up. She tried to cover her face with the back of her hand, but it didn't help much. The tunnel was dark, only slightly illuminated by the dim light from the room behind her. It didn't seem to go very far, and there was maybe enough space for two people before a wall blocked the way. But she supposed there had to be a bend she couldn't see.

The space was thankfully big enough for her to move around and look back at the entrance, but not large enough to really turn around in it. She crawled forward to make enough space for Logan, and reached the back wall where the tunnel bent to both sides. She looked both ways, hoping it could tell her where to go next, but either tunnel was completely dark.

She glanced back at Logan who was climbing in, feet first. He pulled the grate over the opening before fishing something out of his pocket and bringing it up in front of him.

"What are you doing?" she hissed. "Didn't you say we had to leave quickly?"

"I'm just gluing it shut." Logan grunted with concentration. "Won't keep them away forever, but maybe long enough for us to lose them. Just keep going and I'll catch up."

Rena turned and looked down both tunnels again, hoping her eyes had gotten used to the darkness to discern details, but the paths before her were still pitch black.

"Where do I go?" Rena asked.

"Doesn't matter. Both lead to other rooms. We just need to get out of this one."

"What if we get stuck? I can't see, and I won't know whether we're going in circles or not. What if this is the only grate that opens and we never find our way back?"

"Just go forward until you see some light. Like I said, it doesn't matter where we end up, and they didn't consider that people would be crawling around inside these shafts, so the grates aren't welded to the walls. Well, except the ones leading to the outer walls probably. But we're not going there anyway. It would take a whole day to find the correct shafts that lead outside, and who knows where we'd land. Maybe if we had scouted the area beforehand so we'd know where these shafts lead but—"

"Okay, I'm just going to the left."

Rena didn't wait for him to finish his tirade before moving forward.

"Yeah, sure," Logan said, the wild energy sucked out of his voice.

Thankfully, the tunnels were big enough for her to take the turn, even though she had to shuffle around and squeeze past the corner. She could feel the dust caking onto her dress and arms and hands, but at least her disgust was strong enough to override the fear that came with crawling through a dark, enclosed space with no end in sight.

"Aaah!" She cried out and stopped suddenly, her hand having grazed against something she couldn't identify.

"What?!" Logan asked, concern drenching his voice.

"I touched something," she said, worried about putting her hand down again.

"Something moving? There's probably rats and cockroaches in here."

"What?!" she blurted, trying to look back at him, but she could barely see the outline of his body in the dark. "No, no, it wasn't moving. I-it was, I don't know, kind of fuzzy I guess?"

"Dead rat, then. Nothing to worry about. It can't hurt you if it's dead. Let's keep going."

He tapped her twice on the leg, indicating for her to keep moving forward. She stared at his silhouette in disbelief for a while, even if she knew he couldn't see her. Reluctantly, she turned, trying to determine where the supposedly dead rat had been. She wrapped her hand in her sleeve and swiped it over the floor, moving the suspicious object to the side.

"Just a dead rat," she mumbled. "Because those don't carry any diseases at all."

"Less mumbling, more moving," he called out to her.

"We should have just let the guards take us to the holding cells," she called back as she started crawling forward.

"You definitely wouldn't say that if you'd ever been in one before. They don't clean up the dead rats there either."

Chapter Nineteen

After an arduous and sticky journey through the vents, Rena finally noticed a dim light emanating from beyond another grate. As Logan had mentioned before, she had no problem pushing the grate forward and carefully lowering it onto the bookshelf under the exit. She poked her head out to see if anyone was around, but the room seemed empty enough. The layout was almost the same as the room they had just come from, with tall, wooden bookshelves that almost reached the ceiling. Though, there seemed to be a nook in the middle of the room.

Rena scooted forward and managed to shuffle to the side so that she lay on her belly atop the bookshelf. She glanced at the floor, wondering how she was supposed to get down without falling, or taking the whole bookshelf with her.

Apparently, Logan didn't have the same concerns, because he managed to roll himself off the edge, turn mid-air while holding on to the bookshelf, and land on his feet without any problems.

"Here, let me help," he whispered, turning to face her.

She let her legs dangle off the edge, then slowly lowered the rest of her body.

"Careful," Logan whispered, grabbing her waist so she wouldn't fall off the bookshelf.

She landed on the ground with a soft thump, and whispered a thank you.

"No problem," he replied, turning away to look around the room. "We might be alone in here. That's good. Although, we'll need a good excuse to walk past the guards standing outside."

"You want to just walk out?" Rena's head whipped up to stare at him.

"We only have two options. Well, three if we go back into the vents. But, either we hide in here until they've forgotten about us, or we get out fast and hope we don't run into any of the guards who actually saw our faces."

She glanced at the ends of the aisle and tried to gage the likelihood of them being able to hide in the room. There were no cupboards to hide inside, and hiding atop a bookshelf wasn't very safe. If anyone came looking for them, they would have to sneak through the room to stay away from them, but that also seemed extremely risky and impractical. The only other hiding spot she could think of were the vents, and she didn't relish the thought of having to stay in that dark, damp space for hours while hoping the guards would assume they had gotten out.

She sighed and nodded.

"All right, the faster we get out, the quicker we can make sure Asha and Rodrick are unharmed."

"Exactly." He grinned at her before turning away and moving forward in a half crouch.

They reached the end of the aisle and Logan held a hand up for Rena to stop. He leaned forward and peered into the room.

"Okay, I think we're good," he whispered after a while.

"So, what's your brilliant plan for distracting the guards outside the room?" Rena asked in a hushed voice as they snuck through the main corridor.

"You walk out as if you're just a regular scholar, once the guards stop you to interrogate you, I sneak out and surprise them from behind."

"Logan, that's a horrible plan. There might be more than just two guards if there's another room opposite this one. And anyone else in the hallway would hear the commotion."

"It's going to be fine," he whispered and waved her off. "I just need to get behind one of them to steal their sword. Then we can force them into this room and lock them in."

"What? How would we lock them in?"

"We'll figure something out," he replied with a shrug.

"Logan, I'm really not sure about—"

"Shh." Logan suddenly slowed down, holding up another hand to silence Rena.

They carefully stepped closer, and Rena finally saw the area at the centre of the room, filled with long wooden desks instead of bookshelves, although it looked abandoned. The chairs were all placed neatly beneath the desks, as if no one had touched them since the day they had first been placed. Logan slowed down and hid behind the last bookshelf before the entrance, his back flat against the edge of the shelf. He inched his face forward until he could see the foyer, then remained like that for longer than Rena thought was necessary if the area had been empty.

"What?" Rena mouthed, touching Logan's elbow slightly.

He didn't react then sighed and let his head hang, running a hand over his face.

"What?" Rena repeated with more urgency, but before she could lean over to look out into the foyer herself, Logan pushed himself away from the bookshelf and walked towards the entrance.

"What the fuck are you doing here?" Logan cried out, throwing his hands out in exasperation.

Rena stepped around Logan and immediately her body froze. On the desk next to the door sat the man that had tried to arrest them earlier. The urge to turn around and run away overcame her, to scramble back into the shafts and find another empty room, but Logan wasn't moving, and neither was the captain. He just sat on the table, leaning against the wall, one leg outstretched, the other angled up.

"How the fuck did you find us?" Logan demanded.

"Logic and deduction," the captain said dryly. "I know the layout of this place, and where the shafts lead. A bit of chance and guessing to find the exact room you'd end up in, but it seems like fortune is smiling down on me."

The captain slid from the desk and calmly walked up to them.

"So, tell me," he said. "What were you doing looking at the administrator's letters?"

Rena dared to breath again, slow and shallow, as if any unnecessary movement from her part would make the tension in the room explode.

"Why would we tell you anything?" Logan asked, his head held high to look down at the captain. "Just because you found us a second time doesn't mean we're suddenly gonna give in to your requests."

"Don't pretend you've got any power in this situation," the captain said, raising an eyebrow.

"You didn't exactly give me any incentives to tell you the truth," Logan replied, mimicking the captain's facial expression. "Is this how you city folks conduct your interrogations? Where's the torture? Or maybe a bribe? Getting my weight in gold is always nice."

"You know, you're quickly becoming the most annoying person I've ever met." The captain circled them slowly, looking them up and down.

"H-hi," Rena blurted out when their eyes met, as if a switch had been flipped in her. "I'm Rena, uhm, I'm really sorry we ran away from you earlier. It was just a frightening situation. We didn't mean any harm by reading those letters. We're just trying to figure some stuff out." She hadn't meant to tell the captain any of this, but now that she had opened her mouth, she couldn't seem to stop. As if she was personally responsible for breaking up the tension. "We're not colluding or rioting or planning a coup. I promise, we're not going to cause any trouble for the archives, and I'm sorry we took some of the letters with us. We'll give them back as soon as we've had an opportunity to read them. It's really just because we're trying to piece together what happened to my hometown, because we think something strange is going on."

"Stop talking," Logan hissed through his teeth. "Why are you telling him any of this?"

"So that the two of you don't start stabbing each other," she replied, desperation tinging her voice. "And maybe he can help."

"Why would someone like him ever help us?"

"The rest of you are also helping for no apparent reason!"

"And we might have the same concerns," the captain added.

"What?" Logan and Rena asked in unison, their heads turning to look at the man.

He crossed his arms and leaned back against the desk, eyeing them wearily, his jaw clenching and unclenching as if mulling something over.

"I don't exactly know what you people are looking for, or what you're even talking about, but I've done some digging of my own, and I'm not thrilled about the things I've found."

"Do you know anything about Oceansthrow?" Rena burst out, rushing towards him. "O-or maybe Miller's Knee? The towns that burned down?"

"I've heard of them," he answered carefully.

"There's something weird going on, right? That the fires weren't just accidents? Something to do with those crow effigies? And that's why the events had to be kept secret?"

"How will you survive out in the wild if you just tell the enemy everything we know?" Logan interrupted, coming closer to join them.

"He caught us twice." Rena turned to look at Logan. "He can just take the letters off us when he throws us into jail. What does it matter if I tell him now or later?"

"We could have bargained," Logan explained.

"It didn't look like your bargaining was working very well."

"You didn't exactly let me finish negotiating, did you?"

"Maybe I should just have the both of you thrown into jail if this is how you behave," the captain said dryly, looking between them with annoyance.

"I'm sorry, sir," Rena said, turning back to the captain, instantly unsure of what to call him. "O-or maybe my lord? Prince? ... Duke?"

The captain sighed and shifted around, visibly uncomfortable.

"None of that. My name's Finn."

"Hi. Logan, nice to meet you." Logan instantly changed his attitude. Smirking, he held out a hand and waited for the captain to shake it.

Finn looked down at the hand in confusion, his brows slowly knitting together before finally shaking Logan's hand.

"Didn't you just call him the enemy?" Rena asked in a mock whisper.

"I still have manners," Logan replied with a smile.

"Can we get back to the initial subject?" Finn asked, looking away from Logan. "I don't know much about these fires or what purpose the effigies have. But I've heard about the Crow before, and I know that the Royal Council somehow works with them, although, I don't think they want it known."

"So, the figurines represent an organisation?" Rena asked, unable to keep her excitement in check. "What kind? What do they do?"

"I don't know. I haven't figured that out yet," Finn said. "I've got some suspicions, but nothing concrete."

"Anything you'd like to share with the rest of us?" Logan asked.

"You see, I don't think I can trust you," Finn said, glancing at Logan. "I'm going to keep my hard-earned knowledge to myself until I've figured out who you people are."

"Oh, come on," Logan sighed and rolled his eyes.

"I'm from Oceansthrow," Rena said at the same time, interrupting Logan. "My family died in the fire. I just want to figure out what happened."

"Hmmm." Finn looked at her for a beat too long, his jaw clenching, before he averted his eyes. "That might be true, but you could also be lying. And it doesn't tell me who *he* is, or who your other companions are. But none of that matters right now. We need to get out of here before one of the guards decides to go behind my back and tell the administrator about you."

"*We?*" Logan asked and raised an eyebrow. "Since when are we all working together? A second ago you were trying to get us arrested."

"I know I can't investigate this thing on my own," Finn told them. "And I don't exactly trust anyone around here to join me, not for this sort of mission. So, I suppose you lot will do, no matter how irritating you are."

"Why would you trust us if you don't even trust your comrades?" Logan asked.

"Because if they rat me out, the administrator might actually believe them. But if *you* rat me out, I can just have you arrested."

"I love how just and honest the people tasked with protecting our kingdom are," Logan replied with a sickeningly sweet smile.

"Feels like you have a warped sense of reality," Finn said, staring Logan straight in the eyes.

"So why should we trust you?" Logan tilted his head to the side. "Like I said before, you already tried to get us arrested. You might very well be a spy for the Royal Council."

"Don't flatter yourself. The Royal Council doesn't trouble themselves with lowlifes like you. They've got more important issues to deal with than being aware of every cockroach in this kingdom. And if they were actually aware of you, you'd be rotting in jail by now. You don't have to trust me, the same way that it's extremely unlikely that I will ever trust you. We just need to come to an understanding that for the next few days, we're going to work together. We are both investigating the same issue, and I doubt you know as much about the administrator and the Royal Council as I do."

"Well, still," Logan replied, looking off into the distance before glancing back at Finn, "somehow I don't tend to work with people who just held a blade to my throat."

"I think it's going to be fine," Rena interjected, tired of their argument not going anywhere.

"Why?" Logan asked, side-eyeing her.

"A week ago, I didn't know you or any of the others," she told him. "But you still grabbed my hand before running away, and Asha still fought the guards to help us escape, and Rodrick drove us all the way here even though he has no personal stake in the whole matter. So, I don't see why we shouldn't let him into this group too, especially if he already knows more than we do about this whole situation. Maybe all of you will betray each other, or maybe no one will betray anyone. We won't know until the moment arises. And why would they send a spy after us? He's right in saying that we aren't exactly the most important or threatening people to the Royal Council. So, I'd rather believe we're all on the same side, than mistrust everyone and go on this journey alone."

"Fine," Logan sighed, and slid his hands into the pockets of his trousers.

"I'll need to gather some of my things from my chamber before leaving," Finn said. "A ledger with all the irregularities I've noticed while at the archives. You can wait here until I'm back. You should be safe enough if I tell them I didn't see you."

"I don't think we should linger," Logan said, his eyebrows knitting together. "I'm sure you can remember all that important information in that beautiful head of yours. Our best bet is to get out of here as fast as possible and leave town before anyone else starts getting suspicious."

"We need to find Asha and Rodrick first," Rena replied, and turning to Finn asked, "Do you know what happened to them?"

"Last I saw, the woman you were with was busy freeing your other companion. I took most of my men out of the room, and told the remaining guards I'd send for support. If your companions were smart enough, they used that window to escape."

"I'm sure they found a way out on their own," Logan added. "We can just wait for them at the inn. Maybe put a little note on Rodrick's caravan so he knows where to find us."

Rena sighed, uncomfortable with the uncertainty of Finn's words, but there wasn't much they could do from inside the archives without getting caught themselves. She could only hope that Asha and Rodrick had indeed found their way out and were waiting for them at the inn.

"Which inn are you staying iatn?" Finn asked.

"Don't really feel like I should tell you that," Logan answered with a shrug.

"Didn't we decide to trust him?" Rena murmured, turning her face to Logan.

"No," Logan replied, holding up a finger. "*You* decided to trust him. I still think he could backstab us at any moment."

"Whatever," Finn said. "Meet me at the edge of the forest outside the Plains by nightfall. The road that leads to the east. I'll escort you to a side entrance, but you'll have to find your way back to the Plains on your own. There's a hallway on the floor above that leads through the cellar and laundry room, to the backside of the archives. It shouldn't be heavily guarded, and they wouldn't question my passage anyway. Once you're outside these walls, you're on your own. I trust you know how to blend into a crowd and not get caught."

"Of course," Logan answered with a smirk.

"Good. Let's go," Finn said, and opened the door.

Chapter Twenty

It didn't take them long to traverse the upper floor to reach the exit, not passing any guards on their way. Rena kept her gaze on the ground, trying to look dejected in case they did run into anyone and they had to pretend Finn had captured them, but it almost seemed like he had cleared the way beforehand.

The only people they passed had been two boys roughly Rena's age busy stacking sacks of vegetables in the cellar. They had only looked up briefly, and had quickly averted their eyes when they saw Finn.

"You'll have to continue on your own from here," Finn repeated, as they came up to an unremarkable, wooden door at the back of the laundry room.

They had walked through rows of drying sheets and table runners to get to the door – similar to the ones they had seen on the desks in the entrance hall of the archives – obstructing them from the view of any other potential workers.

"Thank you," Rena said. "I really mean it. I hope we'll manage to meet up this evening. I'm going to make sure we're keeping our end of the bargain."

"It's more your loss than mine if you don't show up."

"We should go," Logan said, his hand already on the door handle. "We'll see you when the sun sets, sweetcheeks." He winked at Finn and pushed the door open, grabbing Rena's wrist and heading out.

They stepped out onto a stone pathway, only wide enough for two carriages to pass, the wall surrounding the archives opposite them. To their right, a few workers unloaded wooden crates from a horse-drawn carriage and brought them into the building through tall, double doors.

"Let's go this way," Logan murmured.

He led her to the left, away from the people.

"We just need to get to the crowd and hurry outside. Blend in with the rest of the visitors. It would be too suspicious if we tried to sneak over the wall or something like that. Most of the guards don't know what we look like, we should be fine. Just don't look nervous."

"That's easier said than done," Rena mumbled.

"As long as we don't run, we should be fine," Logan told her.

"Don't you think we stick out just a little bit too much with our dirty clothes?" Rena hissed, pointing at her skirt for emphasis.

"Just pretend it's meant to be like that. Haven't you noticed how unusual some of the people here look? No one cares. People are too self-involved to notice something like that. The worst thing that'll happen is someone will think your sense of fashion is horrible."

"Maybe all of this is easy for you after a lifetime of crime, but I've never even had to consider these things before. When I was back home, I didn't have a habit of sneaking around and deceiving people, okay?"

"You could have stayed home, you know," Logan muttered. "No one's forcing you to be here."

"No, I couldn't have stayed home because it's gone!" Rena burst out.

She stopped, her eyes fixed on the ground, her arms wrapped tight around her chest, trying her hardest not to cry. She pressed her trembling lips together and took in deep, shaky breaths.

"Shit, sorry, I didn't mean it like that," Logan stammered, turning to look at her. "I wasn't thinking. Sometimes I just say stuff."

"I'm sorry I haven't managed to adjust to this massive shift in my life yet, but none of this is easy for me, and everything keeps getting worse," Rena tried to keep her voice calm, to keep her emotions down, but her jaw was trembling and a knot was tightening around her throat. "I had to steal someone's decree, guards are looking for us, we almost got thrown into jail, we don't know what happened to Asha and Rodrick, and it feels like it's all my fault because without me none of us would be here."

"Yeah, no, I know, I know. I'm really sorry." Logan slid a hand over his hair, stepping closer to Rena before stepping back again. "It's not your fault, you know. Don't start blaming yourself for how bad the world is."

"I'm trying my best to keep up with you. But I've never done anything like this, and I just don't have the confidence that everything will be all right. I'm sorry I'm nervous, and I'm sorry I don't have the instincts. I'd also rather be back home with my family than sneaking around some stupid castle looking for stupid letters and ruining one of the only dresses I have just so that maybe I can find out why everyone I ever loved is suddenly dead."

"Fuck, I'm sorry. I didn't mean it like th—"

"And I'm trying really hard to keep it together and just think about what we have to do to find out what happened, but it's hard. And I feel like I'm crumbling, and I don't know what to do, and how to keep myself together, and I miss them so much, and I'm never ever going to see them again even if we find out what happened." Tears ran down her cheeks as her voice cracked around the words.

"Shhh, it's okay, it's okay. Come here, it's okay," Logan said softly, reaching for her. He waited for her to step closer before wrapping his arms around her shoulders. "I'm really sorry I said that. I know what you've been through. It should have never happened. It isn't fair. Sometimes life is way too cruel, and there's no easy way to deal with it."

"I don't know what to do," she sobbed into his shoulder.

"I know, I know," he said calmly, running a hand up and down her back. "You don't have to have all the answers right now. We'll figure it out together, yeah? I know nothing we do will get your family back. I really wish there was a way. You know, if this is too much for you, you can just stop, right? You don't have to go through with this. It isn't your responsibility to fix it. If you want to take a break and deal with your loss first, that's fine. You don't have to force yourself through this if it's too much. I can get you to Rancor and set you up there if you have nowhere else to go. Kalani and Cass would understand. They'd probably welcome you with open arms. That's what the camp's for, after all."

"Thank you," she mumbled into the fabric of his shirt.

"Yeah, no problem. Genuinely, if at any moment, you want to stop, just let me know and I'll drive you straight to the camp. Or somewhere else if you've got someone to stay with. No judgement at all, yeah? Rodrick, Asha and I will keep investigating this thing. And we've got a pretty new face joining the team now, so I'm sure we'll uncover this mystery in no time."

"Not if it's just the two of you," she chuckled and freed herself of his embrace. "If I'm not there to stop you, you'll probably end up stabbing each other."

"Nah. Well, maybe. But I'll make sure to stab him only after we've found out the truth."

"You're the worst." She giggled between two sobs, and tried to find a spot on her arm that wasn't caked in dirt so she could wipe her tears away.

"Our new friend would probably agree with you on that one," he said with a small smile, driving a hand over her hair to flatten it into place.

Rena took a few shaky breaths to ground herself, closing her eyes for a moment.

"We should keep going," she finally said. "I don't want someone to find us here like this."

"We'll just tell them we're jilted lovers who've just had a nasty fight and needed some privacy."

He smiled and stepped away, giving her some space.

"Gross, no," Rena laughed. "You're like ten years older than me."

"Great, that can be the reason for our fight. You've finally come to your senses and want to date an attractive, younger person that can actually relate to you on an emotional level."

"Stop it." She chuckled. "I thought you didn't want to waste any time."

He startled, as if he had completely forgotten what they had initially been doing.

"Right, our escape!" he blurted. "This way!"

Logan took her by the hand and led her around the corner of the building. There was still a crowd in front of the archives, although most people were now heading out instead of in. They walked over to where all of the carriages were standing, drifting through the crowd until they reached Rodrick's caravan. No one seemed to be paying much attention to them, but Rena also forced herself to only look forward and keep her eyes from wandering around.

"Okay, do you have a piece of paper?" Logan asked, patting down his own pockets.

"No," she replied, eyeing him. "Except the letters we stole, I guess?"

"Hmm, not ideal, but we could just rip a small corner off. I need a pen. Do you have a pen?"

He looked around as if he would be able to just magically find one lying on the ground.

"No. Why would I have a pen with me?"

"I don't know. We need something to write the note with."

"This was your plan," Rena told him, "I thought you had it figured out."

"Ah, shit. Okay, okay, it's fine," he replied, driving a hand through his hair again and glancing at the people around them. "I'll figure something out. Wait here for a second."

He jogged over to a group of three middle-aged women in big, colourful, fluffy dresses who stood next to two white draft horses. As Logan came up to them the women turned, wary at first, but they seemed to warm to him quickly. Rena couldn't understand what he was saying, but she heard the raucous laughter of the women well enough.

Rena rolled her eyes and turned around, letting her fingers run over the wood of the caravan as she walked to the back of the wagon. She leaned in close to the door, pressing her forehead against the wood.

"Hey Vincent," she murmured against the door, "how are you holding up?"

From inside the wagon, she heard muffled barking.

"I'm sure Rodrick will come back soon enough to let you out. I'm sorry we locked you in here for so long. It's been a bit of a rough day. I'm not sure what I've gotten myself into." She paused for a while, closing her eyes and breathing in deeply. "I keep thinking that I could just stop and go to my aunt's, but would I really be able to just give up? Now that I know something strange is going on? I think it would eat at me for the rest of my life."

She stopped when she heard approaching footsteps. She pushed herself away from the caravan and turned to her left, expecting Logan to come up to her. As her eyes wandered across the other wagons and the crowd surrounding them, they landed on a spot of bright orange. Behind the wheel of a caravan, sitting in a beam of sunlight, sat a fox, looking at her. The white tip of its tail swayed lazily up and down, but otherwise it didn't move, not even when people hurried past it. No one else seemed to be bothered by the animal. Maybe foxes weren't a rare sight in this city, and people had gotten used to their presence, but something felt different to Rena about this one. It almost felt like she had seen it before, like it was the same one that had been on the crate the day before when they had entered the Plains. Surely there were a hundred of these animals in this city, so why did it feel so familiar?

"All right, let's go," Logan said, suddenly standing in front of her and blocking her view.

"Did you... see that?" she asked as she stepped to the side to look past Logan, but the spot of sunlight where the animal had stood before was now empty.

She looked around, trying to glimpse its red fur in the crowd. She even bent to peer under the wagons, but it seemed to have vanished.

"What?" Logan asked, glancing around.

"There was a fox," she said, still a bit dazed.

"Yeah, they're like plagues in bigger cities," he said. "I don't think they fear humans anymore. And people keep throwing all their garbage onto the streets so it's like a buffet for them."

"I don't know. Something felt different about this one."

"Maybe city foxes look different than the forest foxes you're used to," he said, turning to look at her.

"No, it wasn't anything like that," she said, furrowing her brows, eyes still lingering on the road.

"Well, either way, let's get out of here," Logan said, clapping his hands together.

She nodded. "Did you write the note?"

"Yep, and put it near his seat so he could find it, but still hidden enough so no one else will see. Not like I put our entire plan on that note or anything, but you can never be too careful."

She touched the door of the wagon and whispered a quick goodbye. The dog barked his reply as he shuffled around inside.

Logan turned and walked away from the caravan. Rena glanced around one more time, but the fox had truly vanished. She sighed and turned to follow Logan.

"I don't like it that Vincent's been locked in the caravan for this long," she said, hurrying to catch up with Logan.

"Probably safer than leaving him at the inn all day. Someone could have just stolen him."

"Who steals someone else's dog?" she asked in horror.

"You'd be surprised," Logan replied dryly.

Chapter Twenty-One

They blended into the crowd and Rena kept her gaze fixed on the ground, afraid that if she locked eyes with one of the guards they would instantly know she had to be arrested. The stolen decree felt heavy and warm in her pocket, and anytime someone turned their head in her direction, it felt like they could see it glow through the fabric.

Logan navigated them through the mass of visitors, staying close enough to the other people that someone outside the crowd wouldn't notice them. Rena kept glancing at him, trying to figure out where he had put the pages he had ripped out of the ledgers, wondering how he could exude such an air of nonchalance while carrying such damning cargo.

She only dared look up from the ground when they were already past the last lamp post leading to the archives, and the crowd started to disperse into the Plains. She glanced back furtively, making sure no one was following them. She scanned the crowd around them, frowning, her head movements increasingly noticeable. No one seemed to be following them, no one seemed to even really be noticing them. They had managed to escape, but the knot in her stomach still didn't ease up.

"Shouldn't they close the entire building down if they are looking for someone?" Rena whispered as she leaned closer to Logan.

"Probably don't want to inconvenience their esteemed guests," he said, without taking his eyes from the road ahead.

"But none of the guards even seemed alarmed," she murmured. "Shouldn't they have stopped us? Searched us for any stolen goods? Questioned us if we'd seen anything?"

"Yes, and usually the high-ranking members of the guards don't help the thieves escape. They probably still think we're inside the building. They'd want to catch us without anyone noticing, it doesn't reflect well on their organisation if someone can get into the rooms they're not supposed to. And I'm sure Finn told the guards not to mention the incident to anyone to save his reputation."

"That doesn't seem very efficient," she muttered.

"Yeah, well. With big institutions like this, appearance is often more important than efficiency."

"That's just backwards." She shook her head, not entirely believing Logan's explanation. She was sure the archives were better protected than that, and that probably they had just been lucky and gotten out right before the entire building was closed. Or maybe someone *was* trailing them to figure out where they were going, but they were simply too good at their job for Rena to notice them.

She kept periodically glancing back as they traversed the Plains, until they had reached the inn. She only really stopped once she was back in the room she had shared with Asha the night before, but the feeling of unease never truly went away.

Logan left her alone to get them some fresh clothes, so Rena sat down on the bed furthest from the window, keeping her eyes on the blue sky outside, making sure no one was scaling the building to surprise them. The more she stared at the sky, the more the blue seemed to encroach on her, and the more the silence of the room started to weigh on her.

Her breathing quickened, and soon all she could see was the blue – the overwhelming, bright blue etching itself into her eyes, swallowing any of the other colours. Her heart kept thumping in her chest, the rhythm of the sky embracing her, of the guards approaching.

Any second now, a hand would burst through the blue and drag a body behind it through the window. More hands would follow, creeping in through the cracks around the door. They would know what she had done, would know that she was a thief and a liar and coward who abandoned her family. And oh, how convenient it was that a criminal like her had mysteriously survived the fire, while all of the good people in her family had perished.

Her hands shot up to cover her mouth, caking her face with the greasy dirt from the shafts. The feeling dragged her out of her panic and her hands jolted back again. She shut her eyes, feeling the burning emanating from her eyelids to her head and down her spine. Her tongue lay heavy in her dry mouth as she bit the inside of her cheek, grounding herself in the pain.

She exhaled a shaky breath and opened her eyes again. She couldn't succumb to these feelings. If Maya was still alive, she needed her help, so wouldn't any method that brought her closer to her sister be justified?

Or at least most of them. As long as she didn't hurt anyone, petty theft and dishonesty would be forgiven.

She glanced around the room and was relieved to see a fresh pitcher of water next to the wash basin. She got up and went over to washed her trembling hands. She tried to rub her face clean, but the grime and dust caked onto her skin refused to come off. She rubbed harder and harder until her skin hurt and the water was a clouded greyish-brown. Her hair still felt disgusting, but she would need a bath to fix that issue.

The door opened again, and Rena jerked around, almost pushing the basin over as she stepped back. Relief flooded her body when she saw the familiar face of her companion.

"Good, you're here," Asha said, closing the door behind her.

Rena rushed forward, but stopped herself before getting too close.

"How are you? What happened to your face?" Rena asked, concern expelling her excitement as she saw the dried blood on Asha's temple.

"It's nothing," Asha replied, stepping around Rena to reach the wash basin.

She poured the remaining fresh water from the jug into her free hand and washed her face, a trickle of light pink falling into the murky water Rena had used earlier.

"You seem unharmed," Asha said, glancing at Rena between two handfuls of water.

"Yes," Rena stammered, looking back at the entrance to the room, waiting for it to open again. "Is Rodrick not with you?"

"He's talking to the innkeeper downstairs."

Rena closed her eyes and sighed with relief, and the tight knot in her stomach started to slowly unravel.

"Thank the stars," she muttered, and sat back down on the bed.

Asha put the jug down and started to unlace her arm guards.

"I'm really glad you got out," Rena said, observing how Asha slid her arms out of the leather braces and placed them carefully on the night stand. "I was so worried. I wanted to come looking for you and Rodrick, but Logan said it was best if we got out as quickly as possible."

"He was right," Asha said.

She sat down on the bed next to Rena and took off her boots.

"I'm really sorry we left you alone. Logan just started running, and dragged me with him, and I tried to get back to you when I saw you were fighting the guards, but he wouldn't let go of my hand."

Once Rena had started telling Asha what had happened, she couldn't stop anymore, telling her all about who Finn was, why they had agreed to meet with him, how they had gotten out of the archives, how it still felt to her like the guards could burst into their room to arrest them at any moment.

"Why would we work with someone linked to the Royal Council?" Asha asked, frowning up at her.

She had put her shoes neatly next to the bed and had planted her feet firmly on the ground a shoulder-width apart, propping her elbows against her knees, her hands dangling in the space between her legs.

"We don't really know if he's working for them," Rena stammered out. "I don't think he's a spy, or anything like that, so for now I think we can trust him. I don't really know who the rest of you are either, and I've trusted you so far, so I don't see why I shouldn't trust him either."

"You don't think it's a bit suspicious that he was about to arrest us but then just lets you go and weasels his way into your search?"

"Maybe," Rena murmured, looking down at her interlinked hands in her lap, "but if he actually has information, I think he could really help."

"Fine," Asha said and ran a hand over the thin dusting of black hair that was re-growing on her head. "It's your quest, you can do what you want. I need to go back to Rancor in the morning anyhow."

"Oh... okay." Rena looked up at her in confusion, not having expected their group to split up so soon. "No, yes, of course. I mean, you got what you came for. And you have your uncle to look after. And, uhm, the Sovereign Outcast is waiting for you, right? Of course, you're not obligated to stay with us."

"Yeah, all of that." Asha leaned back on the bed, propping herself up on her elbows.

She looked around the room, her dark eyes clouded in thought, before continuing to speak.

"What, exactly, did that guy say?"

"That he had noticed some weird things going on between the administrator and the Royal Council."

"What weird things?" Asha asked, frowning at Rena.

"I'm not sure. He didn't mention anything specific," Rena answered, brushing her hair behind her ear. "I think he called them 'irregularities.' But he's got a ledger where he recorded everything. That's why he didn't come back with us right away, because he wanted to go get that first."

"Irregularities," Asha repeated.

"Yes," Rena said with a nod.

The door opened with a creak, and Logan stepped into the room.

"Here, catch," he said, and threw a dress at Rena. "Should fit you, probably."

The bundle of fabric hit Rena in the face, and she had to untangle it to figure out where the top and the bottom were.

"Asha!" He exclaimed, throwing a second bundle of clothes on the bed. "Good to see you got out alive."

"Tragedy to see *you* did," Asha said dryly.

"Can't get rid of me that easily," he said with a wink, and took off his shoes while standing.

"I was just telling Asha about Finn," Rena mentioned.

"Finn?" Asha asked, drawing the vowel out, and pushed herself upright again.

"Yeah, the hot guy with the rapier. That's his name," Logan said, almost falling as he tried to take off his right shoe.

"Hot?" Asha repeated, looking at Logan as if he had just declared his loyalty to the Royal Council. "He looked like a sickly child who hasn't seen the sun in a decade."

Logan shrugged, then hopped around until both his feet were free and his shoes were carelessly strewn across the floor. He shook his hand and straightened, turning to face the other two again.

"But isn't it a relief for you to know that there's someone for everyone," Logan told Asha with a devilish grin.

"I don't need *someone*," Asha snarled, staring at Logan as if she was ready to throw him out the window.

"Anyway. Our lovely captain has decided he's part of our team now, apparently," he said, momentarily raising both eyebrows.

"Asha just mentioned she's going to go back to the city of Rancor tomorrow," Rena mentioned, her eyes darting to Asha.

"Oh, come on." Logan threw his hands out to the side in exacerbation. "You're abandoning us already? I thought we were building a bond here. Like brothers in arms, fighting together to overthrow the ruling regime. Isn't that what we all want?"

"That seems a bit extreme," Rena interjected, horrified at his suggestion.

"Okay, okay," Logan replied, holding his hands up in defeat. "Fighting together to find out what happened to the countless lives that were lost to tragedies that should have never happened and that are potentially being covered up, and then maybe figuring out how to better the lives of the people who were affected, which might result in some political changes."

"I'll come to the meeting point with you," Asha said. "See what that guy's all about. I can't guarantee anything beyond that. Like I said, I have obligations."

"Curiosity is winning, isn't it?" Logan smirked. "You'll stay with us, you'll see."

Once again, the door creaked open, and once again a familiar face stepped in.

"Rodrick! Vincent!" Rena exclaimed, rushing to greet them, falling to her knees to pet the dog. "Oh, I'm so glad to see the both of you. I'm sorry we abandoned you. It's my fault the guards were after us in the first place, and I really wanted to go back to help you, but Logan said it wasn't safe."

She looked up at Rodrick who smiled softly.

"Don't worry about it, my child. We're all safe now, so you don't have to blame yourself for anything."

He walked over to the bed and sat down next to Asha with a groan.

"How did you get out?" Logan asked, taking off his shirt, smelling it, then tossing it on the ground with a grimace.

He picked up a new shirt from the pile he had just brought up and slid into it.

"Oh, what and adventure we had," Rodrick chuckled and patted Asha on the knee. "At first our young clerk tried to escort me out of the room when the guards stormed in, but we were stopped by the guard outside the door. I tried to explain to him that I was simply an innocent bystander who didn't know what was going on. I think I almost had him convinced of it when Asha burst out the room."

"Didn't look like they were about to let you go when I got there," Asha muttered.

"Well, never mind that," Rodrick continued, "Asha managed to subdue the guard, and I managed to convince the clerk to let us leave."

"She was scared, I don't think you *convinced* her," Asha interjected again.

"We hurried upstairs to slip into the mass of visitors," Rodrick continued, ignoring Asha's comment. "Luckily enough, we managed to reach the crowd before the next flock of guards stormed past us. I always tried to keep myself between Asha and anyone else, so they couldn't get a good look at her, considering the wound on her face. And then we just walked out."

He finished with a big smile, as if he had been describing a stroll through a forest on a warm, spring afternoon.

"Did you find the note?" Logan asked. "The one on the caravan?"

"Yes, yes, I found the note. Although, whoever wrote it needs to practice their letters. It was barely legible."

"Logan wrote it," Rena muttered under her breath.

"But you did manage to read it. That's literally all that matters," Logan pointed out.

Rodrick chuckled, before he addressed them again.

"Well, I think the important question remains, did you all manage to get what you were looking for?"

"I think so," Rena sighed. "There were some letters between the administrator and the Royal Council that talked about the fires. Logan stole them."

She shot daggers at Logan, but he simply refused to meet her gaze and pulled the crumpled documents out of his trousers pockets and smoothed them out on the bed.

"Better look through these before our meeting tonight?" Logan said, and knelt down before the bed.

"Meeting?" Rodrick asked, frowning at the rest of the group.

Chapter Twenty-Two

As agreed upon, by the evening they found themselves waiting on their new companion at the edge of the forest. They had stayed the rest of the afternoon in their room, discussing Rena's letters, hoping the guards wouldn't find them there. Only Logan dared step out to bring Emmson his documents, but even he wasn't gone for very long.

Rena and Asha were waiting near the road that led away from the Plains, a few steps into the forest so the trees hid them from prying eyes. Logan and Rodrick had stayed with the caravan, which they had stationed further down the road so it wouldn't be visible from far away.

"If he tries to betray us, you run into the forest and let me deal with him," Asha said, her sharp eyes trailing over the tree-line.

"He won't betray us," Rena reassured her.

Even though she really did believe it was unlikely Finn would betray them, she still couldn't keep herself from being nervous, and Asha's attitude definitely wasn't helping. She craned her neck from side to side to catch a glimpse of anyone who might be approaching them. Her hands were clasped in front of her, although she couldn't keep her fingers from playing with the skin on the back of her right hand.

"It still doesn't make sense to me why he would want to help us," Asha muttered, her eyes narrowing at a spot in the far distance.

"It's easier to work on such a big mystery together than to try to solve it on your own. Especially since we might know different things about the situation."

Rena glanced around, but she only saw the deep calm of the forest. All she could hear was the wind rushing through the leaves, the chirping of the birds above them, the low murmur of the city in the distance, but no footsteps coming closer. The tranquillity made her almost more nervous as she would be if someone were approaching. The anticipation crawled all over her body, making her want to pace, to jump, to run through the forest and find Finn before he found them.

"But why us?" Asha continued in a low voice. "He doesn't know us. He barely knows what we are looking for. *I* barely know what we are looking for. At least I can go back to Rancor and continue on with my life whenever I feel like it. But by coming here and deserting his post he's giving up on that privilege, so why risk it? Why not look for allies in his own ranks instead of running away with some vagrants?"

"Because none of them can be trusted." Finn appeared behind them, emerging from deep inside the forest.

Rena spun around, eyes wide, her heart exploding in her chest. She had looked in that direction only a second ago, how could she have not seen him? She hadn't even heard him approach. How long had he been there? Had he been observing them? Hiding behind a tree to listen to their conversation?

Her heart slowly calmed down again, and she looked around to see if anyone else was behind him, but the sun was already setting and she couldn't see very far into the forest.

"I see you got out without any problems," Finn said as he came to stand next to them. "I hope the guards weren't too much of a bother."

"Not at all," Rena muttered, her eyes still trailing the forest around them, before she regained her composure and turned to face Finn. "I was actually a bit shocked by how easy it was to get out. I'd expected that they'd lock the archives or the entire city down to search for us."

"I convinced them that I knew who you were," Finn replied, clasping his hands behind his back. "Told them I was handling the situation on my own. Once they notice I'm gone though, they'll come looking for us."

"Don't you have to report such breaches to the administrator? O-or someone else higher up?" Rena asked.

"Before they realise I never reported it to anyone, we're long gone. How many people saw your faces? Ten? Less than that? Maybe two of those could point you out in a crowd? It will take them a while to figure out who you might be, if they ever do figure it out. If we advance fast enough, they won't be able to catch up. That's also why we should head to Miller's Knee right away since we aren't far from it — before they figure out that's where we're going."

Asha looked at Finn wearily, her frown deepening at his suggestion.

"You think there's something there for us to find," Rena asked, trying to defuse the situation before Asha could say something.

"Who knows? But it's best to take a look before the region is too well guarded."

"And why should we agree to work with you if you're about to put a target on our back?" Asha asked, her hand resting comfortably on the pommel of the sword at her hip.

"You put that target there yourself," Finn answered, staring Asha straight in the eyes, before averting his gaze and looking out into the forest. "I know a lot more about the Royal Council and the rest of the nobility than any of you do. I know who they've got dealings with, and even if I don't, I know how to find out."

"But, as you said," Asha continued, a bite to her voice. "Barely any of them know what we look like. I bet every single last one of them remembers *your* face."

"Trust me, they'll figure out who you are no matter what. At least with me by your side, you'll know what to look out for. But we shouldn't discuss this here. We're just wasting time."

"Convenient, isn't it?" Asha snarled. "To not tell us anything, but have us take you to our hiding spot."

"Asha, please," Rena pleaded, stepping in front of her companion. "I know you don't trust him, but he's right that we shouldn't waste too much time. There's no reason for him to try to lure us into a trap. He basically already had us captive in the archives, he could have just kept us there. I think we can trust him, at least enough to see what he has to say, okay? We can just make a little detour to Miller's Knee, and then get back to the city of Rancor after."

"Cass doesn't usually let people like him anywhere near the camp," Asha said, side-eyeing Finn who was still looking away. "Probably shouldn't even tell him the name of it."

"We'll find a solution once we're on our way," Rena tried to compromise. "He can stay behind in the caravan, or we drop him off in a nearby town."

"I'm not a dog," Finn said, his eyebrows knitting together as he glanced between Rena and Asha.

"Could have fooled me," Asha deadpanned. "Let's go then, since you're so afraid of being spotted."

They walked back to the caravan and introduced Finn to Rodrick and Vincent, although Finn seemed to be much happier with meeting Rodrick than with meeting the dog. He explained his plan to go to Miller's Knee first, and so, without any fail, Rena, Logan and Finn were loaded into the now cramped back of the caravan while Asha stayed in the front with Rodrick and Vincent. Rena and Logan sat with their backs against the door, their arms intertwined so their elbows wouldn't hit against each other, with Finn sitting on the opposite side. He looked around suspiciously, as if unsure whether some of the furniture was about to fall on him or not.

"The caravan is safe to travel in," Rena assured him. "You don't need to worry about it. Just don't touch the oven or the pipes — those are pretty hot."

"First time travelling like a commoner, hm?" Logan asked, a sharp grin on his lips.

"I'm not sure commoners usually travel in such a contraption," Finn muttered as he looked around warily. "You don't even get to see many of these self-drawn carriages in Mellahen, let alone the rest of the province. I don't know who your friend is, but he's definitely not from around here."

"He's a scribe of the land," Rena answered. "And I think he mentioned he used to be a tinkerer, so I'm pretty sure he built it himself."

"Northerner, then," Finn replied, letting his fingers lightly drag over the floor. "Even from its design, it looks more like something from Menakala. I'd say, even almost from the Kano-Raeki Federation."

Logan shot Rena a quick confused glance.

"It just looks like an affluent merchant's caravan to me," Rena replied, pressing her lips together in bemusement.

Finn frowned slightly and shook his head, his eyes trailing up the walls to the ceiling.

"No, the darkened holly oak used in combination with the dark green panelling is specifically used in the North, which of course takes some inspiration from the countries bordering it. Especially considering the grain of the wood, with the thin lines, these planks are clearly from the eastern regions of the Federation. Granted, he could have also just bought the caravan in the north, but it does have a certain... homemade quality to it."

"So, you're also an expert in furniture design now?" Logan quipped, leaning forward and resting his arms on his legs. "We've really caught ourselves a big fish here."

"I just have an eye for detail," Finn muttered, side-eyeing Logan before shuffling around nervously and looking away again.

"Like all the suspicious details you notice while snooping around in the administrator's correspondence," Logan said with a mockingly conspiratorial tone.

"I'm not the one who broke into the archives to *snoop* around," Finn countered, his eyes focused on the row of pans hanging from the ceiling.

"No, but you had to find all of your super important information somewhere," Logan said.

"What exactly did you find?" Rena asked politely.

Finn didn't answer right away, his jaw clenching before glancing at them.

"How about you tell me what you know, then I'll expand on that," he said, his eyes fixed on Rena.

She hesitated at first, but there was no point in holding back information from him. Not if they needed his side of the story to get to the truth. She told him all that had happened over the last couple of days. She told him about the fire, and her family, and the strange bird figurine she found. She told him about how she found her new companions, and about their suspicions for Miller's Knee, and about their journey through the Plains. The only details she withheld were about the city of Rancor and Emmson's business. It was probably more than he had wanted to hear, but talking about it gave it substance to Rena. It made it sound less like just a nightmare. She ended her story by mentioning the letters between the administrator and High Lord Armanid Harkid.

"What did they say?" Finn asked.

"They spoke about the aftermath of the fire in Miller's Knee," she replied, idly playing with the hem of her dress pocket. She was wearing the dress with the red vest again that she had gotten in Halvint, while the one with the green vest had been tied to the top of the caravan to dry. "It mentioned how the town got destroyed and how they were clearing out the place. It said something about 'the complete elimination of the town's memory', which I didn't really understand."

"With major incidents like this, they want to avoid mass panic, so they minimise the risk of news spreading too far," Finn explained.

Rena glanced at him in confusion before her eyebrows drew together into a frown.

"But shouldn't people know that something is going on?"

"It doesn't help anyone if the rest of the province, or the kingdom, becomes hysterical," he explained calmly, as if what he was saying was the most logical thing in the world. "It's easier and faster to deal with this sort of incident while it is still unknown."

"'Complete elimination' doesn't sound like just making sure people don't panic," Logan replied. "Sounds like you're trying to erase it from history."

"I can't tell you more than what I've been told. These sorts of things are under the jurisdiction of the historical academy, and I don't know the intricate workings of that organisation."

"Hmm, then what are you even good for?" Logan mocked, tilting his head to the side to look at Finn.

"But people have a right to know," Rena interjected, heat rising up from her chest. "People died in a horrible manner, and someone's very likely responsible for it. Why would you keep that a secret? Why do they have to die in obscurity? And isn't the job of a historical academy to *write down* history as it happens?"

"Recording history isn't the only thing they do," Finn replied slowly, as if he couldn't really understand what she was upset about. "A large part of their work also consists of regulating the spread of information and public communication. What else did the letters say?"

Rena stared at him for a second, pressing her lips together hard so she wouldn't say anything she'd regret later. She took a long breath, her eyes wandering over the pots hanging above them until her rage had dwindled.

"They mention 'the Lynx' and 'the Crow'," she continued, still a little tremble of anger in her voice, "but I don't know what those are. Some sort of organisation, probably. Apparently, the Royal Council had an agreement with the Lynx *about* the Crow, and that the Crow is responsible for the fires. The letters sounded like the incident in Miller's Knee wasn't the first of its kind. That this Crow group is responsible for more fires."

"I've heard of them before," Finn replied, shifting to cross his legs. His gaze drifted to look at his interlinked hands in his lap, where he methodically pressed and lifted his thumbs against each other. "They're old," he continued, speaking slowly as if recalling something. "There should be three of them. The Lynx is the oldest of them, and the others are offshoots. Sub-groups that disagreed with the opinions or the methods of their leaders. If I remember correctly, they're old religious organisations."

"Religious?" Rena asked.

She knew that in some parts of the kingdom people still held on to the old traditions that related to the old gods, some people even still believed in them. But it had gotten increasingly rare to find anyone who genuinely worshipped in the south.

"At least that's what they started out as a few hundred years ago. I'm not sure they still adhere to those ideals, especially the Lynx. From what I've gathered, they've become more of a business venture over the last century or so. But judging by the effigy you found, I'm not entirely sure that also applies to the Crow."

"The effigies were placed in a circle around the church," Rena murmured, her eyes drifting down to look at her lap where he fingers worried the skirt of her dress.

Slowly, what Rodrick had said that first night came back to her, how the figurine resembled artefacts that had been found in old monasteries. But knowing that there was a connection didn't help her actually understand the situation. It didn't explain the fires, and it didn't explain the connection to the Royal Council, and it didn't explain why any of it had to be kept secret. It couldn't be part of a horrific tradition, because no matter how much people forgot about the old gods, they surely wouldn't have forgotten about something this gruesome.

"But, why are they burning down towns?" Logan asked, vocalising what Rena was thinking.

"I'm not sure why they're doing this," Finn replied. "That's what we need to find out."

"Probably aren't happy that no one prays to their cherished gods anymore." Logan sighed and leaned back, shifting to pull his knees up and lean his elbows on them.

"What does that have to do with killing hundreds of people?" Rena snapped.

"Who even knows?" Logan replied as he idly played with a curl that had escaped his bun. "We'd probably have to ask them about it to find out."

"Where do they live?" Rena asked, turning to look at Finn.

"I don't know," he replied calmly.

"You can't actually go there and just ask," Logan said.

"Why not? If no one else can tell me why they're doing any of this, why can't I ask them? Then we wouldn't have to keep running in circles following tiny breadcrumbs that barely lead us anywhere. They must live somewhere, right? So why not find out and go talk to them? We need to find them anyway if we're going to save Maya."

The two men looked at her in confusion, and Rena's outrage quickly receded as she stared back at them, unsure which part of what she had said had upset them.

"Who's Maya?" Logan finally asked.

She looked at him for an instance, tilting her head slightly to the side. Maya had been a constant in her mind over the last few days, but had she really not mentioned her to Logan? She knew she had talked about her out loud, remembered the pain of opening up, but it must have only been to Rodrick and Asha. How had she spent so much time with her new companions, and never mentioned her sister by name? Never mentioned that she was looking for her?

"My sister," she mumbled, guilt gripping at her heart. "I think they might have taken her."

"That... unusual," Finn said hesitantly. "I've never heard of them taking anyone. It's rare enough that they leave survivors like yourself, but that isn't unheard of."

"I'm not the only survivor?" she asked, her eyes opening wide in anticipation.

"As far as I can tell, there have been reports of inhabitants of these villages surviving because they hadn't been in town when the fire occurred, much like your situation. But I don't know what happened to them after. That they would take someone with them, however." He paused for a moment, his eyes drifting off to the side, his jaw clenching and unclenching as he mulled something over. "I'm not sure if that fits into what I know."

"Did you see them take her?" Logan asked.

"Well, not exactly. I found her ring in the mud outside our house. And I know that doesn't sound like substantial evidence of her survival, but why would her ring be outside? Her body wasn't outside, and nothing else looked like it had been stolen, so I don't think theft was the Crow's motivation. Asha already said I shouldn't blindly follow clues that might only lead me to heartbreak, but I just can't let it go." Her voice drifting off into a whisper, her hand coming up to play with her necklace. "It just doesn't make sense."

Logan took a long breath, then sighed.

"Damn," he said, eyes wide as he looked off in the distance. "Guess we have to go save your sister then."

"I might agree with Asha on this one," Finn said carefully. "It might be foolish to assume your sister is still alive just because you found her ring on the road."

"But if there is even the slightest chance of her being alive, we need to go look for her," Logan interjected.

"It might derail our investigation and put us into further danger if we just run after them blindly."

Rena glanced up at the two men who were staring at each other, not saying anything, waiting for the other to concede. She waited for their argument to continue, hoping that Logan could convince Finn, even though she knew that Finn was probably right. The same way Asha was probably right. That she might lead them down a rabbit hole of pain and suffering just because she had found a ring. The longer the silence went on, the shallower her breaths became, until she felt like she had to hold her breath.

"As Rena said," Logan finally continued, his eyes still fixed on Finn's. "If we want a quick answer to why they're doing this, we need to find them and talk to them. Might as well look for her sister while we're there."

Finn suddenly looked away, turning his head to the side.

"Sounds dangerous," he muttered.

"Yeah, definitely," Logan replied. "Although, I do like a dangerous plan."

He looked over at Rena with a grin and winked at her. She couldn't help herself from smiling back, relieved that he had won, ashamed that she was placing her own desires before the greater good.

"We don't actually know where they are though," Finn said, turning his head back to them, although his eyes never quite reached them.

"I'm sure we can figure it out," Logan replied with a shrug. "We're five very smart and charming people. Finding out where some murderous secret organisation conducts their scheming can't be that difficult for us, can it?"

"Even if we know where they are, that doesn't mean we know how to approach them."

"Hey, one step at a time, buddy, okay?" Logan said, holding his hands out.

"That's how you get yourself killed," Finn answered sharply, finally looking up at him.

"But he's right," Rena told him. "We can't make a plan for how to approach them if we don't even know where they are, or who they are. So, you're right that we need to gather more information no matter what. I think going to Miller's Knee is a good first step, since we're close by. But I think we also need to go back to Oceansthrow, even if it's going to be difficult for me."

"You sure you wanna go back?" Logan asked her. "We could also just drop you off in Rancor, and report back to you afterwards."

Rena sighed heavily and straightened her back, looking at the ground and nodding, trying to convince herself.

"No, I wanna come with you. See what actually happened and what remains of the town."

"The town will probably be crawling with guards and people from the historical academy," Finn said. "I don't know if it's a good idea to go back there."

"We can be sneaky," Logan mentioned.

"The way you were sneaky at the archives?" Finn mocked.

"I think we need to go back, no matter how dangerous," Rena said, determination having settled in her chest.

Chapter Twenty-Three

They abandoned the caravan in a small town near where they suspected Miller's Knee used to be. They had spent most of the evening inching their way closer to their destination, never truly certain which path to take. But, thankfully, Rodrick had such a knack for talking to people that most of the villagers they had approached had willingly helped them find their way, and Rodrick had even found an old farmer who accepted to look after their vehicle while they continued on foot.

And so, as the moon rose higher in the sky, the companions set out to hike through the woods in hopes they would stumble upon anything indicating that a town used to be there.

They found a clearing between the trees, long lanes of grass and underbrush which could have once been a road. Rodrick had brought the lamp that was usually attached to the caravan and illuminated their path — which only made the rest of the forest seem darker and more sinister. The moonlight, even though bright, barely managed to reach them through the treetops above.

At least the dog seemed to enjoy the walk in the forest after the long journey. Vincent trotted along, unbothered by the darkness surrounding them all. He ran ahead on the path before running back, circling each of them, and running off into the distance again. They all seemed to delight in this little game, and even Asha had a small smile on her lips. All except Finn, who stepped away each time Vincent ran up to him.

"If we get eaten by a wolf, we know whose brilliant idea it was to come here first," Logan pointed out, his eyes fixed on the ground so he wouldn't trip on anything.

"There aren't many wolves around here," Rena mentioned. "It's more boars and things like that."

"Well, maybe we'll get eaten by one of those, do you know how dangerous they are?" he said, glancing back at her.

"Shut up, Logan," Asha said suddenly, stopping and looking into the forest to their left. "I think I hear water."

They all stopped and stayed silent for a moment, and true to Asha's word, the faint sound of running water could be heard under the rustling of the wind.

"Shut up, yourself," Logan muttered. "Why should we care about water?"

"You don't think a town called Miller's Knee might have a mill in it?" she replied, moving forward again. "And what do mills need?"

"Wind or a river!" Rena exclaimed, hurrying to catch up with her.

"Exactly," Asha said, turning back around. "So, if I can hear water, it means there's a river, which means the town might be somewhere nearby."

"What an astute observation," Rodrick remarked with a soft smile. "Very well done."

Although the sound of flowing water grew louder the further they walked, they never quite reached it. The road they were on must have run alongside the river, leading them to a wide, empty clearing. They all stopped at the end of the forest, only Vincent running ahead to dart across it, sniffing the ground wherever he went.

The moonlight illuminated the area in front of them, showing how the clearing was covered with grass and bushes and even some young saplings. Rena couldn't image that a town had stood here only a few years ago, but the shape of the clearing also looked too deliberate to be a natural occurrence. To their left, the moonlight glinted in the waters of a brook.

"So, this is really it?" Logan said, frowning slightly. "A bunch of nothing?"

Rena felt the same, even though she knew she couldn't have expected anything else.

"Let's split up and search for clues," Finn said, looking out over the vast expanse. "We'll cover more ground that way."

"Yes, sir," Logan replied with a mock salute.

"I'll stay here and make sure no one's approaching us from behind," Asha said, crossing her arms and looking back at the road.

"Thank you, Asha," Rena said.

They fanned out onto the clearing, keeping their eyes on the ground to catch any glimpses that could indicate anything other than vegetation used to be here. It didn't seem real to Rena. An entire town had been here, with shops, and farms, and homes. Kids used to run through streets, neighbours used to greet each other. And now she couldn't even find the foundation of any buildings. She thought about how this was the same fate that awaited Oceansthrow. That not a single hint would remain of it.

She stopped and looked out over her dimly illuminated surroundings. She could see her companions getting further and further away from her, and suddenly she felt so alone, like the ground was about to open underneath her feet and swallow her. Erase her like it had erased the town and everyone who had ever lived in it. Her fingers grew ice cold as her vision turned blurry, a tear running down her cheek. She would become one with the dirt, grass and mushrooms and trees growing out of her body, and no one would ever find her again.

Vincent came running up to her and pressed his wet nose against the palm of her hand. He paced circles around her while sniffing at the ground, then sprinted off again towards the orange dot of Rodrick's lamp in the distance. She took a deep breath and shook her head, wiping away the tears with the palm of her hand.

She let her eyes wander over the field surrounding her again, her vision having adjusted to the low light. She tried to make out any patterns in the ground, to see where the foundations of buildings could have been, but there was nothing. Her gaze caught on something at the edge of the clearing to her right, something that looked too regular to have occurred naturally.

She walked up to it and saw six flat, stone slabs set into the dirt. She crouched down and noticed that names had been carved into the stones. The cuts that formed the names looked older, worn, with moss growing over them, but underneath the names something else had been carved into the stone. Something newer, like it had been carved over and over and over again.

A SEARING FAITH

"Hey, Rodrick?" Rena called out.

"Yes, my dear?" Rodrick called back from further ahead.

She waved him over, and as he approached, she said, "Do you know what that symbol means?"

She let her fingers run over the deep grooves of two triangles, one right side up, the other reversed, their tips superposed with a dot in the space they formed, and a thick horizontal line running through the dot and the points where the triangles met.

Rodrick came closer and looked down at the slab.

"Hmm, let me see," he said and crouched next to her, groaning with effort. He set his lamp down on the ground next to him, and ran a hand over the slab, ridding it of the moss and dirt. "Well, how odd. The intertwined triangles usually represent Tavuu'Moda, the god of chance. Well, people say chance, but Tavuu'Moda is heavily connected with survival and with perseverance and those concepts. He actually has a twin sister called Kaepi'Pari who is the god of good fortune. Very interesting distinction, but that is a story for another time. You usually only find these symbols on old buildings, like churches or monasteries. In some sects it was almost like a ritual to pray while carving the symbol, although usually a piece of wood was used for this, to create a sort of good luck charm that could protect the wearer. I'm not sure what it is doing on a gravestone, however. Maybe to wish the deceased a safe passage into the afterlife, if the carver believed in such a concept."

He frowned and hummed, running his fingers over the horizontal line.

"Although," he continued pensively. "The symbol is a bit odd. I have seen this variation with the line through the triangles before, especially here in more southern and eastern regions. But this dot in the middle is new to me. Quite peculiar that they added this. I wonder if it could be a local variety."

"So, you think whoever carved this was praying for the people buried here?" Rena asked.

"That would be the most logical explanation to me, yes."

"But then it means that it wasn't the Crow, right? They wouldn't pray for the people they killed to have a safe passage to an afterlife, would they? That sounds a bit twisted."

Rodrick didn't say anything for a while, simply observing the stone in front of them with a serious expression.

"We won't know until we find out who these people are," he finally responded.

He looked up again as if searching for something.

"Logan!" he cried out. "Come here, my child."

"What's up?" Logan asked, jogging up to them, Vincent running after him.

"You've wandered through these parts of the kingdom quite a bit, right?" Rodrick asked, pushing himself back up, one hand on his back, the other on his knee.

"I've been here and there, sure. Why?"

"Have you ever seen this symbol before?" Rodrick asked, pointing down at the stone slab.

"The triangles?" Logan asked, tilting his head to the side as he looked at it. "Not sure. Maybe. It does look a bit familiar, but I'm not exactly sure where from."

"Maybe you've seen it on buildings?" Rodrick asked. "Are there any bigger churches in the area? Ruins of old monasteries maybe?"

"Well, most buildings like that were either torn down or repurposed for something else. I know that in the north they treat these buildings differently, right? More like historical artefacts? Don't touch them and keep them how they are? Here you don't see many of them anymore. People have no use for sentimental keepsakes like that. Although, now that I'm thinking about it, there's some old buildings on the hill formations above the Baedan border. Might have been a monastery before, but I'm not sure. I've only been to that region a handful of times, not much going on there. I went up to those hills once, like 5 years ago."

"I will copy it into my notebook and we can ask around, see if any other people recognise it."

Rodrick pulled his leather-bound notebook and what looked like a small, cylindrical piece of wood out of his breast pocket, and flipped to an empty page. Rena had never seen such a stick before, and she wasn't sure what he needed it for, but when he dragged it over the page it left a mark — like charcoal, but lighter in colour — and he drew the symbol onto the paper.

"We could ask some of your acquaintances," Rodrick said and closed his notebook. "I'm sure someone has seen it before."

"Sure, we can try," Logan said hesitantly, but it was clear that he didn't really believe that it would work.

Asha suddenly jogged up to them, quickly followed by Finn.

"We need to leave," Asha said, her shoulders squared and tense.

"What?" Rena blurted, worry instantly bursting from her chest and filling her entire being.

"Someone's coming," Asha replied, stepping away again and waving for them to follow. "We shouldn't stay here to find out who. Follow me, we'll go the long way around to get back to the caravan."

Chapter Twenty-Four

They disappeared between the trees with Asha taking the lead. Rena tried to glance at the people who were supposedly arriving at the clearing, craning her neck to look behind the trees.

She didn't see much at first, then spotted shadows moving on the path leading to the clearing. Three people stepped into the clearing but from this far away she couldn't recognise any faces. Their silhouettes looked like they were wearing tight, dark trousers, and a thick dark cloak that almost made them look like a capped mushroom.

Logan grabbed her arm and dragged her forward, making sure she didn't fall behind.

"Who are they? Do you think they're guards?" she whispered, looking to the side and letting Logan guide her forward. "How do they already know we're here?"

"They don't look like guards to me."

"What?" she asked, and almost tripped over a root growing out of the ground. "You think so? Who else should it be?"

"Shh!" Asha shot a glare over her shoulder.

"Sorry," Rena whispered back.

"I must agree," Rodrick whispered. "I'm not sure they looked like guards."

He came up to Rena's other side, leaning in closer so they could hear him. Vincent was in front of them, only a few paces behind Asha and Finn.

"You really think so?" she whispered back, shocked. "Do you think it might be the Crow? Why would they be here? Do you think they're following us?"

"Maybe they're scouting out their old arson locations for some new inspiration," Logan added.

"Logan!" Rena almost cried out.

"Sorry," he said ruefully.

"Well," Rodrick continued. "The Tavuu'Moda triangles did look like they had only recently been carved into those gravestones. It might not be that outlandish to think those who perpetrated this atrocity came back."

Finn whipped around to stare at them, flinching aside for a second when the dog almost ran into him.

"Will you shut up?!" he hissed at them. "We are clearly sneaking away from a potentially dangerous situation. How do you folks not understand that silence is of the utmost importance? And yes, they looked like guards. Why would anyone come back to the scene of a crime, years later, when there is nothing left of the town?"

"Shh!" Asha shushed them more forcefully, putting her finger in front of her mouth.

"Sorry," Rena whispered again before shutting up.

The forest in front of them was dark, and they didn't dare re-ignite Rodrick's lamp, but by staying close to the path Asha managed to navigate them out. No one seemed to be following them, and no one seemed to be waiting outside the forest either, so they walked back to the nearby town as if nothing had happened. Rena clung to Logan's arm, hyper-aware of her surroundings, trying to see from the corners of her eyes if they might not be alone after all.

But luck was on their side, and they didn't meet another soul until they woke up the old farmer to get Rodrick's caravan back. Rena wished they could have stayed with the farmer for the rest of the night, ask him for a place to sleep and maybe a bath, but the others were keen to get away from this part of the province and from whoever roamed the ruins of Miller's Knee.

Rena lay on the floor of the wagon and tried to rest, even if it was quite impossible with the noise and the rattling and the heat. They drove all the way back to Halvint, to the inn she and Rodrick had stayed in that first night. Darian wasn't happy to see them arrive so late, but when he recognised them — only briefly glancing in confusion at the new additions to their group — he shooed them into a room and told them to come talk to him in the morning.

It was a cramped room with eight beds — two of which were already occupied by other patrons. The mattresses weren't comfortable, but after the long journey in the caravan, anything even slightly soft was a blessing to Rena. The linens smelled familiar to her, almost like home, and a wave of melancholic sadness flooded her whole body as she buried her face into the blanket and tried to fall asleep.

Rena woke with a start, breathing heavily, sweat running down her back. It took her a moment to realise where she was, her throat too dry to swallow. Her vision was still blurry – the light burning her eyes – and she had to blink multiple times to be able to see anything.

"You okay?" a voice asked from her left.

She slowly turned her head and saw that Logan, Asha and Finn were looking at her with concern. She nodded and shifted in her bed, sitting up straight and pulling the blanket up to hide most of her body.

"I'm fine," she managed to croak. "Just a nightmare."

"I'll fetch you some tea," Asha said and stood up.

Rena wanted to protest, but before any words could leave her lips Asha had already stepped out of the room.

"Sorry about the nightmare," Logan said with a grimace. "Must be tough to be this close to home again."

"Yeah," she muttered and dragged her knees up so she could plant her face in the blanket.

She had dreamt of the fire again, but this time, a giant crow had swooped in and stolen Maya from right in front of her. No matter how ridiculous that image was, the memories of her sister's screaming and the fire's smell didn't want to let go of her heart. Her jaw trembled as she breathed in, the images not leaving her mind.

She lifted her head and took in a deep breath, before turning to Logan and Finn – who were sitting opposite each other on the bed next to hers – and flashing them a hesitant smile.

"Good morning," she managed to say in a shaky voice.

"Morning, sunshine," Logan replied, and returned her smile softly.

Finn muttered a greeting and the door creaked open again. Asha stepped in with an earthen mug which she handed Rena, who accepted it with a mumbled *thanks*.

"Why are you all up already?" she asked after having taken a careful sip of the tea.

"Because it's a beautiful day and the sun is shining," Logan replied with a wide smile, looking past her through the window at the sky outside.

"We're not all sixteen anymore," Asha said dryly as she sat down on the bed next to Logan's. "Our bodies decide for us when it's time to be awake."

"They woke me up," Finn mumbled groggily, as if he didn't actually want to be conscious yet.

Rena pulled the blanket up to her chest, feeling cold in only her undergarments. She looked around the room, noticing the other lodgers had already left. She turned to her right and saw that Rodrick was still asleep, the dog curled up on the bed at his feet. She turned back to face the others, wrapping her arms around her legs and letting her head drop onto her knees.

"What are you guys doing?" she asked, the memories of her dream still tugging at her mind.

"Scheming," Logan replied, raising his eyebrows as his smile grew wider.

"Trying to figure out what the best strategy is for the journey ahead," Finn answered, throwing an annoyed look at Logan.

"Same thing." Logan shrug and waved him off.

"What the idiots are trying to say," Asha began. "Is that we have decided Rodrick and I will go to the city of Rancor to talk to Ocassian about this situation. The idiots will go to Oceansthrow to figure out what's going on there, and we hope they don't get killed, and manage to come back with some valuable information."

"So little trust," Logan said in a low voice.

"In you? Always."

"And what about me?" Rena asked.

"That is for you to decide," Logan told her, his voice growing softer again. "We can't force you to go back to Oceansthrow. We definitely wouldn't want you to relive all of that if you aren't ready for it. So, if you want to visit the ominous Sovereign Outcast with Asha and Rodrick instead, you can do that, or you just stay here and take a day off."

"What about Darian?" she asked. "Didn't he say he wanted to talk to us?"

"You slept through all of that, my dear."

"What did he say?"

"Like a bunch of stuff," Logan replied, waving his hand around vaguely.

Asha sighed and closed her eyes in annoyance.

"The authorities have already come to take a look at Oceansthrow," she finally explained. "Someone from Halvint actually contacted them to get help, because they still believe these people are here to help us. A flock of guards arrived two days ago and told everyone they weren't allowed to get close to Oceansthrow anymore because they've got it all under control. And yesterday, some lady in a fancy blue dress arrived to tell them the fire was just a tragic accident because someone left the oven on overnight."

"Going by the description of the dress, that was the envoy from the historical academy," Finn added.

The image of the scholar they had stolen the decree from flashed into her mind – her dark blue uniform with the golden inscriptions running up the skirt.

"And she said the fire was because someone left the oven on?" Rena asked, unable to wrap her mind around such a blatant lie. "But... an oven fire wouldn't spread throughout the entire town. People would have noticed and evacuated."

"Apparently she mentioned something about wind direction," Logan said with a shrug. "And how someone left their hay out to dry, and the fire spread too quickly for people to do much about it."

"But that doesn't explain how no one survived," Rena snapped.

"According to her, people got trapped by the collapsing buildings and it was just really bad luck. And you survived, so you can't say that everyone died."

"They're using me as an excuse?" Rena cried out, a cold shudder running down her spine imagining what the envoy might have said about her.

"Apparently they're looking for you," Asha said dryly.

Rena opened her mouth to reply, but didn't know what to say. She had wanted to talk to someone in a place of authority from the start, but now her body revolted against the idea of it, and she didn't quite understand why. These people might just want to talk to her, to let her know what was going on. As Finn had said, it didn't help if the entire kingdom knew what had happened, it would just cause mass panic. Maybe the historical academy was trying to find the Crow, and would reveal the truth once they had brought them to justice.

She looked at her companions – worrying her lower lips with her teeth – and decided that it was too much of a risk to talk to the envoy. Not before she knew what exactly they had done to her hometown. Not before she knew how much they were hiding.

Her mind returned to what Logan had told her, to the excuses the envoy had given. An oven fire that supposedly destroyed the entire village, helped by the wind and dry hay. It hadn't even been windy that day, and the season for hay drying had barely started. Anger started bubbling up in her, low in her stomach, spreading its tightness throughout her body until she was digging her fingers hard into the blanket.

"And people believe this?" Rena snapped, instantly embarrassed about her outburst.

"Darian didn't seem to believe all of it, but what can you do, right?" Asha said, sarcasm dripping heavily from every word. "At least he isn't ratting you out to the historical academy."

"I don't know what you all think the historical academy would do," Finn said slowly, his eyes wandering from one person to the next with suspicion, "but they wouldn't harm her."

"Sure, they wouldn't", Asha replied, dragging out the first syllable.

"It is simply part of their job to assist in these investigations, of course they would want to speak to the only survivor."

"Better not talk to them so we don't have to find out if they would or wouldn't hurt anyone," Logan interjected, leaning back against the mattress. "Anyway, apparently there's also another group of shady people roaming around town that Darian couldn't really place."

"Shady people?" Rena asked, frowning at Logan's change of topic.

"I don't know," he said with a shrug. "He mentioned something about a group of people arriving yesterday morning that no one in town has ever seen before. I'm not actually sure it really means anything. Maybe Darian's just being paranoid. Could just be some creeps who like looking at tragedies, or the kinda guys who're trying to solve weird mysteries on their own. There's some odd people out there, but hey, life wouldn't be fun without them."

"Aren't we the kind of people who are trying to solve this mystery on our own?" Finn asked, confusion in his voice, but his question was only met with a blank stare from Logan.

"I don't fault Darian for being careful," Asha said, ignoring the other two. "Better to be paranoid about things like this."

"What?" Logan asked, breaking out of his daze. "You really think the ominous Crow would come back to check on the situation when the place is crawling with guards? Wouldn't that be the stupidest decision they could take?"

"They might be working with the guards, that's why they aren't afraid of being caught," Asha replied.

"As in, the guards know who's setting these fires but refuse to apprehend them?" Rena asked, her eyebrows knitting together.

"Wouldn't be the first time," Asha deadpanned.

"No, I won't believe that," Rena replied, shaking her head emphatically.

Asha sighed.

"I know it sounds terrible, but that is just the way the world works."

"She's sixteen, give her a break," Logan murmured.

"I don't want her to run into their arms thinking they can help us when all they'd do is try to silence her," Asha replied, a bite to her voice. "What have they done until now? Absolutely nothing. If this has really gone on for years, how haven't they done anything about it? The letters showed that they know who's responsible for it, and yet they're still allowed to roam free two years later to burn down another village?" She paused to look each of them in the eyes. "I know it's a hard truth to believe, Rena, but I'd rather break your heart right here than have you keep hoping that any of them would be willing to help people like us. I went through enough pain figuring that out, you don't have to go through the same years of agony. They're rotten, every last one of them."

She ended her tirade by looking at Finn, who stared back at her, unblinking, his jaw clenched.

"Listen, Asha," Logan said and sat up, squirming around and running a hand over his hair. "I'm with you on most of this, but we could try to phrase it a bit less bluntly."

"I'm sorry," Rena blurted out, and stood up from the bed to stare into Asha's dark eyes, her blanket falling to the ground. "I know you mean well, but I won't believe the guards, and the administrator, and whoever else, know who burned down Miller's Knee and haven't done anything about it this entire time. Maybe I was naïve thinking they would help us. Maybe I don't completely understand the reality of the world we live in. But you're telling me my entire family is dead, and it could have been prevented, but the ones who could have done something just ignore it? For what?"

Asha broke their eye contact, and hung her head low, running a hand over the short cropping of tight coils re-growing on her head.

"Either money or power," she replied, the bite taken out of her voice. "It's always just money or power with these people."

"Maybe some of them," Rena conceded. "But not all of them. Finn's here, isn't that enough proof. There have to be others who didn't know and wouldn't just accept it. And if you consider how many people are needed to dismantle and entire town, I refuse to believe that all of them knew what was going on and not a single one of them cared."

"Those probably just got silenced," Asha replied with a sigh.

"You are all just a bunch of miserable grouches," Rena shouted, her voice cracking. She curled her hands into fists, her nails digging hard into the flesh of her palms. "Everything is bad and horrible and forsaken in your eyes. I'm tired of it. There's good in this world, and people care, and not everything is a calamity."

Her voice had risen to the point where it felt to her that the people outside the building must surely have heard her. Her heart was hammering in her chest and ears, her head growing dizzy. The others didn't say anything. Logan and Asha simply stared at her, dumbfounded, while Finn was focused on flattening the linens in front of him.

"What's going on?" a groggy voice muttered from behind her.

"Goodbye, I will see you at lunch," Rena exclaimed, heat rushing to her cheeks, too nervous to look at Rodrick.

She turned around, grabbed her dress, and stormed out of the room. She slipped into her dress in the hallway, and walked barefoot over the coarse, wooden floor until she was halfway down the hallway.

She turned around again, then instantly changed her mind and swivelled to continued walking away, spinning around a few more times before she simply stopped. Her breaths were coming in quick and ragged and she had to shake the energy out of her body before she could calm down.

She hadn't meant to explode like that, wasn't used to it, but it was as if her body refused to believe in a world where human beings would deliberately put their own comfort before the lives of others. Some, certainly – she wasn't naïve – but not everyone. Not so many that a secret organisation could murder hundreds of people over decades and no one did anything about it.

The door behind her opened and closed again.

"Rena, wait," Logan called out, jogging to catch up.

She turned to look at him, and crossed her arms, quickly averting her eyes so she wouldn't have to look him in the eyes.

"I'm sorry we upset you," he said in a soft voice, coming to a halt in front of her.

"I shouldn't have yelled like that," she muttered.

"You barely did," Logan replied with a short chuckle.

"I'm not oblivious, you know," she said. "Even before the fire I knew that life wasn't always easy and that those in power weren't perfect and sometimes made horrible decisions. They do teach us how the Royal Council was created because we used to have only one monarch ruling the entire kingdom and they could do whatever they wanted and that included bad, selfish things. Just because I'm from a small town doesn't mean I'm ignorant. But it's a giant leap from 'sometimes the nobility is corrupt' to 'none of them actually care about us'. I can accept that the authorities are trying to cover this up because they haven't caught the perpetrators yet, and that they don't want it to tarnish their reputation, or cause mass panic, even if it kind of breaks my heart. But to know who did it and just let it happen? That's horrible."

"I know, I know," he tried to reassure her, his hands lightly touching her shoulders. "We got a bit carried away. Asha's gone through some stuff with her family, you can't blame her for having such a negative outlook on life. It's been a rough couple of years for her. I'm sure at least some of the nobility care. The administrator sounded upset about what happened to Miller's Knee in the letters, right? At least a little bit. I'm sure she's also upset about Oceansthrow. I don't think anyone can look at this situation and not be upset one way or another. We just need to find the right people who'd be willing to help us."

"Do you think Finn will know who the right people are?" she asked anxiously. "He's probably well connected, right?"

Logan chuckled and shrugged.

"He might know some of them. But we don't really know who he is, and if he's just the third son of some old house that barely even owns land anymore, and he only got his position because of some favour, I don't think he'll have a lot of bartering power. We could also just bribe or blackmail someone if we don't find anyone willing to help us."

"Isn't this what you are all complaining about?" Rena scoffed and rolled her eyes at him. "That nobility is corrupt and doesn't play fair? How is blackmailing them into helping out any better?"

"Hey, they started it," Logan said, raising his hands in defence.

The door creaked open once more and Asha stepped out into the hallway. Their eyes met, and Rena froze, anticipation and remorse gripping her tight. Asha stepped closer, keeping her eyes fixed on Rena, but didn't say anything for a while. Rena had to look up at her, feeling Asha's imposing presence as their argument flooded Rena's mind again.

"I didn't mean to be this harsh," Asha finally said.

"I'm sorry I called you a miserable grouch," Rena blurted out at the same time.

The right corner of Asha's mouth twitched up for a second.

"You don't have to apologize for that. Some people might agree with you."

"Runs in the family," Logan muttered under his breath as he pretended to look at the end of the corridor.

Without looking at him, Asha hit his shoulder with the backside of her hand.

"What I wanted to say," Asha continued, choosing her words carefully. "Is that I apologise for how I expressed my view of the world and for trying to drag you towards my way of thinking with not enough regard to how that might make you feel."

"Thank you," Rena replied and shot her a soft smile. "And I'm sorry for my outburst. That wasn't very conducive to a healthy discussion. I know you mean well. Maybe one of these days we'll have a few hours of rest where we can discuss everything in more detail and try to convince each other without shouting."

"Are you done?" Finn called out from the other end of the hallway as he stepped out of their room. He had already put on his entire uniform, sword dangling from his side, and he had slicked his blond hair back with water.

"Really?" Logan answered. "You couldn't have waited five more minutes?"

"Asha said to give her two," Finn said as he approached.

"Did you count the seconds?" Logan asked, shaking his head at Finn.

"We're only wasting time waiting around here." Finn stepped up to them, looking at Rena and Asha.

"It's okay," Rena said before Logan could add anything more. "We're good now."

She smiled at Asha who nodded back once.

"Are you coming with us, Rena, or are you going with Rodrick and Asha?" Finn asked.

"You really don't have to if you don't feel up for it," Logan piped up. "Don't force yourself for our sake."

Rena sighed and looked at her three companions.

"No, I'm coming with you," she said with more confidence than she really felt. "I need to know what happened to Oceansthrow. Just let me get my shoes."

Chapter Twenty-Five

They left town after Rodrick insisted on an early lunch, and approached Oceansthrow by foot – having made plans to meet up again in Halvint before nightfall. The closer they got to her hometown, the more Rena's stomach twisted and turned on itself. She started having trouble breathing again, but forced herself to take in deep breaths so the other two wouldn't notice.

By the time they reached the end of the road, her fingertips were ice cold, her back was drenched in sweat, her lips were numb, and she desperately wished she could sit down and rest for a moment.

"Let's just pretend we're curious farmers from somewhere close by, who came to check out what actually happened," Logan said. "I'm sure the historical academy hasn't been to all of the tiny villages around the coast yet to tell them not to come here."

"Do I look like a farmer to you?" Finn frowned.

"We can just pretend you're our weird cousin who ran away to join the guards and now dresses in ridiculous clothes to pretend he's made it in life."

"My clothes aren't ridiculous!" Finn exclaimed. "Your plan just doesn't make any sense."

"My plan is perfectly fine."

"I think I'm going to be sick," Rena muttered, a wave of nausea suddenly hitting her.

She stopped walking, her vision going blurry. Logan stopped and turned around, crouching in front of her to look her in the eye.

"Okay, okay, look at me," he said. "Deep breaths."

He mimicked taking long and deep breaths. Rena looked up from the ground, and tried to look him in the eye, but couldn't focus. She tried to breathe, but her jaw trembled too much and she could feel the heat of bile rising up her throat.

"We're here with you, okay?" Logan said softly. "Do you want to sit down? Should we take a break?"

"We don't have time for a break," Finn noted, standing to Logan's side.

"Do you even have a heart behind those ridiculous clothes of yours?" Logan snapped, turning to glare at him. "Don't you see she's struggling? Even you have to recognise this is a difficult situation."

Finn's jaw clenched, and he quickly stepped back again, looking away from them.

Rena's palms turned clammy; her mouth too dry to swallow. She pressed her lips together, biting down on the inside of them, and closed her eyes for an instant before opening them up wide.

"He's right," she said shakily. "We don't have time for a break. I didn't come with you to slow down the investigation. We should keep going."

Logan stared at her. She could focus enough to see the green streaks colouring the brown of his eyes, but it took an enormous amount of effort to not just let her vision go blurry again. She nodded slightly, hoping he'd understand her.

"Okay." He nodded and stepped back. "But promise me that before you faint you tell me you want to take a break, yeah? No falling over without giving us a warning first."

"Sure," she chuckled weakly.

They advanced slowly, until they finally emerged onto a wide plane of dirt and ashes. The ground had been trampled into mud, and even at the edges barely any grass remained. The only building still left standing was the burnt ruing of the church in the middle of the clearing. A big pile of rubble indicated where the tower used to be, but astonishingly enough, the main building next to it had not completely collapsed in on itself, with the roof still intact on the rightmost side.

Horse and wheel tracks ran from both roads towards the church, next to piles of neatly sorted and stockpiled debris. Three people were currently next to the church, loading a horse-drawn carriage with pieces of wood from one of the piles.

"They really took everything away," Rena muttered, exhaustion flooding her body.

The bile was retreating, her stomach unclenching, as if the anticipation was worse than seeing the reality of the situation. But that wasn't it. Visiting Miller's Knee had prepared her for this. Since they had seen what had happened to the other town, she had tried to imagine what her own home might look like, although it had almost felt impossible to picture nothingness. But standing in front of it, being faced with the reality that Oceansthrow was gone, made her feel as if she, too, couldn't exist anymore.

"I'm sorry," Logan whispered weakly.

She sighed heavily.

"I knew they'd take the remains, but I thought at least some of it would still be here."

"Yeah, they really worked quickly," Logan said ruefully.

"It's just ... gone. I lived here my whole life and now nothing's left except the stupid school."

"Once those guards are gone," Finn interrupted in a low voice. "Let's get closer to the church and look at what remains."

"Come on, give her a second." Logan shook his head slightly.

"I said once they're gone. That's multiple seconds."

Rena pointed to the other end of the clearing where the second road led into the forest.

"Over there," she said. "That used to be my father's friend's house. He had a few goats in his backyard and he used to make cheese from their milk. It wasn't the fancy kind you see in bigger towns or cities, just regular goat milk cheese, but he made it with love and he always gifted us some and that made it special to us." Her hand moved to the left. "And there used to be a soap shop run by this old lady called Maggie. When she was young, she travelled all over the kingdom, and even up to the Kano-Reki Federation and further north. I'm not even sure which country is higher north than the Federation."

"It borders the nation of Yarrik and the duchy upon Elizar, although they might merge soon," Finn informed her.

"Shut up," Logan muttered.

"And Maggie gathered all these recipes for soaps and then settled down here, because her family was here," she continued, ignoring her companions, her finger travelling further to the left. "And my house used to be on that side, not too far from the forest. My uncle's house was right down the street. Every week we used to all gather together and eat a big meal. Everyone got their turn to decide what we should cooked, even the little ones. It would have been Maya's turn to choose this week. She would have probably asked for some cod again. She always asked for cod."

"I'm really sorry," Logan murmured.

She stopped for an instant – her hand falling to her side again – as she looked out over the vast nothingness, and it felt like it was spilling out of the ground and winding its way up her legs and over her body, swallowing her whole.

"I thought I would start crying when I saw this, or faint or be sick," she said softly. "But I just feel empty. Like this place. Stripped of everything that used to be here."

"The guards are leaving," Finn noted.

"Stop it," Logan muttered.

"Looks like one of them stayed behind," Rena said, her eyes wandering over to the only building that still stood. "I think he's guarding the place."

"We'll need to distract him somehow," Finn replied. "I don't see how we would be able to sneak up on the church without him noticing."

"Leave it to me," Logan said, stepping forward.

"What? No wait!" Rena exclaimed, instantly ripped out of her melancholic state.

Logan jogged up to the guard, waving and calling him over as he approached the church. Rena couldn't hear what he was saying, but the guard didn't seem alarmed. Logan shook the guard's hand when he reached him, not letting go of it for a good while.

"I'm terribly sorry for your loss," Finn murmured, his head tilted slightly towards her.

"Thank you," she replied in the same tone of voice, not able to take her eyes from Logan's performance.

"I apologise if I come across as heartless, I simply don't want us to miss our window of opportunity. I know this must be a difficult time for you."

"No, you're right. We probably don't have much time before the next crew arrives."

Even though Rena couldn't see the guard's face, she certainly could see their shoulders tremble from laughter as Logan's patted them on the back.

"What is he doing?" Rena whispered and squinted at the spectacle.

"I don't know," Finn said hesitantly. "It just looks like they're talking and … laughing. He might actually be pretending to be a curious farmer."

"How does this keep working on people?" Rena sighed.

"Him pretending to be a farmer?" Finn asked, confused.

"No, in general," she replied, waving a hand around vaguely. "Him just walking up to people and having them instantly trust him."

Finn didn't reply for a while, observing Logan's wide movements as he explained something or other to the guard with great enthusiasm.

"It's the smile, probably," he finally replied pensively.

"You really think that's all it takes?" she asked, dumbfounded as she stared at the scene unfolding a few metres away.

Logan put a hand on the guard's shoulder and they spun around to inspect the piles of debris next to the church. He patted the guard on the back, staying a step behind them, before his arm suddenly slid around the guard's throat.

"What is he doing?!" Rena exclaimed. "He's going to hurt them!"

She picked up the hem of her dress and ran up to Logan.

"Stop it!" she cried out. "What are you doing!?"

Logan looked up at her in confusion and let the guard slip out of his grasp.

"What?" he asked.

"You could have hurt him!" she exclaimed, stopping right in front of him, the unconscious guard laying on the ground between them. "H-he's not dead, is he?"

She glanced down at the body in horror and took a small step back.

"He's fine, just sleeping," Logan replied with a groan, stretching his arms over his head.

"We should hide the body," Finn said as he came up next to Rena. "We don't know when the next troop will arrive."

"Are you sure he's fine?" Rena asked, hesitantly crouching to look at the guard's face.

"Yes, stop worrying so much," Logan dismissed her. "He's going to wake up soon enough. Let's just put him in between the piles here and tie him up."

Logan leaned down and turned the unconscious body around until he could grab hold of the guard's legs and dragged the body over the ground.

"I wouldn't exactly call that hidden," Finn remarked.

Logan stopped and looked up at him, annoyance written all over his face.

"Oh yeah, do your beautiful blue eyes see another hiding spot in this great vastness of nothing? Does your highness want to drag him all the way to the forest? Maybe we should dig him a hole and hide him there, if we're already at it."

"You are absolutely infuriating," Finn sighed, pinching the bridge of his nose. "If a new troop appears, they will find him straight away if you just put him there. What kind of advantage does that give us?"

"You guys deal with your mess," Rena said, stepping away from them. "I'm going to go look at what remains of the church."

"Yes, great observation. Do you also have a follow up plan?" Logan continued without reacting to Rena's departure. "Or do you want to sit down and think about it for an hour?"

"We could put him inside the church," Finn's voice echoed faintly as she circled the ruins of the building. "The right side looks intact enough for people to enter."

"As if that isn't the second place these guys will be checking. How does that help us more than putting him down here?" Logan argued.

As Rena's eyes swept over the scorched beams sticking out beneath the rubble, the memories of the fire came back — of the collapsing church as she entered the town, the hand sticking out, reaching for help, the bodies of her mother and brother lying lifeless in their destroyed home. The searing scent of that evening clawed its way down her throat again as if she was still surrounded by burning bodies. She stopped in front of the back side of the church, bile rising again as her vision went blurry. Acid shot up her throat and she vomited up the delicious lunch

Darian had prepared for them against the remains of the church. She braced herself against the wall, sweat forming around her mouth as she struggled to breath and her stomach tensed again. Soon her stomach felt as empty as the rest of her body, and she spit out the last remains of bile, before pushing herself away from the acrid smell.

She wasn't happy that she hadn't managed to keep it in, but at the same time it was almost a relief that it had finally happened. That her body had finally managed to expel this feeling from her. She stumbled back and dug her nails into the palms of her hands until pain was all she could feel. She forced her eyes shut and took in long, deep breaths, dragging her mind from the fire towards happier memories. Towards her new life, and the warm, soft fur of Vincent.

Footsteps approached from her left, and she opened her eyes again.

"Anything interesting on this side?" Logan asked as he walked around the corner. "Couldn't see much from the other side, but the room seems stable enough for us to enter." He stopped and wrinkled his nose. "Oh. Are you okay?"

She nodded and wiped her mouth, wishing she had brought something to drink with her.

"I'm fine now," she said weakly.

He regarded her for a moment before nodding.

"I checked the guard's pockets," he continued, "but there wasn't anything in them. Not even a letter with orders or anything like that. He's definitely from Mellahen though... unless these people all stole official guards' uniforms, but that seems highly unlikely."

Rena slowly unclenched her fingers, the pain remaining a dull, pulsing ache in her hands.

"Let's look inside," she replied, her voice hoarse.

She approached the part of the old building that had collapsed. She could see into the room from where the collapsing roof had torn a hole in the wall. Spots of light covered the ground from the broken windows and roof, illuminating the piles of ashes and rubble inside the church. Footsteps lead to and from holes in the wall, towards the almost intact, left side of the room. She squeezed through the hole, making sure not to touch the walls or the beams, and stepped into the ruins of the church. She had to crouch until she reached the part where the roof hadn't collapsed. The smell of fire filled her lungs, but this time she was certain it wasn't just in her mind. She tried not to look at the ground too much, too scared to find a part of someone's body again.

She remembered this part of the building. It was the smallest of the classrooms, where they had looked after the little kids that didn't have the attention span for a learning environment yet. Along the wall to her left stood a row of closets filled with blankets and toys, although most of them had collapsed, and their contents had spread on the ground. A few of the tables were still standing untouched, covered in ashes, although the ones at the very back had been pushed forward, forming a half-circle around the back wall.

Logan came up behind her, glancing around the room.

"Well, someone was definitely in here," he noted.

"They moved some of the tables," Rena remarked. "I don't think the destruction from the fire could have piled them up like this."

"Yep, definitely looks deliberate. Nothing else was touched though."

She glanced around at the rubble surrounding them.

"Wait, what's this?"

She stepped closer to the back wall. Fresh marks had been carved onto the surface, two interconnected triangles with a horizontal line and dot in the middle.

"Yep, that's definitely the same one we saw in Miller's Knee," Logan remarked, following her to inspect the symbol carved into the wall.

"What is this?" she blurted out, anger rising in her voice. "Who would do something like this? People died here not even a week ago, a-and some random strangers came in here to carve symbols into the walls to ... to what? Pray to some old god no one has thought about for hundreds of years?"

"I honestly have no idea," Logan sighed. "I'm sure they must have some reason for it."

"They destroy the entire town, leave their stupid figurines everywhere, then carve some triangles into a wall, and that's supposed to make sense? Is their god smiling down on them now? Are they happy? Did they achieve everything they ever wanted? Should we applaud them for their little ritual?"

"I don't think so," Logan said hesitantly, side-eyeing her with concern.

"I just don't get it," she muttered, the white-hot rage dissipating as quickly as it had appeared. "All this destruction and pain for what? For some old belief system that disappeared centuries ago?"

She turned around, her gaze wandering over a pile of rubble to her right. She stopped, her eyes landing on a flash of white between the black and brown debris.

"What's that?" she asked, her mind slowly realising what she was seeing.

Logan turned, and instantly spun her around.

"Don't look at it."

Rena froze, her eyes going wide as she stared unfocused at the exit Logan had turned her to, ice cold shivers running over her body. Of course, the school wouldn't have been empty when the fire erupted. Of course, someone would still have been inside when parts of the roof collapsed.

Footsteps quickly echoed from outside, and Rena blinked quickly to get her eyes to focus again.

"Someone's coming," Finn hissed, stopping just outside the hole in the wall.

"Guards?" Logan asked.

"Looks like it. Another wagon to pick up materials. We should leave."

Chapter Twenty-Six

"Let's get out of here," Logan said in a hushed voice. "We can head towards the forest. With the right angle, they won't see us leave."

Rena's shoulders tensed, too aware of the body lying behind her. She wanted to run, to disappear, but at the same time it felt impossible to move. She stared straight at Finn, eyes wide. He stared back, his eyebrows drawing together into a confused frown, before he averted his eyes and stepped back.

Logan gently grabbed her wrist and tugged at it.

"We need to go," he said calmly.

Rena looked over at him, her head turning before her eyes, and forced herself to nod. She took only shallow breaths until they had stepped out of the church, feeling like the air inside the building was infested.

On the other side of the church, horses whinnied as they approached and stopped, and heavy boots landed on the ground.

"Dijani? Dijani?" someone called out.

"Where the fuck did he go?" another voice said, barely audible.

"Let's go this way," Logan whispered, nodding towards the forest.

He hurried straight for the trees – still holding on to Rena's wrist – and made sure the intact part of the church was between them and the arriving cart.

"Hey," someone shouted behind them, much closer than what Rena was comfortable with. "Hey!"

Rena glanced back at where the voice had come from. One of the guards had rounded the corner of the church and had spotted them. Confusion only kept him in place a short while before he pushed forward and started running towards them.

"Run!" Logan yelled, dropping his hold on Rena's arm, and without waiting for his companions, he picked up speed.

Rena's mind instantly jumped into action, her body pushing past the stiffness of her muscles, as she lifted the hem of her dress and started running. Logan disappeared between the trees, Finn only a few steps behind. Rena tried to follow, tried to weave the same path between the trees, but she had to keep one eye on the ground and the other on the guard that was closing in, and soon she had lost sight of both men. She ran in the direction she thought their footsteps came from, but the forest muffled and spread sounds, and she didn't have time to stop and figure out where she had to go.

She kept running, even after she couldn't hear the guard behind her anymore, even after she couldn't hear her companions in front of her anymore. She slowed to catch her breath, to let her heart drop to its usual cadence again, until she was only walking. She let the bottom of her dress drop, only holding it up enough so it wouldn't drag over the ground and get caught in the underbrush.

Finally, she stopped and looked around, unsure of where she was. She knew these forests well enough, but even she couldn't tell the difference between one random gathering of trees and another. At least it was only early afternoon. She still had plenty of sunlight to find her way out. She tried to picture a map in her mind, to chart their path on it, and thought she might not be too far from the road that led from Halvint to Mattak. She would have to find her way further east, but she first had to figure out where east was. She looked at the ground, trying to discern where the shadows fell, but she had forgotten how to read them. She examined the bark of the trees, to see where the moss was growing, but little pockets of it sprouted everywhere. She looked up at the branches, trying to see where they were densest.

All of her observations were vague, nothing that told her for certain where east was. She crouched down for an instant and buried her face in her hands. Her whole body ached, and although she felt like crying, she forced herself not to. There was no need for it, she would find a way out. The forest wasn't that big. Even if it might take her more than a day, she would manage to get back to Halvint.

She stood back up, took a deep breath, and continued on her journey. She didn't have a way to tell the time, she just knew her legs were getting heavier and her feet started hurting. The feeling in the pit of her stomach that she had gotten lost grew larger, but she decidedly ignored it. She started singing all of the songs she could remember, and once she had gone through her whole repertoire, she started over. She ignored the voices telling her that she had passed a specific tree twice already, ignored the heaviness of her tongue begging for water. She marched, and marched, until a branch poked through the fabric of her shoe and almost made her trip.

She decided that she had advanced enough to deserve a break, and so she sat down on a rock and untied the laces around her ankles to let her feet breathe. She was used to walking through the woods in these thin, canvas shoes, but usually she didn't have to run in them or hike through the underbrush for hours. She massaged the soles of her feet, trying to soothe the knots that had formed in her muscles.

Something rustled nearby, and Rena froze, her eyes slowly scanning the area around her. If the guard had followed her for this long, she would have surely heard him earlier. Even Logan and Finn would have been more noticeable. So, the only thing that remained, was a wild animal. She slowly straightened her back and moved her head, but she didn't feel observed, so she didn't think it could be a large predator.

Another rustle. Rena turned in one quick motion and saw the flash of something orange disappear behind a grove of trees. She laced her shoes back up and stood. She waited to see if the animal would appear again, but nothing moved. She carefully pushed off the boulder and stepped closer to where the animal had disappeared, curiosity overtaking her. She looked back at the rock — to remember what it looked like so she wouldn't lose her progress in the forest — and then stepped behind the trees. With her dress in one hand, and her other hand grazing the trunks, she carefully stepped away from the clearing.

Another rustle sounded, and Rena whipped around to see a white tail disappearing into a bush. Had that been a fox? She felt silly that the first thought that flashed into her mind was wondering if it had been the same fox from the archives. She was on the other side of the province now. It was absolutely impossible for the fox to have followed her here.

She knew she shouldn't chase the animal further into the forest, no matter how curious she was, no matter how much she couldn't shake the feeling it had to be the same fox. She stepped forward, her body moving on its own. She reached the bush, approaching it carefully, and leaned down to peer through the branches. When she couldn't spot any glimpses of red or white fur, she stood and inspected the forest floor, but there was nothing there.

She took a deep breath and forced herself to turn away, to not follow a random wild animal deeper into a forest that she was trying to escape, not with how much she was struggling to find the right path. She only moved a few steps before she heard the animal behind her again.

She slowly turned to see the fox standing in front of the bush, looking straight at her. For a moment, they simply stared at each other, neither of them moving. Rena opened her mouth slightly to say something, then realised how little sense that made. She stepped closer and the fox jumped back, disappearing into the bush again. When it noticed Rena wasn't following, it peeked its head out to look at her.

Rena stared at it for a while, blinking in confusion, then decided to turn back to her rock. She had to be very dehydrated if she thought a wild animal was trying to communicate with her. She didn't have time to figure this out, she needed every second of daylight she had to find her way back to Halvint. She shook her head to clear her mind, but before she had reached her previous resting place, the fox jumped up on the rock. Rena stopped again, unsure of what was going on.

"What?" she muttered, as if the fox would be able to understand her.

The fox jumped away again, disappearing behind a tree to her left.

"I don't know what you want," she shouted, and raised her arms in defeat.

It didn't appear again, and it didn't answer, but Rena knew she had no other choice but to follow. She had some difficulty stepping through the bushes as her dress kept getting snagged in the branches and briars, but the fox was never far away, always a few steps ahead, waiting for her to catch up. It led her through the thickest parts of the underbrush, but Rena kept going, even if she could feel the million cuts forming on her legs. Soon she was out of breath, and her legs hurt from the effort, but the fox never stopped running ahead.

At some point, the horizon grew brighter as the tree canopy thinned. Rena picked up her pace, the edge of the forest coming closer. The fox ran ahead and didn't stop, not even to check on her. It simply ran out onto the road and disappeared between the trees on the other side.

"Wait! Don't leave!" Rena cried out, scrambling out onto the path.

She wanted to follow it, to figure out who or what it was, but she had finally found her way onto the road and couldn't risk getting lost in the forest again. She crossed to the other side and stood at the edge of the treeline, peering in, hoping to see a glimpse of the red fur, but the fox was gone. She didn't understand what had just happened — why this wild animal had led her to safety. She had never seen any creature act like that. Maybe a dog — if you trained it well — but definitely not a fox.

The feeling that it had been the same fox that she had seen in the Plains had solidified in her mind, but that didn't help much with explaining why it had acted this way. She turned around and started walking north. She didn't want to think about the fox anymore. There was enough unusual stuff going on around her, she didn't also have the time to figure out why a wild animal was trying to communicate with her.

She reached Halvint not long after and headed straight to the inn to see if Logan and Finn were waiting for her, but Darian told her that he hadn't seen them since they had set out. He gave her something to drink, and allowed her to wash her legs so the cuts from the underbrush wouldn't get worse. She waited in the inn for a while, but with every passing minute she became more restless, and so she decided to walk through the streets to distract herself, hoping that maybe, somehow, she would run into her companions. But the town was empty, except for some kids who were playing in the town centre.

Halvint was slightly bigger than Oceansthrow, with a handful of extra shops. She visited all of them, but none of them kept her mind from imagining worse and worse scenarios for what could have happened to Logan and Finn. There wasn't much she could do but wait, either for them to finally show up, or for Asha and Rodrick to come back so they could go look for the other two together. The nagging feeling that she was all alone again slithered its way into her mind, and no matter how much she told herself that it was extremely unlikely that all of them had been apprehended at once, it never truly wanted to go away.

She went back to the water pump in the town centre and sat down on its raised platform. It was close enough to the inn that she'd see anyone approaching it. She pulled her thick, brown hair to the side and started braiding it, undoing and redoing it over and over just so her hands had something to do. Her eyes wandered between the streets in front of her which led towards the town centre, forcing her body to remain still so she wouldn't attract any unwanted attention.

A man appeared and hurried diagonally across the court, crossing behind her so she couldn't get a good look at him until he had passed. He had been carrying a sack or crate, something hidden by his body now that she was able to glance at him. He was wearing black trousers that only reached his knees, with thick laces running down the rest of his legs, and dark red tights underneath. Over his shoulders, he wore a thick cape that reached his waist, made of greyish brown fur, and that was draped over his arms.

At first, she didn't think much of him, only keeping her eyes on him because she had nothing better to do, but as he got further away from her, the silhouette of the strangers arriving in Miller's Knee flooded her mind. She stood instinctively, but stopped herself before moving. She looked around quickly, unsure if she should follow him while she was alone.

She felt bad for judging this stranger based on a faint hunch she had, but what if she was right, and she had finally found the first real lead that would bring her closer to Maya? She could always find her companions later, but she might never see this man again. Her friends would surely understand her decision.

Before she could lose sight of the stranger, she moved forward, slowly at first, then hurrying to catch up when he had disappeared between two buildings. He led her to the outskirts of town, where the fields and farmhouses stood. Rena had to stay further and further away as the opportunities to hide behind something in case he ever turned got sparser, but he never did turn around. They headed straight to one of the farmhouses, one she knew grew onions and shallots and other such bulbs. He didn't enter the small shop at the front or walk into the main building, however. Instead, he walked around the farm, taking the small path between the main building and the fence of the field, and headed towards a smaller, detached building in the backyard.

Rena pretended to examine the prices listed in front of the shop, then strolled over to look at the fields, slowly making her way towards the back of the farm. She was certain she wasn't allowed back there, but no one seemed to notice her, or care enough to say anything. She scanned the area through the corners of her eyes, and when she was certain no one could see her, she hurried closer to the building and hid behind the wall facing away from the farmhouse. Crouching near some windows, she wondered how she could look inside without being spotted.

"Hey," Logan suddenly whispered from beside her.

She startled and turned around in shock, not having heard him approach.

"What?" she cried out, pressing her lips together instantly, then continued in a quieter voice. "What are you doing here? Since when have you been behind me?"

"A while," he replied with a wink.

"Why didn't you catch up?" she asked, hitting him lightly on the arm.

"It was fun watching you try to follow him without getting caught."

"Unbelievable." She shook her head, then searched the area beyond his shoulder. "Where's Finn?"

"Lost him in the woods somewhere," he replied nonchalantly. "Tried to look for him, but then I saw this guy and followed him."

Her gaze kept wandering over their surroundings, as if Finn might suddenly show up.

"Should we be worried?" she asked hesitantly, concern already blooming in the pit of her stomach.

"I don't know," he replied with a shrug. "Depends on who this guy is."

"I mean, about Finn."

"What? Nah, he'll be fine." He waved her off. "He wanted to go on an adventure, now he'll find out what that means. We can start getting worried in the morning."

She frowned at him, trying to decipher if he was being serious or not.

"What if the guards caught up to him?" she asked.

"Then it's his own fault for being so slow," Logan muttered and stepped closer to the nearest window, peeking up slowly to peer into the house.

She scowled and sighed, but didn't argue with him. She had to tell herself that everything would be fine, and that they'd find Finn waiting for them in the inn later.

She followed Logan, but didn't dare look inside the building. Her discomfort grew with every passing second, certain that someone would spot them at any moment.

"What do you see?" she whispered.

"It's a bedroom with two beds and a table in the corner. Someone's definitely been sleeping here."

"What else?"

"There's a stack of parchment rolls on the table, and a sort of nest made of fabric with a bird figurine on it."

"What?"

Rena shot up to look through the window, and true to Logan's word, a bigger and more detailed version of the figurine she had left in Rodrick's caravan lay propped up on a pile of red, orange and yellow fabrics.

"What is this?" she asked, dumbfounded.

"Looks a bit like an altar to me," he replied, tilting his head to the side. "Like something they used two hundred years ago in the North. That's also what their clothes look like, like they raided one of the museums in Jodash."

"How do you know that?" she asked, glancing over at him.

"I've been around," he replied with a shrug.

"That doesn't make any sense."

"I've been to museums before," he replied defensively.

"To steal things?" she asked hesitantly, narrowing her eyes at him.

"What? No!" He shook his head, looking at her as if she had just stabbed him. His face lit up an instant later, and he tilted his head from side to side. "Well, once, yes. But I mean I've been to museums as a regular citizen before."

She peered back into the room for a moment, before turning her head back to Logan.

"People can just visit those?"

"Yeah?" he replied, squinting. "What did you think they were for?"

"To keep things safe?" she replied sheepishly.

"No, it's so people can go and look at stuff."

"Why?"

"Because it's interesting to look at?" he replied slowly, as if he wasn't sure about it anymore himself.

They stared at each for a while without saying anything, both wildly confused by their exchange.

From inside the house, a door creaked open.

"Shit, get down, someone's coming!" Logan hissed at her, his right hand pressing her head down below the window.

Chapter Twenty-Seven

Rena sat down – her back flush against the outer wall of the house – as someone stepped into the room behind them. She looked out over the fields in front of her, with eyes wide open, not registering any of the landscape, too busy holding her breath and listening to the footsteps resonating behind her. Whoever had entered the room walked around for a bit, then stopped. Rena forced herself to take very shallow breaths so she wouldn't faint. A moment later, the person started walking again, and the door creaked shut.

"I think they left," Logan whispered and slowly stood back up to peer into the room.

Another door opened, further away, and Logan dropped back down to the ground.

"Shit!" he hissed as he sat next to her.

People exited the house, their footsteps crunching on gravel as the door creaked shut. Rena's heart hammered in her chest, her hands digging into the dirt beneath her, her vision going blurry as her eyes opened wider. She could barely hear the footsteps over the blood rushing through her ears, but she was certain they would be discovered any second now. That the entire group of strangers had noticed them, would round the corner, and confront them about why they were hiding behind the house. But a second passed, then a second more, and Rena had to start breathing again or she would faint. She slowly turned to glance at Logan. He squinted at the distance in front of them, the tip of his tongue poking out between his teeth.

"Okay, follow me," he whispered and suddenly jumped up, turning to face the house.

"What?" Rena hissed. "Wait, where are we going?"

"Inside. Come on," he said, waving for her to follow.

Her hand shot up to grab at his arm, keeping him from leaving.

"No! Someone might still be in there!"

"We'll be careful," he said, poking up to peer into the house. "If the house was crawling with people we would have noticed by now. Aren't you curious about what they're hiding?"

He crouched back down to look at her, his free hand still on the windowsill.

"I'm more interested in staying alive!" she grumbled. "And shouldn't we wait for Rodrick and the others?"

"It's going to be fine," he said, nodding to reassure her. "Let's go around back."

He got back up and shook his hand free out of her grip. He turned – not waiting for her to join him – and snuck along the side the house, his left hand trailing the wall, stopping at each window to peer into the house before continuing on.

Rena looked back towards the road, unsure of what to do. She hadn't really had a plan when she had started following the stranger, she had simply wanted to not lose sight of him. But breaking into someone else's house when it was unclear whether it was empty or not? Without having notified their companions about it beforehand? That sounded extremely risky to her.

Logan had disappeared behind the corner and was leaning back, insistently waving for her to come closer. She looked at him for a while, wondering if she could still back off, and then stepped forward.

The back of the house had two doors, one that obviously led into the house, and another at the bottom of a flight of stairs that probably led to a cellar. Logan snuck over to the window next to the first door and looked inside.

"The coast is clear," he whispered, hurrying to the door to gently press the handle down. His free hand lay on top of the crack between door and doorframe as if to keep it from rattling. He slowly pulled, but it didn't budge. He frowned and tried to push, but nothing happened either. He took a step back and stared at it, placing his fists on his hips.

"It's locked," he said, dumbfounded.

"Yes, I can see that," Rena hissed.

"Let's try the other one," he replied and turned around.

He practically flew down the flight of stairs while Rena stayed near the door, keeping her ear close to the window so she could hear any potential movement in the house. She concentrated on the noises around her, but all she could hear was the wind rustling through the fields and forest around them. Not long after, Logan came back up to her, his frown deepening.

"That one's locked too," he said.

"I think we should just leave," Rena pleaded. "Luck clearly isn't on our side right now. It would be a mistake to force it and expect nothing bad to happen."

"Oh, come on, where's the fun in that? We could try the front door. I don't think I heard them lock it."

"No!" she said, shaking her head emphatically. "That's much too dangerous. Someone might be waiting on the other side. O-or someone could see us from the farm!"

"Yes, but breaking one of the windows definitely makes more noise," he answered, raising his eyebrows as if that would convince her.

"We also shouldn't break any of the windows!" she insisted, desperation in her voice.

"You have too many rules." He sighed and looked around at the house, pursing his lips in contemplation. "I've got one more idea," he finally said. "Just let me try it. If it doesn't work, I'll concede."

Rena didn't answer right away, they just stared at each other for a moment, each hoping the other would give in and realise the error of their ways. Rena caved first.

"Fine," she murmured, and Logan instantly turned around and walked back down the stairs.

Rena nervously looked around, crouching down further, hoping no one would notice her from the surrounding fields. She quickly turned and peered into the house, into what looked like an empty kitchen with an open door that led to a hallway, before ducking back down and joining Logan at the bottom of the stairs.

"What are you doing?" she hissed at him, a look of horror on her face.

"It's an old door, we can just take off the hinges." Logan groaned with concentration.

He was standing upright, his brown, curly hair undone, trying to thread the piece of fabric that usually held his hair up under the pin of the upper hinge.

"Aren't they going to notice that?" Rena asked

"Yep, but hopefully we'll be gone beforehand."

He managed to wedge the string underneath the pin, wrapping it around a few times before slowly pulling it up. As the bolt slid upwards, the knuckles of the hinge sprang apart and Logan unwrapped his string to repeat the procedure at the bottom of the door. Rena looked back nervously, certain someone would emerge at the top of the stairs at any moment and discover what they were doing.

Another pop, and the second hinge was unbuckled. The side of the door protruded, but didn't jump out of its frame. With the tips of his fingers, Logan pulled the door forward, making the wood groan and the metal lock creak. Rena's body froze as her heart hammered in her chest. If there was someone in the house, they'd definitely hear all the noise. The door inched out of its hole little by little until it lurched out with a final groan.

"Okay, great. Help me out," he said, stepping aside so Rena could grab hold of the side near the handle.

"Hold on to it," he instructed. "We need to slide the door to the side for the bolt to pop out. Then we just need to make sure the door doesn't fall on us."

There was barely any space between the edge of the door and the surrounding wall, and Rena really didn't know how they were supposed to slide the door out of its frame.

Rena gripped the handle tight, her other hand flat against the door, but both her palms were so sweaty that she was scared it would just slip out of her grasp. The door groaned and creaked and she felt the strain on the bolt, how it resisted the unnatural movement and threatened to break the wood and the frame.

The bolt suddenly popped out of its socket and Rena almost fell into the room with the door, only keeping herself upright by pressing her shoulder into the frame.

"Perfect!" Logan exclaimed with a wide smile. "See, that wasn't so difficult."

Rena was too scared to answer him, too afraid of what lay beyond. She wanted to flee, to run back into the forest and scream away the tension in her body. She wasn't made for this life.

"I'll hold the door up, you go inside," he told her, motioning for her to move.

Her body obeyed automatically. She squeezed through the hole they had created and walked into a dark room. It looked like any regular cellar. One wide room with well-organised shelves, crates, and barrels.

"Help me out for a second," Logan whispered, motioning for her to come closer. She held the door upright while he squeezed his way into the room.

"We can slide the bolt back, close the door as best as possible, and hope no one'll notice it," he said in a hushed voice.

"I don't think it's just going to hold upright without fastening it to anything," Rena answered.

"I'll just tie the hinges together with my string," he told her. "Gonna hate having my hair just floating around untamed, but sometimes you gotta make sacrifices."

As Rena held on to the door, Logan wrapped the string over the uppermost hinge and carefully pulled it closer. He managed to shut the upper half flush and tie the string to the second part of the hinge, but the bottom part of the door stood out slightly, letting a trickle of light pass through its corner.

"All right, that should hold for a little while," Logan murmured.

They stepped away from the door, and turned around to face the darkness. The room didn't have any windows, and any light trickling in from around the door wasn't strong enough to illuminate much of anything. Still, Logan moved forward, and Rena had to follow, holding her hands out in front of her so she wouldn't bump into anything.

Suddenly, a creak above them, and Rena instantly froze.

"Wait!" Rena hissed, her head turning to the ceiling. "There's someone upstairs."

They both paused in the darkness, straining their ears to hear what it could be.

"I don't hear anything," Logan murmured.

"I swear there's something upstairs," she muttered, her eyes still fixed on the ceiling above them.

The creaking sounded again, faint, but rhythmic enough that it might have been footsteps.

"There!" Rena hissed, pointing to where she thought it had come from, her arm falling instantly when she realised Logan wouldn't be able to see it anyway.

"Okay," Logan said slowly. "Sounds like it's only one person. That's not much of a problem. We'll just need to be careful, no need to panic."

"What? No!" Rena exclaimed. "We can't walk around upstairs if there's someone else in the house! What if they aren't alone?"

"Doesn't sound like it's a group of people. If whoever's upstairs sees us, I'll just take them out."

"What if they have weapons?" Rena insisted.

"We have the element of surprise," Logan explained. "It's going to be all right. Now come on."

He slowly crept forward, the floor faintly groaning beneath his feet.

"I hate this plan," Rena mumbled, reluctantly following. "I'm starting to think I hate all of your plans."

"But they get results," Logan replied in a sing-song voice. "You'll see."

Her eyes had adjusted well enough that she could see faint light emanating from around the door leading into the house. When Logan reached it, he put one hand on the handle and one on the crack between door and frame again. He gently pressed the handle down, pulled, and this time, the door actually opened. He managed to open the door without making any noise, and to Rena's relief, no one was waiting for them on the staircase beyond the cellar.

"Okay, let's go," Logan whispered, opening the door wider, signalling for Rena to go first.

She took a deep breath, poked her head out to make sure they were truly alone, and then stepped onto the stairs. Lifting the hem of her dress with one hand, she placed the other on the wall — to stabilise herself and make her footsteps as soft as possible — but she couldn't keep the wood beneath her feet from faintly creaking. She held her breath as she ascended, keeping her ears focused on any other possible sounds emanating from the house.

When she got close to the top, she stopped and craned her neck to look over the edge of the floorboard. In front of them was what looked like the front door, with an empty coat hanger fixed to the wall on her left. To her right, just beyond the end of the stairs, was another door. She turned and looked out into the rest of the hallway, and saw another five doors – one standing open at the end of the hallway, which she recognised as the entrance to the kitchen.

"Where should we go?" Rena asked in a barely audible voice, scanning the corridor for any clues.

"I don't know," Logan replied, stopping on the lower steps. "Probably the room we saw from outside."

She closed her eyes one more time to listen for any footsteps, and only moved when she was certain she couldn't hear anything. She tiptoed forward to the first door on her left and bent to look through the keyhole, but she couldn't see much except for two unmade beds. She used Logan's technique to slowly open the door, but it opened inward, and she almost fell into the room.

She stepped inside, slowly at first until she was certain no one else was there. She hurried the rest of the way in, waving for Logan to follow.

She turned and slowly walked over to the strange alter they had seen from outside. She reached for the figurine, her fingertips grazing over the lines meticulously carved into its front, a familiar pattern under her skin by now. Rena wished she could read the words, know what these people felt so strongly about to carve it into their effigies.

Logan stepped in and quietly closed the door behind him.

"It looks exactly like the little statue I found," Rena said, not looking up from the figurine. "Just bigger and better made, but the inscription's the same. I think. Difficult to tell when I don't know what it means."

Logan reached out and touched the fabric surrounding the effigy, rubbing it between his fingers.

"Great choice of fabric colours," he said with a hint of sarcasm in his voice. "Doesn't feel disrespectful at all."

She looked over at the red, orange, and yellow carefully laid out so they would swirl together, forming the mockery of a fire.

"It's terrible," she said, picking both the figurine and fabrics up, and wrapped one in the other. She walked over to the bed closest to them and stuffed the bundle under the blanket, ensuring it was completely hidden. "I don't want to see it anymore."

"Finally, some rebellion from you," Logan said with a smirk. "I like it."

"What do the parchments say?" she asked, nodding at the pile of paper remaining on the table.

Logan picked one up and unrolled it, holding it up to the light so they could both look at it. He frowned for a while before picking up a second, then a third. None of them seemed very long, but they were all composed of blocks of tightly written text next to woodblock prints.

"I have no idea what any of these mean," Logan finally said, putting the roll down again. He rubbed his fingers together as if they were covered with residue. "Pretty sure they're old, though. I don't know if we should really touch them. They look like they'd tear very easily."

"This one's just a big drawing," Rena said, spreading one roll out with her fingertips.

"Let me look," Logan said, craning his neck. "Oh, nice! Like those giant tapestries that tell a story."

Rena frowned up at him, not knowing what he was talking about.

"Did you see those in your museums too?" she asked, a slight hint of mockery in her voice.

"Yes, I did," he confirmed, sliding the picture closer. "I'll take you to one of the good ones one day, then you'll see how fun they are."

"So, do you know what this is?" she asked, looking at the image again.

"Hmmm." He tilted his head from side to side. "Not exactly. But most of them were legends about heroes and the monarchy, before the Royal Council existed. The really old ones also like to depict the gods and all the hubbub around them. Especially the ones in this style, you know, the weird, lanky figurines and the big swirls and the tiny text running all around it."

Rena hovered her hand over the image, tracing the air over the contorted figure of a woman who held an orb between her hands, lines radiating out from the centre and curling in on themselves at the edges of the image.

"I suppose the life of a simple farmer isn't interesting enough to put in your museums," Rena muttered.

"There actually is a museum of rural life in Jodash," Logan mentioned, looking over at her for a moment. "But I've found it to be a bit inaccurate. More digestible fairytale than what's true to reality."

"They could just come down here and talk to us," she remarked, slightly annoyed. "No need to put lies in a museum."

"Oh, but my dear friend, museums are full of them," Logan said, waving his hand around with a flourish. "Wouldn't want the citizens to know what's actually going on in the kingdom, would you?"

"Right," Rena sighed. "Nothing is the way I learned it would be, got it. So, do you know what this one's depicting?"

She lightly tapped her finger twice on the image.

"No idea, I really don't know anything about the old religion," Logan said, driving a hand through his curls. "Maybe Rodrick will know more. We should just take it with us."

Logan rolled the parchment back up and slid it into one of the pockets of his trousers.

"You know, you don't have to steal everything," Rena muttered, but let him take it anyway.

She riffled through the rest of the parchments, but none of them seemed to be written in a language she could read.

Footsteps echoed from the back of the house, clearly coming closer. Rena froze, crumpling the parchment in her hand, her eyes opening wide as she stared at the door. Her blood ran ice cold at the prospect that someone might enter at any moment, that they might have pushed their luck too far. Somewhere in the house, not far from them, a door opened.

Rena's hand slowly lowered as she silently put the parchment back on the table. The door closed again and the footsteps faded to the other side of the house where they had come from.

"I think we're good," Logan whispered, daring to move again.

"We shouldn't be here," Rena said firmly, her eyes still fixed on the door.

"I think we can find out more if we stay a bit longer," Logan remarked, inching closer to press his ear against the door.

"Logan, stop it!" Rena objected. "We don't know what they'll do if they find us."

"They're in the back of the house," he said, leaning away from the door again. "If we avoid that part, we're going to be okay. Let's just go across the hallway."

Rena sighed heavily, and closed her eyes.

"Fine, but after that we're leaving!" she said against her own better judgement.

"I promise," he whispered and quietly opened the door.

He peeked out for a second before slipping into the corridor and tiptoeing to the other side. Rena followed him with a heavy heart and closed the door as carefully as she could, her eyes constantly darting to the closed doors at the other end of the house.

They entered a smaller bedroom that only held one bed and a wardrobe. The bed looked freshly used but not unkempt. Rena quietly closed the door before stepping in, looking around at the almost empty room.

"I don't see anything unusual here," Rena remarked, her eyes trailing over the sparse furnishing of the room.

Logan knelt to look underneath the bed, then stepped over to the wardrobe and opened it. Rena glanced over his shoulder to see what might be inside, but it was empty except for a pile of towels.

Logan sighed and closed the wardrobe again.

"Yeah, I don't think there's anything to find here," he said and turned around, hands on his hips, eyes wandering over the walls of the room. "This isn't very helpful."

"No, it isn't," Rena agreed.

The dull footsteps sounded again, coming closer.

"Fuck," Logan hissed under his breath, grabbing Rena's wrist and dragging her to the corner between the wardrobe and the door. They pressed their backs against the wall, and dread rose in Rena as the footsteps came closer and closer.

The door opened, stopping a hand-width away from Rena's face. A person walked in, wearing the group's uniform of black trousers and dark red tights with a loose white shirt, forgoing the cloak the stranger had worn outside. A rather plump woman, with short curly brown hair and warm beige skin. She walked straight towards the bed, holding a pile of folded laundry in her arms.

Logan stepped forwards, pushing the door closed, and before the woman had the chance to fully turn towards him, he had wrapped his arm around her throat. The woman tried to fight him off, the pile of clothes falling to the ground as she clawed at Logan's arm, but soon her movements became sluggish and her arms fell to her sides and her knees buckled. Logan gently let the body drop to the ground, making sure she didn't hit her head on the bed's frame.

"I don't like it when you do that," Rena muttered as she stepped closer.

"I don't exactly enjoy it either," he replied and bent down to move the woman around. "But she'll wake up soon enough. We need to tie her up so she doesn't come after us."

He dragged the unconscious body closer to the bed and picked up one of the tights from the pile of clothes that had fallen to the ground. He pushed the woman around until she lay on her side with her arms wrapped around the leg of the bed, and then used the tights to tie her up.

Rena sighed and crossed her arms, her right hand worrying the fabric of her sleeve.

"I told you staying wasn't a good idea," she said, unable to keep her irritation out of her voice.

"Yeah, well," Logan started, pausing to tie the woman's legs together. "We aren't hurt, so nothing *bad* happened, either."

"Right," Rena muttered, and let her eyes wander over the spilled pile of clothes at her feet.

She stopped, and frowned at the only fabric that stood out from the pile. A white and green dress similar to the one she owned. Time froze, a cold creeping over her back, as she recognised the swirling flowers that had been meticulously embroidered into the fabric. The same pattern she had run her fingers over so often as she helped her mother fold their laundry.

"This is Maya's," Rena murmured, crouching down to pick up the fabric.

"What?" Logan asked, looking up at her.

"This is my sister's dress," Rena said, looking up at him in distress.

Logan stared at her, his hands still hovering over the knot he had just tied. His eyes wandered down to the dress in her hands, his mouth opening slightly as if he wanted to say something, but no words came out.

Rena's vision went blurry as her eyes filled with tears.

"Why do they have her dress?" Rena asked, desperation in her voice.

"I don't know," Logan said quietly, eyes wide in shock as he stared at it. "A-are you sure it's her dress?"

"Yes, I'm sure!" Rena cried out. "My grandmother embroidered those flowers, no other dress looks like this!"

"I'm sorry," Logan said defensively. "I really don't know why they have it."

"Do you think she's here?" Rena asked, her eyes growing wider, a mix of hope and fear rising in her. "We need to find her!"

She scrambled up, clutching the dress close to her chest. Without waiting for Logan, she turned and hurried from the room.

"Rena, wait!" he called out after her.

She stopped in the hallway for a second, evaluating where they might be keeping her sister, then rushed over to the first door to her left. She didn't wait to hear if anyone else was still in the house, didn't wait to make sure no one was waiting for them. They had taken Maya, and that was all that mattered.

She burst into the room and frantically looked around. One long table stood in the middle of the room with eight chairs standing around it. One side of the table was covered in loose papers, books, and rolls of parchment. The other side was empty except for another pile of clothing. Along the wall to her left stood two large cupboards. On the far wall beyond the cupboards was a fireplace that still held ashes from the previous night.

Rena rushed into the room, and opened each of the cupboards, but of course Maya wasn't anywhere to be found. She frantically whirled around, looking for any hidden doors or compartments she might have missed.

"Rena, come on, stop!" Logan said, coming to a halt next to her. "I doubt they'd keep her here."

"We need to check the other rooms," Rena replied without looking at him.

She tried to shoulder past Logan but he grabbed hold of her arm.

"She isn't here!"

"You don't know that," she yelled and yanked her arm out of his hold.

She hurried out into the hallway as the front door creaked open, and Rena found herself looking straight into the bright green eyes of a woman she had never seen before. She had an old scar running over her nose and under her left eye, and her light brown hair was almost the same colour as the pelt she had draped over her shoulders. The woman stared at her, her eyes growing wider before her face contorted in anger.

"Who are you?" the woman growled.

She stormed forward, her hand disappearing under her cape before re-emerging with a dagger, its tip slightly curved upwards. Rena quickly stepped back until her back hit the wall next to the open door to the kitchen, clutching Maya's dress tightly to her chest. The woman rushed towards her and raised the dagger, but as soon as she had passed the door to the parlour, Logan jumped out and grabbed her wrist – the sudden halt in movement turning her around to face away from Rena.

Rena used the opportunity to slide into the kitchen. She thought about closing the door, but didn't dare leave Logan behind. She frantically looked around for anything she could use, and her eyes landed on the cast-iron pans hanging from the wall. She grabbed the biggest one with one hand, refusing to let go of the dress, and rushed back to find Logan prying the dagger out of the woman's hand. From afar, Rena saw two more people, wearing the now familiar outfit, rush towards the building. She ran forward and threw the heavy pan at them, almost losing her footing. She tried to close the door before the men could reach it, but she wasn't fast enough. One of them slammed into the door and sent Rena flying backwards. The distraction was enough to break Logan's concentration and the woman ripped her arm out of his grip, spun him around, and held her dagger to his throat.

"Who the fuck are you people?" the woman demanded again.

"I wouldn't even think about hurting him," Asha said from the front of the house.

Rena's head whipped up, eyes wide, at the sound of her friend's voice. Asha stood behind the man who had burst through the door, her golden sword at his neck.

Chapter Twenty-Eight

"I would suggest you put your dagger down," Asha growled, glaring at the woman who held Logan at knife-point.

Her own sword slid forward, tilting the chin of the man in front of her upwards, a thin trickle of blood running down his neck. Behind her, Kalani appeared in the doorframe, with Vincent, and an out of breath Rodrick. The dog growled at the tension in the room, but never left his owner's side.

Rena scrambled upright again and took a step back. Kalani stopped only a few steps past the door, her sharp, dark brown eyes fixated on Logan and the woman. Rodrick held on to the doorframe with one hand, his other hand on his thigh as he regained his breath. He looked up at Rena, his eyes full of concern, as if asking her how she was doing. She nodded slightly, pressing her lips together, hoping this would convey she was unharmed.

She craned her neck to glance past Kalani and Rodrick, to see if anyone else was behind them. On the ground, the second man lay unconscious, spread-eagle, the cast-iron pan she had thrown lying next to him.

"Have you seen Finn?" Rena asked, her eyes still search the area outside the house.

Asha quickly glanced over to her, her frown deepening for a second.

"No?" she replied in confusion. "He left with you, why would he be with us? Did you lose him?"

"We had to run into the forest and we got separated," Rena explained. "I thought he was with Logan, but apparently he lost him."

"I didn't lose him," Logan replied, his head still titled up by the blade. "I'm sure we'll find him once we actually look for him."

"Sounds like you lost him to me," Asha deadpanned.

"This is not a stage show! You will take us seriously," the woman behind Logan hissed, the blade cutting into his skin. Blood started to run down Logan's neck, mirroring the man Asha held captive.

"Okay, okay, okay." Logan chuckled nervously, raising a hand in defeat. "How about we all calm down, yeah? There's no need for anyone to get hurt."

Kalani stepped further into the hallway and stood next to Asha. She reached a hand out towards Rena and waved for her to come closer. Rena glanced back at the woman whose bright green eyes were full of rage, frantically darting back and forth between Asha, Kalani, and her.

"Who are you and what are you doing in my house?" the woman demanded, her nostrils flaring in anger.

Rena slowly stepped back until she was close enough for Kalani to grab her arm and drag her away from the woman.

"We could ask you the same?" Kalani said, determination carved across her face. "And don't pretend like this is your house. I know the farmer rents it out to whoever's willing to pay. But usually, these visitors aren't responsible for the death and destruction of an entire village."

"Do you actually believe those insolent rumours that we're responsible for that tragedy?" the woman spat out. "What, just because we're outsiders that don't adhere to the norms of these lands? The people in this town spew nothing but lies. They can't wrap their tiny minds around structures that don't resemble their own."

"It seems awfully convenient that you just happened to show up right after the fire happened," Kalani replied, tilting her head slightly. "I can't fault them for being suspicious of you."

"It seems awfully convenient to blame the outsiders you don't understand for it. Where's your proof that we have anything to do with it? Or are you just blaming us because we're the easy scapegoat?"

"They had a shrine dedicated to one of the figurines Rena found in—" Logan started, but the woman's grip on his throat tightened, and his sentence gargled to a stop.

"Shut it," the woman hissed in his ear.

"What did you do to Maya?" The words burst out of Rena without her consent, her fingers digging into her sister's dress.

She couldn't stand waiting for this game to resolve, for them to coax tiny shreds of evidence out of this woman who clearly didn't want to comply.

Kalani turned towards Rena without taking her eyes off of the woman.

"Who is Maya?" she asked calmly.

"My sister."

"Your sister?"

She turned her head to look at Rena, her eyes darting momentarily to the dress.

"We found her dress here," Rena stammered out. "In a pile of clothes. I've been looking for her, because I found her ring during the fire, and I knew she still had to be alive. I'm aware it's barely any proof at all to just find a ring somewhere, but they have her dress! Why would they have her dress if they don't also have her somewhere!"

Rena held the dress out for Kalani to see, who stared at it with a deep, sunken frown, the muscles of her jaw clenching.

"What did you do to her sister?" Asha growled, grabbing the man's hair with her free hand, before kicking him in the back of the knees so that he fell down to the ground.

"I don't know. I don't know!" the man yelped, fear splitting his face into a grimace.

"Bullshit, you don't know."

"I should have you all skinned alive for breaking into our house and stealing our things," the woman cried out, the blade at Logan's throat digging deeper into his skin.

"Whoa, whoa, whoa." Logan was starting to panic, leaning back against his assailant to alleviate the pain. "Easy on the blade! We're not stealing anything, I promise! We were about to put it back where we found it!"

"But this isn't yours," Rena exclaimed. "This is Maya's dress! You can't just pretend it isn't hers. So why do you have it? What have you done with her?"

Rena felt a hand land on her shoulder, and she jerked back in fear before realizing Rodrick was trying to comfort her. Vincent stood at her feet, his body between her and the strangers, baring his teeth at them.

"That is none of your concern," the woman hissed in response, her gaze nervously flicking down to the dog.

"I think it is time both sides set down their blades so we can discuss this issue peacefully," Rodrick said calmly. "Surely you can see my friend here is very worried for her sister, so I implore you to help us find out what happened to her."

"I said, it is none of your concern."

"My good lady," Rodrick began, but was interrupted by a loud, dull thump from their left.

Their heads all turned simultaneously towards the noise, towards the room where Rena and Logan had tied up the other woman. Logan used the distraction to slip out of his assailant's grasp, slide behind her and slam her head into the wall. Her body instantly went slack and fell to the ground, blood trickling out of her nose.

Vincent jumped forward and towards the unconscious woman, but before he could reach her, Rodrick whistled and the dog circled back to him.

The noise from behind the door grew louder. The woman they had tied up earlier must have woken. She cried out, although it wasn't clear what she was saying.

This time around, the man Asha was holding used the distraction to try to get away, but Asha's grip on his hair was still tight enough that he couldn't stand up. She slammed him onto the ground, pushing his face into the wooden floor. She dropped her sword an arm's length away and used her free hand to pin the man's arms to his back, kneeling on his back to keep him from getting up.

"I'm sorry, I'm sorry," he tried to say, his face squashed against the floor.

"Shut up," Asha spat out before turning to look up. "Logan, who the fuck is in that room?"

"Yeah, sorry," Logan replied, stretching his neck from side to side, one hand pressed against his wound. "We tried breaking in without getting noticed, but that kinda failed, as you may have noticed."

"Logan choked her out, then tied her up," Rena added.

Logan shot her an annoyed look as if she had betrayed him.

"Fantastic, this is going great," Kalani sighed, placing her fists on her hips. "Two unconscious cultists and two terrified ones. Truly the best conditions for a productive conversation." She sighed and drove a hand over her face. "Logan, go get the one from outside before someone sees him. We need to figure out what to do next."

"Yes, sir," he replied and stepped past them.

"Is there a cellar in this house?" Kalani asked, looking around. "We should bring them down there until we know how we'll proceed."

"We kind of broke the door when we entered," Logan said sheepishly, stopping at the entrance to the house.

"Of course, you did," she groaned. "Just go grab the body and fix the door downstairs. We shouldn't be staying here for much longer anyway. I'll grab the other one."

Logan bowed to Kalani with a flourish, his left hand covered in blood, then left the building.

Kalani ran a hand over her braids and pulled them over her right shoulder, strands of white running through the black hair. She carted her fingers through them as she looked around the room before her gaze landed on the unconscious woman. She looked at her for a moment before bending down and dragging her towards the stairs.

Rena used the opportunity to open the doors to the other rooms, but of course they were all empty. Crestfallen, she returned to Rodrick and Asha and crouched down, holding her hand out for Vincent to sniff.

"Rena, my dear, are you all right?" Rodrick asked.

Her hand ran over Vincent's fur as he nuzzled his head into her hand.

"Yes, thank you. I'm not hurt," she replied in a haze. "Don't really know how to feel about the dress, though."

"We'll find her, don't worry," Asha told her.

Rena looked up at her, and their eyes met. Asha's eyes were almost black, and they burned with such a passion that Rena could do nothing but believe her whole-heartedly. There was no doubt in her mind anymore. Maya was alive. They would save her. She wasn't the only one who had survived the fire.

"Thank you," Rena whispered, and kept her eyes on Asha's until Logan broke her concentration dragging the unconscious body into the house.

Kalani joined him, and together they lifted the man up and carried him down the stairs, coming back up a few minutes later to carry the second body down.

"I almost expected not to see you again, Asha," Rena said, turning back to Asha and shooting her a soft smile.

"I had half a mind set on staying at camp," Asha replied. "But this whole situation kept nagging at the back of my mind. My uncle's doing fine anyway, there are enough people able to fawn over him in Rancor. He doesn't need me right now."

"Thank you," Rena said sincerely. "For coming back."

Kalani came up the stairs again and walked over to Asha, squatting down to look at the man beneath her knee.

"If you cooperate, I'll tell her to get off of you," she said, tilting her head to the side.

The man didn't say anything for a while. He simply looked up at her, breathing heavily, spit drooling from his open mouth.

"Or maybe we should go talk to your comrade in the other room," she suggested.

When the man still didn't answer, Kalani straightened and strode to the first bedroom on the left, Logan right behind her. Hesitantly, Rena got up and followed them in.

The woman had managed to untie the tights around her legs and was now lying on her back, feet propped against the bed frame, trying to lift it up enough to get her arms out from under it.

"I wouldn't try anything stupid," Kalani warned, sitting on the bed, quashing the woman's hopes of escape.

Logan picked up one of the white shirts still lying on the ground and pressed it against the wound on his neck. Rena slowly stepped into the room, scooting aside to let Rodrick and Vincent in after her. Asha stayed in the hallway; her knee still firmly planted on the man's back.

Vincent slowly trotted up to smell the woman, who turned around in panic to scramble away until her back hit the bed.

"Please don't let it hurt me," the woman begged in a shrill voice.

"Sure, if you tell us what we want to know," Kalani said sweetly.

"What? I can't help you, I don't know anything," the woman stuttered, her eyes fixed on the dog.

"Where's Maya?" Rena asked, her voice filled with tired sadness.

"I-I don't know any Maya," the woman replied, firmly shaking her head.

"The girl who had this dress on. Where is she?" Rena asked, holding the dress up. "She looks like me, just shorter hair and a bit darker skin."

"I don't know anything about that."

Kalani kicked her thigh, making the woman jump.

"Answer her," Kalani said firmly.

"I'm sorry," the woman stuttered. "I really don't know anything. I just do what I'm told and they told me to fold the laundry."

"But the dress doesn't look anything like the rest of your clothes," Rena pleaded.

"I didn't question it."

"Now that's a load of bullshit," Logan remarked.

"There really is no use lying to us," Kalani said, leaning forward to place her elbows on her knees, interlacing her fingers. "We just want to know where her sister is. I don't think that's an unreasonable question to ask. Do you?"

"I'm not allowed to talk to people like you," the woman said, arrogance seeping into her voice.

"You see your friend over there?" Kalani asked, pointing towards the man pinned under Asha's knee. "He doesn't seem too comfortable to me. If you help us, we help him. If you don't help us, well…"

The woman looked at her companion, his face still crushed against the floorboards, mouth hanging open.

"There is nothing you can do to us that would make me abandon my faith," the woman insisted, and turned her face away.

"Oh boy," Logan sighed and shifted around uncomfortably.

"Right, you guys are *that* kind of people," Kalani noted, and leaned away again.

"But, you're okay with this?" Rena asked, a tightness wrapping around the pit of her stomach as anger started bubbling up in her. "With destroying whole villages and killing hundreds of people? Even if you're not the one setting the fire, you're okay with what the others are doing?"

"Y-you have no proof of that," the woman sputtered out, her voice growing higher and faster and more desperate. "If, hypothetically, we were responsible for these fires, and this is by no means an admission of guilt, there would be a righteous reason, more sacred and important than any individual human lives lost along the way, even if their deaths would be tragic."

"What are you even talking about?" Logan asked.

"My entire family is dead because of you," Rena said quietly, her fingers digging tightly into the fabric of her sister's dress.

"But don't you see? Modern life would have been the death of them anyway."

"What?" Rena muttered.

"This life we're living is just a distortion of what it should be. This isn't how any of us should exist."

"Wait, is that what you're fighting against?" Logan asked, pushing away from the wall. "Modern life as in, the new technologies? The lights and machines and the train?"

"I-is my family dead because you don't like ... that they're building a trainline?"

"No, no, no. You misunderstand," the woman said, shaking her head violently. "No one said anything about the gas lamps or the train. I quite fancy the train, actually. Maybe one day I'll be able to ride on it. Maybe one day we'll *all* be able to ride on it! But that is exactly the problem. That all these people in power keep us regular folks away from everything that is good. That they are the ones deciding what we are allowed to do, and what our lives are supposed to look like, which province gets help, and which get forgotten. A-and they're pretending like their system is fair and that it is for the best and that we have a say in it. But we all know none of that is true. They are building this on the ruins of a once great and sacred system, and are spitting in the face of our history."

"But what does any of that have to do with burning down villages?" Rena yelled, her breath coming in heavy, ragged gasps.

"There is a divine reasoning behind it that you would not understand."

"Because you aren't explaining it!"

"Rena," Rodrick said calmly, placing a hand on her shoulder. "My child, there's no use getting worked up. It doesn't seem like you are going to be able to reason with her."

"But ..." she started, looking over at him, her eyes filling with tears.

"I know, I know," he said, patting her shoulder lightly.

"He's right," Kalani said, getting up off the bed. "This is just a waste of time." She stepped around until she was facing the woman. "How about you tell us where you brought her sister? And let's stop pretending like you don't know." She turned her head to the corridor and spoke louder. "The both of you, all right? You either tell us now, or someone gets hurt."

"I can't," the man groaned.

The woman pressed her lips into a thin line and turned her head away.

"Asha," Kalani said, turning her torso to their other captive.

Asha leaned more of her body onto the man's back until he groaned in pain.

"I can't," he said through ragged breaths.

"The two of you remember those scrolls you have near the altar, right?" Logan suddenly interjected, coming to stand next to Kalani. "The really old ones? The ones that look important and irreplaceable and like they mean something to you? Would be a shame if something happened to them, don't you think?"

The woman's head whipped around to stare at Logan with wide open eyes.

"You wouldn't dare," she whispered.

Logan glanced at Kalani with a smirk.

"Got them."

Kalani reciprocated his smirk and turned to look at the woman.

"Hmm, I do think we would dare. Go get them for me, Logan, dear."

Logan came back with the scrolls and dropped them on the bed. He picked one and handed it to Kalani, who unrolled it and tried to read it.

"Take your hands off of them!" the woman shrieked. "These aren't for you. You have no right to even look at them!"

"What is this?" Kalani, frowning down at the scrolls in confusion.

"We don't really know," Logan said.

"It's written in a language we can't read," Rena added. "But there's also some with drawings on them. We think maybe it has something to do with the old gods. Some legends or something like that."

Rodrick stepped forward and joined the other two near the bed.

"Let me take a look," he said and leaned closer to Kalani.

"Can you read this?" Kalani asked, handing Rodrick the parchment.

"Put them back!" the woman yelled, pulling frantically at her restraints.

Vincent hunched down and started growling. The woman's movement slowed down, her eyes fixed in fear on the dog.

Rodrick took the parchment from Kalani and held it close to his face, squinting at the writing.

"Hmm, I don't think so. It doesn't seem very familiar to me. I do have an acquaintance in Hemmankem who is an expert in old languages, however."

"Right," Kalani said, taking the parchment out of Rodrick's hands again.

She turned back to the woman and squatted in front of her, holding the scroll aloft.

"I don't need to know what's written on this to figure out you care about it. So why don't you help us out? Then nothing will happen to them."

"You will not break us," the woman sneered, keeping her head held high.

"All right," Kalani responded and started slowly ripping the parchment in two.

"Oh," Rodrick exclaimed weakly, stepping forward, but Logan held him back.

The woman's eyes grew wide in horror as she stared at the paper in front of her.

"How many of these can you fathom losing?" Kalani asked, holding the two pieces of parchment in both hands and letting them glide to the ground.

"There's also a fireplace in the other room," Logan mentioned.

The woman's eyes darted to Logan, filled with panic and rage, a tear rolling down her cheek.

"We don't need to go to those extremes," Rodrick interjected. "They are historical artefacts after all."

"That decision is entirely up to our two friends here," Kalani said, tilting her head to the side. "We only want to know one thing. Where is Rena's sister?"

Rena stepped forward, holding the dress tightly to her chest.

"Please," she whispered, trying to meet the woman's gaze.

"You don't understand what you're doing!" The woman spat the words, her wild eyes only on Kalani.

Kalani waited a moment before shrugging, then waved for Logan to bring her another scroll. She unrolled it and frowned, then ripped that one too.

"Stop, please," the man in the corridor exclaimed. "I'll talk, I'll talk."

"Michael!" the woman shrieked, finally looking over at her companion.

"Please don't destroy the scrolls," the man groaned, his voice full of pain. "Please. I can tell you where she is."

Kalani stood back up, letting the fragments of parchment fall onto the woman's lap.

"Finally, someone who's reasonable," she said, turning towards the corridor. "Asha, get him up."

Asha heaved the man up by the lapel of his shirt and marched him into the room.

"Michael, you know what Inkra will do to you if you tell them anything," the woman said, shuffling around and fighting against her restraints.

"Her wrath will be greater if they destroy the scripture," Michael answered weakly, falling to his knees before Kalani.

Rena strode towards him, and knelt down in front of him.

"Michael! It's Michael, right?" she asked, trying to meet his eyes. "I don't know who Inkra is, and I'm truly sorry if we're the reason you get into trouble with her, but I need you to tell me where my sister is. Is she all right? You didn't hurt her, did you?"

"I don't know, we're just the clean-up crew," he said between heavy breaths, glancing at her. "We only arrived after the fire, I swear. We didn't even meet the first crew, they had left before we arrived. Most of the stuff is theirs. It's always like this, they leave their mess lying around and we have to deal with it."

"But you said you knew where she was," Kalani replied, crossing her arms in front of her chest.

"Yes!" Michael replied, nodding enthusiastically before tapering off into uncertainty. "Well, there are only a few places where they could have taken her."

"That doesn't sound like you know exactly where she is," Kalani said, raising an eyebrow.

"No, no, no, I do! It's north-east of here, just over the border in Baedan! It's the most likely place where they would bring her if she's still alive. It's our closest base from here."

"I will have to report this treason to Inkra, Michael," the woman hissed, struggling against her bindings.

Logan sat on the bed next to her and placed a hand on her shoulder, pinning her down.

"Inkra will understand," Michael said and nodded solemnly. "She would have done the same."

"I think I know the place," Logan replied, looking up at Kalani. "There's an old, abandoned monastery in the hills near Tarkot's Bridge. We talked about it earlier. I remember it having some of the same symbols we found at the ruins of Miller's Knee and in Oceansthrow. Seems quite plausible that they might be connected."

Kalani looked at Logan for a moment before her eyes snapped to Michael's a second later, unblinking, nodding slowly as if in thought.

"All right, apparently we're crossing the border today." She stepped out into the corridor. "You're coming with us, Michael. Rodrick, we're taking your wagon. Horses would be faster, but we'd have to find some first."

"Wait, no, no, no," Michael exclaimed, shaking his head violently. "You can't take me with you. I told you where it was, you don't need me anymore. And your comrade clearly knows what I'm talking about. I wouldn't be any further help to you!"

"Serves you right, Michael," the woman spat.

"I promise we won't hurt you," Rena said softly, trying to reassure him. "Maybe you can talk to the people at the old monastery and tell them to release my sister. I'm sure they'd listen to you more than us. Please."

"Let's go, we're wasting time," Kalani said, clapping her hands together.

Asha heaved Michael up by his lapel again. She had to stabilise him while standing as his legs buckled under him.

"What about her?" Logan asked, patting the woman on the shoulder.

"Tie her up properly, then leave her. Someone will find her sooner or later."

Chapter Twenty-Nine

They left the house soon after. Logan had managed to tie the woman's legs together again, and gagged her with one of the tights — even though the woman tried to bite him multiple times.

Kalani led the way out and instructed them to surround their prisoner as they walked into the village. Asha let go of him, but still kept an arm around his shoulder so it wouldn't look too suspicious. They moved swiftly without running, heading to the northern road where they had left Rodrick's wagon. They managed to cross the village without any major incidents. Michael didn't even try to run away or call for help, he simply walked alongside them and murmured something Rena couldn't uderstand.

Rena was on edge until they reached the wagon. She was just waiting for someone to catch up with them, constantly glancing around to make sure no one was following them. But soon she sat on the front bench of the wagon next to Rodrick, Vincent at their feet, the rest of their crew in the back, and the wagon rumbled to life.

She still clutched her sister's dress, her fingers twisting into its fabric. Tears filled her eyes and fell in thick drops down her cheeks and onto the dress. She didn't want to hope, didn't want to get her heart broken once more if their new journey didn't lead them to Maya. Maya, who was only a year younger than her, who had never been afraid of the forest or the dark, even when Rena had still been scared. Maya, who had loved the night and the stars and the moon and listening to the wind glide over the ocean. Who had always had a mind of her own and who loved tinkering with things.

She pressed the dress against her face and took in a deep breath, but the fabric didn't smell like her sister anymore. It didn't even smell like the fresh laundry she was used to, as if any remnants of her old life had been denied to her.

A sound echoed above the noise of the wagon, slowly getting louder, a fast, rhythmic tapping.

"Halt!" someone called from their left.

Rena looked up in panic. Guards on horseback had appeared on both sides of the wagon.

"Good afternoon, what seems to be the problem?" Rodrick called out in a friendly voice without stopping the wagon.

"I said halt!" the guard shouted again. "Stop your vehicle right away!"

"We are simple merchants on our way up north, there is no need to yell at us," Rodrick said, shooting the guard a warm smile. "Is there a reason you need me to stop? I ask because it is quite the ordeal to get this beauty started."

"On the orders of Captain Silac, each traveller on these roads has to be inspected."

From behind, another mounted guard appeared, manoeuvring their horse in front of the wagon before stopping in the middle of the road. Rena glanced behind and was shocked to see another three guards riding after them. What horrified her even more, was that accompanying them with a drooping, bloodied right arm, was the woman with the piercing green eyes that they had left in the cellar of the farmhouse.

She turned to Rodrick, leaning closer to him.

"There are more behind us," she hissed. "And the lady who held a knife to Logan's throat is with them."

Rodrick nodded once without taking his eyes off the road ahead. He seemed to think for a while, his face growing serious.

"Hold on to something," he instructed, and leaned over to crank a lever down.

The wagon lurched forward before Rena could actually follow his instructions, and she was thrust backwards, all the air being expelled from her lungs as her back hit the wagon hard. Rodrick steered straight forward, towards the guard that had planted their horse on the road in front of them. The wagon shook violently and Rena scooted forward, only managing to not drop off the bench by pressing her foot into the wooden panelling in front of them.

Rodrick didn't budge from his path, and for a second Rena was truly afraid they were about to run into the guard and their horse. She closed her eyes and brought the dress up to her face – but no collision came. She dared peek out again, and saw that the road ahead was empty.

The shaking of the wagon was so violent it almost felt like the vehicle was about to fall apart. But it still wasn't fast enough to outrun a horse, and soon the two guards re-appeared next to them.

The one next to Rena tried to grab her, grasping for her leg, but the shaking was so uncontrollable that he couldn't hold on to her. She tried to kick him away, but it just made her slide further down the bench, and she feared falling off. Next to her, Rodrick had the same problem, with the other guard trying to get a hold of his steering wheel. Vincent snapped at the guard's hand, but never quite manged to bite him.

The guard next to Rena finally got a grip on her, his hand digging into her sister's dress. She tried to kick him, to throw him off his horse, but instead she slid from the bench and fell onto the footrest, Vincent yelping as her shoulder pushed him aside. As Rena's back hit the floor, the shock made her lose her grip on the fabric. The guard discarded the dress right away, throwing it onto the road behind him. Rena tried to push herself upright again, tried to get away from the guard's hand, but he managed to get a hold of her ankle and yanked her back — not enough to pull her off of the wagon, but enough that her legs were dangling off the edge. She tried to grab onto the wagon so she wouldn't fall, to claw her way back up, but there was nothing she could do. She fell off, tumbling hard to the ground, and all the air in her lungs was violently expelled. She rolled forward a few times, then landed with her face in the dirt.

A deafening noise erupted from behind, and she turned to see the wagon veering off the road before crashing into a tree. She tried to scramble upright, but slipped on the muddy road and fell down again. One of the guards pulled Rodrick's limp body from the wagon, but Vincent leapt from the remains of the caravan to the guard, teeth burying into the leather armour of the guard's arm.

The back door of the wagon burst open and the rest of her companions rushed out. Asha jumped out first, sword ready, a stream of blood running down the side of her face and neck. Logan was right behind her with a heavy-set cast-iron pan in his hands, the towel he had used to bandage his wound a deep crimson red.

Rena scrambled back up again, even though her back and her legs hurt like nothing she had ever felt before. The horse in front of her stopped and the guard dropped down to the ground. She turned around and tried to run away, but she was quickly surrounded by the other horses.

A loud metallic *thunk* resonated behind her, and she turned to find the guard lying on the ground, Logan next to him with two hands around the cast-iron pan.

"Run!" he yelled at her.

"I can't just—," she stammered out, eyes wide with panic.

"Just run!" he shouted, pointing at the forest.

A horse came up beside them, and the guard tried to grab Rena. He was yanked back from the other side and fell off of his horse.

"Forest! Now!" Logan cried out before turning away from her and taking hold of the horse's reins.

And so, she did. She ran past Logan, only stopping to pick her sister's now mud-covered dress off the ground, and disappeared between the trees. She lifted the skirt of her dress and clutched it tight to her chest, bundling it up with her sister's dress so she wouldn't lose it.

She didn't know for how long she ran, or where she was running to. She only stopped because her legs became weak, her foot caught on a root, and she fell to the ground.

She was out of breath, her mouth dry, her heartbeat hammering in her chest and her head. She tried pushing herself back up, but her body couldn't take it anymore.

She scooted closer to a tree and lay next to it, hoping that no one would find her there. She wished the fox would show up, that it would lead her to safety again, but she waited and waited and it never came. Her eyes became heavy, impossible to keep open anymore.

Footsteps approached, slow, tedious. Rena's eyes shot open, and she held her breath, waiting. A figure appeared from behind a tree, staggering towards her, and tripped over a protruding root, collapsing on the ground.

"Oh my stars, Logan!" she cried, scrambling up to hobble to him. "Are you all right?"

She rushed towards him, and knelt down. With great effort she pushed him over onto his back, his head dangling to the side, his hair caked in mud and blood covering his face.

"Logan?" She pulled him onto her lap, pulling his long hair to the side. "Logan, wake up!"

She tapped him lightly on the cheek but he didn't react. The side of his throat and face was smeared with blood — even the front of his shirt was covered in it.

"Please," she whispered, trying to shake him awake, but he still didn't move.

Her trembling hand pushed his shirt up where the fabric was torn and a dark stain was forming. A wide gash ran above his ribcage — a trickle of blood running over his skin and dripping down on the forest floor. It didn't look deep, like the sword had barely grazed him, but if she didn't stop the blood from flowing and get the wound cleaned, Logan might still die before they could ever reach safety.

She would need to get help, but she couldn't just leave him unconscious in the middle of the forest. She got up, laying his head down gently on the floor, and ripped a wide piece of fabric from her dress. She tied it around his waist as best as she could — the fabric staining red instantly. She straightened and went to get Maya's dress, tying it around her shoulders.

She knelt down and grabbed Logan under the armpits. She leaned back and dragged him over the floor, but his shirt caught on the underbrush and Rena fell backwards. She scrambled back up and untangled the fabric, determined to at least get him to the road. She wouldn't abandon him in the forest, no matter how difficult the journey would be.

A voice pierced through the calm of the forest, a shout far away. Rena dropped into a crouch, making herself as small as possible. A second shout, coming closer. Rena tried to determine where the person was, or what they were shouting, but her heartbeat was too loud for her to hear anything besides it.

"Logan!" the voice shouted again, and Rena perked up as she recognised the voice.

She shot up, craning her neck to see if she could find anyone coming closer.

"Logan!"

"Asha?" Rena finally shouted back, stepping away from Logan.

"Rena?"

Through the trees Rena could finally see someone approaching them and she rushed forward. Asha didn't look as bad as Logan, although a streak of blood and dirt ran over her face and skull.

"Are you all right?" she asked with urgency, grabbing Rena's shoulder and looking her over.

"Come quickly," Rena begged her, grabbing her hand and dragging her towards Logan.

"What happened?" Asha asked, kneeling down to inspect Logan's body, turning his face from side to side.

"I don't know. He stumbled towards me and then just fell. I can't get him to wake up."

Asha opened Logan's eyes and then lay her ear to his chest.

"He's alive, but we need to get him to Halvint," Asha said, getting back up.

She picked up Logan's right arm and pulled him up.

"Get the other one," she groaned as she slung the arm around her shoulder, her free hand wrapping around Logan's waist.

Rena hurried to Logan's other side and wrapped his arm around her shoulder, although the difference in their heights meant that Asha had to carry the majority of Logan's weight.

"Where are the others?" Rena asked, her eyes fixed on the ground as they dragged Logan back to where they had come from.

"The fucking guards got them. I barely managed to escape myself."

"Should we go after them?" Rena asked, looking over at Asha with panic, almost tripping over a root because of it.

"We can't. We'd only endanger ourselves."

"But we can't just let the guards take them away," Rena pleaded, Logan's arm weighing heavy on her shoulders. "We don't even know where they'll bring them or what they'll do to them! Not if they're working with the Crow."

Asha groaned as her knees buckled, but she managed to catch herself before falling.

"We'll figure something out," she grunted, straightening and readjusting Logan's arm on her shoulder. "We need to get Logan to safety first. The best course of action is to get him patched up in Halvint and then go to Rancor and talk to Cas. We can't go after them without help, anyway. We'd just get ourselves killed."

A tightness was starting to grip around Rena's chest, making it hard to breath. The thought of Rodrick and Kalani being imprisoned — or worse — because of her, because she dragged them into this mess, clawed its way into her mind, taking over her whole body, and pooled itself into her stomach. They didn't even know where Finn was. He might be dead because of her, or they had fallen into his trap and he had been the one to alert the guards. She shook her head, dispelling the thoughts from her mind. It was no use spiralling.

"Okay," Rena said weakly, turning her gaze back to the path ahead. She pressed her lips together so she wouldn't throw up.

She had to trust Asha. They had to save Logan first, to make sure he didn't lose too much blood and his wounds would heal correctly. They would find people in the city of Rancor to help them rescue the others, and once they were all back together, they would find the old monastery and stop the Crow.

A strange warmth rose in her at the thought of seeing her sister again.

The Heart Pyre Audio Drama

A Searing Faith is based on the award-winning, interactive audio drama *The Heart Pyre,* in which listeners can vote for how the story continues after each episode.

If you want to participate in determining how Rena's adventure continues and want to find out when season two starts, follow *The Heart Pyre* on social media, visit www.theheartpyre.com, or sign up for the newsletter.

Season one is available on every platform on which you find podcasts. If you liked *A Searing Faith*, find the audio drama on your favourite platform to listen to the bonus content.

Newsletter

Subscribe to my newsletter to stay up to date with new releases and special offers!

Newsletter Sign-up

Acknowledgments

I wanted to thank Maria May for the amazing cover illustration. Working with her was a delight and I am so happy with how the cover turned out.

I wanted to thank Maria Tureaud who edited this book. Her feedback was invaluable in turning this story into what it is.

I also thank Chelsea Beam for her invaluable editorial feedback on characterization.

I wanted to thank everyone who listened to *The Heart Pyre* and who voted for how the story should continue after each episode. Rena's story would not have turned out the way it did without all of you. Also a big thank you to all of the other creators in the audio drama community, who welcomed me with open arms and taught me so much about writing and creation.

And, finally, I wanted to thank my family and friends for all the support and understanding in the months it took me to write this book and the first season of the audio drama.

About the Author

Audrey Martin is a writer from Luxembourg. She has a degree in English Linguistics and Literature, and also a second degree in 3D animation, which she definitely totally has any use for. She loves stories in all forms, be it books, video games, comics, audio dramas, old folk tales, movies, or anything else you can think of. Language and stories is what connects us all as humans, to the present and to the past. As a writer, Audrey likes writing about the weird and the dark, about injustices and about how we can retain our hope until the end, about regular people who got thrust into unusual situations and about the hubris of humankind.